Margaret Yorke

A Case
to Answer

LITTLE, BROWN AND COMPANY

A *Little, Brown* Book

First published in Great Britain in 2000
by Little, Brown and Company

A CIP catalogue record for this book
is available from the British Library.

ISBN 0 316 85192 2

Typeset by Palimpsest Book Production Limited,
Polmont, Stirlingshire
Printed and bound in Great Britain by
The CPD Group, Ebbw Vale (Wales)

Little, Brown and Company (UK)
Brettenham House
Lancaster Place
London WC2E 7EN

A Case to Answer

1

She was invisible.

For a long time Charlotte did not realise what had happened, for the onset was gradual. Approaching pedestrians headed straight towards her when she walked along the street, not deflecting from her path, so that she was forced to step aside, even sometimes apologising, though no one answered. She must also be inaudible, she reflected.

There were moments, such as at the check-out in the supermarket, or against the grille in the post office, when she was perceived, but usually the cashier or the clerk made no eye contact with her. After all, it wasn't necessary for the transaction; why should they bother? And it wasn't as if the post office staff in Granbury had known her before her transformation, for she had moved there only after Rupert's death and, small and dumpy, unremarkable in every way, she was patently a person of no consequence.

Until Jerry called.

He came one evening after dark, ringing the doorbell hard. Charlotte had been listening to the radio and she thought it was the milkman, wanting to be paid. Even he never looked at her, merely taking the money, and asking if she required the usual at the weekend. But instead of him, a young man stood on the doorstep. He looked straight at her out of large eyes whose colour, though the porch light shone down upon him, Charlotte could not see. A new helper for the roundsman, she supposed.

'Are you from the milkman?' she said, and smiled.

'No,' said the caller. 'I'm a young offender. Thank you for smiling,' and he held out a plastic identity card of what she later thought might be dubious authenticity.

'Oh,' said Charlotte, unaware that she had done so, and only briefly startled. 'I never buy anything at the door,' she told him firmly. Such youths had rung her bell in the past, but never one with such a pleasant, open countenance. 'I hope you'll mend your ways,' she said, and added, 'You shouldn't be calling on people after dark. You could alarm someone.' Of a nervous disposition, she nearly added.

'I suppose that's true,' said Jerry. 'Well, thanks,' and, hefting his shabby satchel stuffed with unattractive merchandise on to his shoulder, he turned away and walked down the short path to the gate.

Charlotte was still smiling as she closed the door. What was his crime, she wondered: simple theft, shoplifting, perhaps? Rupert would have given him short shrift, probably even reporting his visit to the police, declaring that such pedlars might be testing to see if houses were unoccupied so that they, or accomplices, could break in. Surely that nice young man wasn't on such a mission?

The thought worried her as she returned to her radio programme and her tapestry. Rupert had died six months ago, suddenly, of a heart attack, and after only two years of marriage, she had become a widow for the second time.

*   *   *

That old bat – well, she wasn't so old – was on the ball about the darkness, Jerry thought, walking down the road, for that was when, unnoticed, you could sometimes find a door or window unlocked and slip inside to help yourself to anything available; there was always something lying around even if you found no cash – a radio or an easily detached video recorder. Jerry enjoyed the excitement of such raids; he wasn't into drugs or nicking cars. He'd done several opportunist operations like this with Pete. It was Pete's scam; Jerry did the sweet-talking at the door while Pete went round the back and sneaked inside to take whatever he could find. The woman had seemed all right; a bit more talk and he'd have got her to buy a few things from him. Still, he'd soon find someone else to dazzle with his sales pitch; Jerry's artless expression and steadfast gaze had got him out of many a past scrape.

While Jerry was knocking on doors and doing his best to sell dusters to whoever answered, Pete was testing for easy entry. Pete was small, slim and agile, and he nipped quickly round the rear of houses while Jerry was busy switching on the charm. They'd mocked up a licence and bought a few dusters and dishcloths at a warehouse sale. As a decoy, Jerry was a useful partner.

Pete, sticking close to the wall of the house, then sliding past the garage, was round at the back before the door was opened. There was no way of knowing, in advance, how many people were at home, so he was alert for movement indoors. Watching the houses was not part of his and Jerry's routine, for that could attract attention; you had to take your chance, nip in fast while the householder was at the door, kept busy by Jerry and his patter.

These recently built houses were less easy to approach unseen than the older, individual ones with well-planted gardens offering cover to prowlers, and unless Jerry, at the front, had a sale, any snitch had to be swift. A security light came on as he tried the back door; it was unlocked, and he stepped inside; the exterior light illuminated the kitchen as Pete glanced quickly round. Two pans were draining by the sink but there was no purse or handbag visible, nothing to be quickly taken, and then he heard footsteps. Jerry had failed to detain whoever had opened the front door. Pete did not wait; he fled as swiftly and silently as he had come, but he'd remember this house, maybe visit it again. A good few folk locked their back doors at dusk, but not, it seemed, whoever lived here.

He was luckier further down the road, collecting a watch and a transistor radio left ready for the taking. Neither was missed until the following day.

The railway station at Becktham had recently been modernised, its ironwork painted vivid red and blue, even a coffee bar established on the up-line to London. Trains carried commuters back and forth, running frequently at peak times and maintaining a good service throughout the day; a number of Granbury's regular travellers found it worth driving the extra miles to use this route rather than the nearer station at Nettington, where the car park was filled to capacity soon after nine o'clock when the first cheap fares operated. Charlotte Frost had forgotten about the young offender when, one morning some weeks later, she inserted her Fiat between a Discovery Range Rover and a blue Honda; she had planned to catch the 9.05, but thought she might not manage it when she arrived at the booking-office, for a large man in a dark suit who was making a complicated booking with his credit card seemed impervious to the fact that there were other passengers queuing up behind him. Buying his season ticket, Charlotte deduced, mildly irritated by the delay but content to catch the train due fifteen minutes later, for she had no morning appointment and was planning to visit an art exhibition before meeting Lorna. She decided that the man was insensitive, pompous and boring; he was entitled to receive whatever attention he required, but his was an intricate transaction; couldn't he have arrived earlier? Standing behind him, her exact fare ready, she wondered about his life. Was his wife bullied into meekness or was he a lamb at home? He was clearly prosperous; was he a city magnate or a lawyer? While she pondered, rapid footsteps pounded up behind her and a breathless woman, streaked blonde hair in some disorder, saw the hold-up ahead, came to an enforced halt behind Charlotte, and stood shifting from foot to foot. She was not merely impatient; she was frantic. The man still stood there, slowly conducting his negotiations while the new arrival chafed.

'The train will be coming. I've got to get to work,' she told the air, or Charlotte.

'Go ahead of me. It doesn't matter if I miss this one,' said Charlotte, standing back.

'Oh, thank you,' gasped the woman, barely looking at Charlotte as she took her place.

At this point the man's business was concluded and he moved ponderously on. The distressed blonde bought her ticket in seconds, speeding off as the train's arrival was announced, and Charlotte's good deed was rewarded, for the clerk produced hers promptly and she, too, was in time to board it. Taking her seat – there was still space, though the train would fill up at the next stop – she wondered briefly about the distraught woman who, like the man, had not allowed enough time to catch her train. Perhaps she had had to take children to school, or the washing-machine had flooded, or some other domestic disaster had delayed her. Charlotte would never know.

She travelled up to London in a different carriage, but, glancing out of the window when the train stopped at Denfield, twenty minutes into the journey, she saw the woman hurry along the platform, still in a rush.

Charlotte enjoyed the exhibition and afterwards took the Underground to South Kensington, where she was to meet Lorna, her stepdaughter, who was a partner in a residential letting agency based nearby. In the cloakroom at the restaurant where they were to meet, Charlotte, who had arrived first, added cautious dabs of blusher to her pale face; she was determined that Lorna should deliver a good report to her brother: they, after all, had lost their father, while she was an interloper, marrying him after the death of their mother, whom Charlotte had never met.

Charlotte had known Rupert slightly for several years; she had worked for a charity which the company he ran had sponsored, not only financially, but also by providing training and work experience. Meeting at a fund-raising function, each had felt the other to be an old friend, when they were really little more than acquaintances, but Rupert, now widowed, had walked her to her car after the event, and somehow or other they had arranged to meet for dinner the following week. He had collected her from the house where she had lived since soon after her husband's death. One thing had led to another, and because he was now the chairman of his company, Rupert had insisted that they marry. To be openly lovers, he had said, would provoke gossip, and living together without marrying would be even worse. Also, he wanted to give her the security marriage to him would offer. In fact, he loved her, and it had been easy for her, after her first astonishment, to love him in return. Their two years together had been happy, though for Charlotte they were demanding for her new role involved many duties. Rupert's house was large; its grounds were occasionally used for village events; and there were the visits of his children and grand-children. In addition, there was the garden, which delighted Charlotte, but it took up time and energy. She adapted as rapidly as possible, doing all she could to make friends with his family; then, abruptly, one fine summer's day, everything changed when Rupert collapsed and died at a meeting in London.

Lorna had suggested that they meet today. After their father's death, his children had rearranged Charlotte's life. By the terms of his will, apart from the pension she inherited, she was to continue living at White Lodge, which was left to his children, for as long as she wished, but if she were to move she was to be re-housed, rent-free, in a style befitting her status as his widow. Felix, Rupert's son, soon told her that White Lodge must be sold as it was much too big for her on her own, which was true, and, bustled briskly along by him, she was speedily installed in a three-bedroomed modern house in Vicarage Fields, a small development in the grounds of the former vicarage in Granbury.

Charlotte could not object; it was appropriate and comfortable, but it was not hers: after her death it would revert to Rupert's family.

Granbury's vicar, whose territory now included three other churches, lived in a modern house in one of the other parishes.

Charlotte's son Tim, who was in the navy and serving overseas when Rupert died, thought she should have asked for a cash settlement and bought somewhere of her own. She still had money left after paying off the mortgage from the sale of her house when she remarried, but she had gone along with her stepchildren's arrangements because events had been too rapid for her to think things through calmly. In any case, her capital, in a building society account, had not appreciated as much as house prices. White Lodge was soon sold; probate was not long delayed and it had all happened very quickly.

Number Five, Vicarage Fields, was comfortable, warm and freshly decorated. It was furnished with pieces Charlotte had kept from her former home, and a few new things swiftly bought from John Lewis. Though Lorna urged her to take anything she wanted from White Lodge, Charlotte asked for nothing; she did not want bad blood between herself and Rupert's children lest in future they disputed her right to any items.

Now, buffeted by the speed of her metamorphosis, she felt herself to be in limbo, invisible, without status, and without even her own identity, for she had a new name, one which had been hers for only two years.

What did Lorna want, she wondered, entering the restaurant, following the waiter to the table which the younger woman had booked. It was an Italian trattoria, and she did not seem to be invisible to the waiter who showed her to her seat; Italians, she reflected, were fond of their families and respected their grandparents.

Lorna, arriving at the restaurant in a rush, gave her a fleeting kiss, summoned the waiter to order a bottle of the house white wine, and dutifully asked about Charlotte's family. Tim was still aboard his ship somewhere in the Mediterranean while Victoria, his wife, and their children were carrying on their lives ashore in Dorset. Jane was working for a publisher in New York.

Jane hadn't liked Rupert's son, Felix. Charlotte had been aware of that, early on, but the two had rarely met and she could see no reason for the hostility. Felix, dark and saturnine, not much resembling his father, had an arrogant manner which Charlotte did not care for, but she attributed it to a sense of insecurity, for though he seemed successful in his career, it did not match his father's. In New York, Jane was living with a man she had met through her work, a writer, Ben, a lot older than she was, separated from his wife but not divorced. Charlotte had never met him; photographs showed a thin, pleasant face, and Jane expressed herself as very happy.

Lorna was relieved to learn that all was well with Charlotte's family; if any one of them were having a crisis, either domestically or to do with their work, she would have felt inhibited about asking for Charlotte's help, the reason for today's invitation.

Over fruit salad for Lorna, and zabaglione for Charlotte –

she was touched that Lorna remembered how much she liked it and insisted that she have it – this was revealed.

'Felix and Zoe have broken up,' Lorna said abruptly. 'Zoe's gone off with some photographer she met through work.' Zoe, Felix's wife, was a journalist working for a women's magazine. 'The kids are in a mess,' she added. 'Imogen's pregnant and has run away from school. She was missing for a while, but she turned up at Zoe's mother's, and Nicholas can't be found.'

'Oh dear,' Charlotte said, inadequately. Imogen and Nicholas were twins, aged just eighteen. She'd sent them fifty pounds each on their birthday several weeks ago. Imogen had sent a card, thanking her, but she had yet to hear from Nicholas.

'The thing is,' said Lorna, plunging on, 'with Zoe having bunked off – she's in Los Angeles with her photographer who's on an assignment there – I wondered if you'd have Imogen to stay for a while, till she sorts herself out a bit.'

'Oh,' repeated Charlotte, now thoroughly dismayed.

'She's always liked you,' Lorna tried, as a lure.

Charlotte and Imogen had seldom met, but Charlotte knew that Rupert had thought the plain, plump girl was overshadowed by her elegant, hyperactive mother and her handsome twin.

'I suppose this pregnancy is a desperate gesture,' she said.

Lorna was aware, not for the first time, of Charlotte's sharp perception.

'Yes,' she said. 'I think so. But Zoe hasn't come back. Says Imogen must decide for herself what to do, and she's got to fulfil her contract.'

'So she has been told?'

'Yes.'

'What does Felix have to say about it?'

'He's hit the roof. Furious,' said Lorna. 'And he's furious with Nicholas, too, but he says he'll turn up when he's out of money.'

'When do you want Imogen to come to Granbury?' she asked, making an effort not to sound as reluctant as she felt.

'So you'll have her, then?' Lorna's face lit up in relief.

'For a while,' Charlotte said. 'She'll be bored with me,' she added, on a more hopeful note.

'She needs a bit of looking after,' Lorna said, feeling rather sheepish now that her objective had been achieved.

'Where is she now?' asked Charlotte. Imogen was a pupil at a boarding school in Sussex and Nicholas was at a sixth-form college in Oxford.

'She's with Zoe's mother, but she can't stay there. Zoe's mother's going on a Baltic cruise on Saturday,' Lorna said. 'Imogen can't stay in the flat alone in the state she's in.'

Maybe not, thought Charlotte grimly, but she can return to it when her grandmother's cruise is over.

She asked when that would be, and Lorna seemed vague.

'Oh – two weeks or so, I suppose,' she said. 'Imogen will know.'

Charlotte told herself that Rupert would want her to care for his granddaughter in her hour of need, and what if it were one of her own grandchildren in this extremity? Wouldn't she expect someone, in the family or outside it, to rescue her? The fact that her own grandchildren were still under ten was irrelevant.

'When do you want her to come?' she asked again.

'Could you take her back with you today?' Lorna asked. 'After you've done whatever you've planned this afternoon?'

Today was only Thursday.

'I suppose the grandmother has things to do. Packing and

so on,' Charlotte said. She had been wondering why she had
been asked to lunch in London when all this could have been
settled on the telephone.

'Precisely,' Lorna said.

'Why can't Felix have her?' After all, she was his daughter.
And Lorna was her aunt.

'Well, you know he's away a lot,' said Lorna. 'He's abroad
now.' Felix was a director of a company with interests in West
Africa and spent a lot of his time travelling. 'Besides,' she added,
'he's so angry. He needs time to cool down. He'll telephone, of
course.' She'd make him. There was no need to tell Charlotte
that Felix, too, had been playing away from home. 'He's always
been so disappointed because Nicholas got the looks and poor
Imogen is so ordinary,' Lorna went on. 'He had this notion,
like all fathers, I suppose, of a pretty little adoring daughter.'

'I've never thought her ugly,' Charlotte defended Imogen.
'Nor did Rupert.'

'No – well – she was very upset when he died,' Lorna said.
'That probably didn't help her state of mind.'

It didn't help me, either, Charlotte thought.

'I'm sure she was very fond of your mother,' she said aloud.
Poor girl: she'd been through quite a lot before this break-up
of her parents.

'Yes,' agreed Lorna. 'I can't have her at the moment,' she
added. 'I've got a lot of work on just now and Brian's in the
middle of a big case.' Lorna's husband, Brian, was a solicitor
specialising in company law.

When their father remarried, and so quickly, she and Felix
had been amazed and even shocked. At first they resented
Charlotte. After all, their father could have afforded a housekeeper, they reflected, reckoning that they could provide him

with all the affection he might need, and unwilling to acknowledge that he might want a sexual relationship. Though Brian had disagreed, they and Zoe had decided that Charlotte had caught him when he was vulnerable. Lorna's attitude had altered during the brief marriage when she saw its success, and when she realised that Charlotte did not want to usurp her mother's role. She was quiet, undemanding, dependable and self-effacing, and Lorna trusted her to do her best for Imogen in the short term.

'Does Imogen know about this plan?' Charlotte asked. 'What if she won't agree?'

'She has agreed,' said Lorna. There was no need to describe Imogen's hysterical reaction to the idea, but after she had calmed down she had seen that there was no better alternative.

'What about the young man involved?' Charlotte asked.

'She won't say a word,' Lorna replied. 'Nicholas may know who he is. Some boy at the school, I suppose.'

What a pickle, Charlotte thought, agreeing to meet Imogen at Marylebone. The grandmother would despatch her there in a taxi; only the train they would catch need be decided. It had all been well thought out. She had been skilfully manipulated into a position from which she could not extract herself without seeming to be very disobliging.

She reached Marylebone well before the time of the train she had selected as convenient; always well organised, she had a timetable in her handbag. Emerging from the Underground, she saw that Imogen was already standing below the departure indicator board, her shoulders slumped, as though beneath the burden of her long straight hair, a large holdall at her feet. She wore a navy fleece jacket and baggy tracksuit trousers. Remaining invisible for a few minutes more, Charlotte studied her as she approached. She looked lost and dejected, and she was very young. Poor unhappy girl, I must make her feel welcome, Charlotte told herself, advancing. She's having a bad time now and there is worse to come, whatever she decides to do about her present predicament.

'Hullo, Imogen,' she called, as she approached, and the girl turned a pale, mutinous face towards her.

The woman with the mane of tangled hair who had been so desperate at the ticket office that morning got into their carriage when they stopped at Denfield on the way back. Still in a rush, she sat down across the aisle from Charlotte, who was in the gangway seat of a set of three, with Imogen, separated by a vacant seat, next to the window, staring out. The woman did not notice Charlotte. Invisible again, thought Charlotte, who throughout her lunch with Lorna had been looked in the eye across the table but whose gaze Imogen had steadily avoided after first greeting her with a sullen 'Hi.'

The woman left the train ahead of them, but Imogen, even with her holdall, was close behind her, not waiting for Charlotte as she ascended the stairs and crossed the bridge over the track.

'You wait here with your bag while I get the car,' Charlotte told her when at last she halted, looking indecisive, outside the station buildings. The girl had dozed off during the journey, drooping against the window, scarcely stirring. Charlotte, who had brought a book, read it with determination if not wholehearted comprehension. She did not view the days or weeks ahead with optimism. Lorna had declared, before they parted, that it was up to Charlotte to get Imogen's story out of her and talk her through the choices that were before her.

'After all, you're not related. You can be objective,' Lorna had said. 'There's not a lot of time in hand,' she added.

Meaning if the girl was to have an abortion, Charlotte thought.

'Any decision has to be hers,' was her reply.

'Of course,' Lorna had agreed.

Now, as if she had not heard Charlotte's instruction, Imogen trudged along behind her with her bag, and heaved it into the boot of Charlotte's Fiat. The woman with the hair was ahead of them, still walking down the parking lot, but as Charlotte started the engine she drove past them, rather too fast, in an old red Metro.

Her working day was a short one, Charlotte reflected; she had spent the journey gazing out of the window and she, like Imogen, was a troubled soul.

2

That evening Lorna telephoned her brother Felix, now in Germany.

'It was OK,' she said. 'Charlotte was only too pleased to help. Imogen will be safe with her. I'll call her soon and see if they've had a good talk, and you should ring, too.'

'Wretched girl,' said Felix. 'She's done this just to get at me. And Zoe, I suppose.'

'I doubt it,' said Lorna. 'The running away from school, maybe, but not the pregnancy bit, but she'd have been sacked anyway, when they found out. That's probably pure accident.'

'Or impure,' said Felix. 'I thought girls knew it all these days – safe sex, morning-after pill and all that.'

'They do, in theory,' said Lorna. 'It's the hormone bit that's unpredictable.' And peer pressure, and other unforeseen things, uncomfortable ones like emotions.

'Do you think she'll get rid of it?'

'How do I know?' Lorna replied. 'If she talks to Charlotte, I'm sure all the pros and cons will be fully aired. Charlotte is very sensible.'

'And she owes us,' Felix said.

'Oh, come on, Felix. She made Dad very happy and she's taken nothing that was ours.'

'The house,' said Felix. 'There's nearly three hundred thousand tied up in that house, bringing nothing in, and she's only sixty-five.'

'It'll hold its value – even appreciate,' Lorna said. 'And she's going to see to its upkeep herself. You're just thinking of the settlement you'll have to give Zoe.'

'It had crossed my mind,' said Felix.

Lorna did not remind him that she owned half of Charlotte's house.

'What about Nicholas?' she asked. 'Have you tracked him down?'

'No. I've left messages with his flatmates,' said Felix. 'But he hasn't rung back.'

'I hope he hasn't run off somewhere, too,' said Lorna.

'No. The flatmate was so cagey that I think he knows where he is,' said Felix.

'Did you leave a message about Imogen with the flatmate?'

'No. We don't want her foolishness broadcast all over the place,' said Felix. 'I just said I needed to speak to him urgently.'

'Well, he'll ring eventually,' Lorna soothed. 'You could let him know where Imogen is,' she added.

'I'll go down to Granbury when Charlotte's had a chance to talk to her,' Felix decided. 'Make her see some sense.'

'That's up to you. I thought you were going to go to LA to try to win Zoe back,' said Lorna.

'I thought about it,' he answered. 'But what good will it do, if she's made her mind up?'

'Can it do harm?' asked Lorna. 'At least it shows you want her back.'

'But do I?' Felix said, in bitter tones. 'If I persuaded her, she might take off again.'

They could go on talking in circles like this all night.

'Look, I've got to go now,' Lorna said. 'Think it over and talk to me again.' And you might say thanks, seeing that I've sorted out your daughter, however temporary the solution, she thought.

Felix, hurt and angry, did not want to end the conversation. 'I suppose you've got things to do,' he said.

'Something like that. People to feed and so on,' said Lorna, whose husband was even now preparing dinner for the family.

'Don't give me that,' said Felix. 'I know Brian's the cook in your house.' But he laughed as he said it.

'Take care,' said Lorna, and hung up.

After her good lunch, a snack was all Charlotte wanted for her supper, but she had a pregnant mother in her care. Nourishing fare must be offered.

It had not taken her long, after she married Rupert, to get used to catering again for others than just herself, even though it was some time since her own family had left home, and now, just as easily, she had resumed the solitary's pattern of minimum supplies. There were no remains of a leg of lamb or roast chicken in the fridge to fall back on, but there were fresh vegetables, eggs and cheese. She suggested an omelette, and Imogen, who had not said a word since they met, merely obediently following her like a silent shadow, nodded.

Despite her resolution to be patient, Charlotte was exasperated.

'Imogen, I realise that you are very unhappy and going

through a bad patch in your life, but you haven't lost the power of speech, have you? I know you to be normally well-mannered. Please show me that you haven't changed and reply so that I can hear you.'

'Yes, I'd like an omelette, please,' said Imogen. Then she burst into tears, and rushed upstairs.

Charlotte, who was tired after her day in London and the unexpected way in which it had ended, sank down at the kitchen table in defeat. She would not follow the girl. Let her cry or sulk or both, and if she were hungry, eventually she would reappear. She had put Imogen in the nicer of the two spare bedrooms, where the bed was already made up, as it always was in case, however unlikely it might be, an unexpected guest arrived. Imogen had dumped her bag and then, after Charlotte had taken clean towels for her from the airing cupboard, had gone across to the bathroom, but had soon emerged and followed Charlotte downstairs.

I can only do so much for her, Charlotte decided, and poured herself a whisky. Must I take her omelette up to her, she wondered, while she ate a cheese sandwich. After she had finished it, with no sign of Imogen reappearing, she decided that she should, so she whipped one up, adding parsley and tomatoes, made some toast and laid it all on a tray which she carried upstairs. She knocked on Imogen's door and said, 'I've brought your supper up.'

There was no reply, and during the few seconds before she decided to try the door, she wondered what she would do if it was locked and Imogen refused to open it, imagining slit wrists and overdoses, so it was a relief when it yielded to her hand.

Imogen was lying on top of the bedspread, fully dressed but without her heavy trainers, which were neatly placed below the window. Her face was tear-stained and she was fast asleep, a deep, exhausted, natural sleep. There was no glass of water or paracetamol packet at her side.

Charlotte took the duvet off the other bed and draped it over her. Then she drew the curtains against the night and tiptoed out, closing the door quietly, taking the tray with her.

Pete, returning to Vicarage Fields on a further opportunist expedition, had seen a number of lights on at Number Five, which he had marked down on his earlier visit with Jerry as a likely target. Figures passed to and fro, two women, and at last the lights went out, but he decided to leave that one tonight and try another time. He turned back out of the close and into the High Street, off which it led, continuing until he came to Meadow Lane and into Church Street.

Meadow Lane was a quiet road with a few old cottages which had been renovated and were now much sought after by couples moving out of London. Charlotte would have liked one of these pretty houses with their established gardens, and Apple Cottage had been for sale when she moved, but at a far higher price than Number Five, Vicarage Fields. She had seen for herself that this ruled it out before Felix had explained that a modern house cost far less in upkeep; with an old place, he said, you were always having to find money for repairs. There was no argument.

Pete remembered that there had been a very elderly man at one of these houses; Jerry had said the man had spoken to him firmly, advising him to go to the Job Centre and look for real work. He'd gone and done it, got a job, though not through the Job Centre, and he'd said he wouldn't go out nicking any more. Stupid twit, thought Pete. On his previous visit, he had been able to get to the rear of this cottage under the cover of various bushes and shrubs while Jerry sweet-talked the old man, but the back door had been locked. However, Pete had seen that there was no burglar alarm, and that there was a window with a half-light which looked easy to force; he had decided to try it one night. With luck he could reach inside and open the latch. Now was as good a time as any.

He walked up the road with his usual loping stride. Pete did not swagger, as Jerry often did; he was thin but muscular, appearing to pose no threat but in fact wiry and strong. People remembered Jerry, but they overlooked Pete. Reaching the cottage, which was some distance from the nearest street light, an advantage for anyone seeking unlawful entry, Pete opened the gate and went across the short front lawn to the side of the house, which was in darkness. Though his eyes had adjusted, he stumbled at first, almost tripping over the stone border to a flower bed, but immediately a bright security light blazed, and he ducked into the shelter of a large bush. Nothing happened, and he moved cautiously on; cats could set those things off, he reminded himself as he edged round to his target. Another light came on, and Pete swore under his breath. The place was wired up like Fort Knox. He moved close against the wall, calculating that this would remove him from the orbit of the sensor and that the light would soon go out. The window he was aiming for was only a few yards away and he inched towards it, stretching up with his knife to force it open. Pete had done plenty of breaking and entering in his young life, and this should be an easy one. He balanced on the sill, reaching in for the catch of the main window which, after a struggle, he managed to unfasten. Soon he was crawling across the drainer by the sink, lowering himself on to the floor. He felt his way to the door and opened it: a getaway route was vital, in case the householder should wake up. All this time the outside light was illuminating the interior, but now, abruptly, it went off, and Pete switched on the torch he carried, revealing a pine table, pine fitments round the walls, an electric cooker and a large refrigerator. Hoping to find cash, he opened a few drawers, but saw only cutlery and rolls of plastic bags, foil, J-cloths in a pack, and, in one, a stack of tea towels. He moved on to the door, opened it, and crossed the stone-flagged hall, entering a large room where there were two armchairs in faded blue linen covers and an oval oak dining-table with four wheel-back chairs set round it. Two matching chairs stood against the wall, and there was a flat-topped desk in one corner. Pete hurried over to pull out drawers, looking for cash, a pension book, credit cards – anything of value.

A slight sound made him turn at the same moment that Howard Smythe, a retired naval captain, eighty-six years old, turned the main light on as he entered the room, and, holding aloft a golf club, demanded to know what he was doing.

Pete's pencil torch was too slim to serve as a weapon, and he looked round for one, grabbing a heavy paperweight and advancing towards the old man who was blocking his way out. Pete flung it at him and Howard Smythe was forced to duck. Pete pushed past him while he was off balance, but the old man did not fall. He hooked Pete round the ankle with his number four iron and had the satisfaction of seeing the boy trip, crashing to the ground.

Pete was young, with quick reflexes, but Howard Smythe was tall. He stood over him, golf club at the ready, well aware that a householder, in such circumstances, must not use inappropriate force, even in self-defence, or he would be the one to be arrested.

'You miserable little wretch,' he said, as Pete, his face pressed against the thick Indian carpet, tried to struggle to his feet. 'Lie down,' he added, and, still wielding the golf club, pushed him hard between the shoulder-blades with his slippered foot. 'Now crawl,' he ordered, and made Pete move on hands and knees across the room until Howard could reach the telephone, which was on the desk.

The police took fifteen minutes to arrive. They found that the back door was open and by then both captive and capturer were feeling the draught which blew across the hall and into the sitting-room. Captain Smythe, in his ancient Jaeger dressing gown, was sitting in a large wheel-back chair which he had placed across the intruder's legs. Every time Pete, still lying face downwards on the floor, started to wriggle free, a sharp tap on the shoulder from the golf club caused him to subside.

'It was a good sight,' said PC Dawkins, first on the scene, after he had charged his prisoner at Nettington Police Station. 'The little toe-rag hadn't had time to take anything. Kept complaining that he'd got his face full of fluff off the carpet, if you please.'

Charlotte, though tucked away in Vicarage Fields, heard the siren of the first police car that hurried to the scene; sounds carried strangely, and when the church bells rang she could hear them clearly, their peals funnelling across a gap between trees and buildings. Oh dear, she thought: trouble somewhere. She sat propped up in bed, spectacles on, reading a short story by Carol Shields. Short stories were just right for reading in bed, she found; you could finish one and then compose yourself for sleep. Tonight, however, after she closed the book, her mind began to dwell on the presence and the problems of her uninvited guest. At some point they would have to discuss Imogen's plans, if she had any, and if her visit lasted more than just a few days she should see the doctor.

Eventually, Charlotte went to sleep, and did not wake when Imogen, in the early hours, crept downstairs and made herself a hearty fry-up. Charlotte only discovered that the girl had done this in the morning. Imogen had washed up the plates and cutlery she had used and left them to drain, but the last two eggs had gone, much of the milk, the end of a loaf and the two remaining bananas.

She must be feeling better, Charlotte decided, taking bread out of the freezer, and putting on the kettle for her coffee. What was she going to do about her? When would Imogen deign to appear downstairs? And if she did, what then? She couldn't simply hang about all day doing nothing. If she were younger, useful or interesting tasks could be devised; Charlotte remembered school holidays with her own children and the activities that had occupied them – tennis, swimming, going to museums. But that was a long time ago, and Imogen was not a child.

At this point in her thoughts, the telephone rang. It was Nicholas.

'I think you've got my sister there,' he said. 'I'd like to speak to her.'

There were no preliminaries, no lead in to the conversation, so Charlotte wasted no time either.

'I'll see if she's awake,' she said. 'Just hold on, Nicholas.'

Irritated by his belligerent tone but relieved that at least he had now surfaced, she went upstairs and tapped on Imogen's door, then opened it.

'It's Nicholas on the telephone,' she said, addressing the bed, where a humped bundle under the duvet was all that could be seen. 'I'll tell him you're coming to talk to him, Imogen.'

There was a grunt, and then some mumbled words.

'What did you say?' asked Charlotte.

'I said, haven't you got a cordless?' Imogen growled. They were virtually the first words she had uttered within Charlotte's hearing.

'No, I haven't,' Charlotte snapped. 'But you can take it in my bedroom, to be more private. It's just across the landing,' and she went from the room, leaving the door open and going down the stairs.

'She's on her way,' she said to Nicholas.

'Thanks,' he managed.

'Where are you, Nicholas?' she asked.

'Nowhere important,' he replied, and at that moment Imogen's voice cut in on the other instrument. Charlotte replaced hers firmly. She could dial 1471 after they had finished their conversation, and learn the number he had called from. It might be necessary to tell Felix that his son had made a move; she'd think about that.

How had Nicholas, reported to be missing, known where his sister was?

3

Half an hour later, Imogen left the house.

After talking to her brother, she sprang into action. Charlotte heard her running a bath, and while she was in the bathroom Charlotte dialled to discover Nicholas's number. By its length, she knew the call had come from a mobile phone, so she was none the wiser as to where he was. Soon, Imogen appeared, dressed in clean jeans and a white sweater under the heavy fleece jacket she had worn on the journey yesterday. She had washed her dark hair, which hung damply round her shoulders.

Charlotte offered her the hair-drier, but Imogen said no, it would be all right, thanks. She had to go out and she didn't have time.

Charlotte managed not to ask where she was going.

'When will you be back?' she enquired, instead.

'I don't know,' said Imogen. 'Maybe I'll phone you.'

'Please do. I need to know about meals,' Charlotte said. 'Do you know my number?'

Imogen didn't, and Charlotte wrote it down on a piece of paper.

'Thanks,' Imogen said, still not looking Charlotte in the eye.

'Have you got any money? Or a phone card?'

'I've got a mobile,' said Imogen, patting her jacket pocket. 'It wasn't turned on. That's why Nick had to ring you,' she added, grudgingly, rightly interpreting Charlotte's expression.

Everyone except Charlotte seemed to have one these days.

'Enjoy your walk,' was all she said, as the front door closed behind the girl.

Wherever she went from Vicarage Fields, Imogen would have to go into the High Street, but unless Charlotte followed her, there was no means of finding out which way she turned after that. I'm not her keeper, Charlotte told herself; but she was. Imogen had seemed animated at last, however. Making contact with her brother had brought her to life. Perhaps she was going to meet him somewhere now, but she hadn't taken her luggage, such as it was, so she must mean to return. Charlotte went upstairs into the spare bedroom where the girl had spent the night, expecting to find the bed unmade and discarded clothes flung about the room, but it was scrupulously neat: the bedspread was tidily arranged, tucked up under the pillows; the only sign of occupation was the plain wooden-backed hairbrush and a black comb placed neatly parallel on the dressing-table. In the bathroom, the same high standards prevailed: Imogen's peach-coloured towel hung on a hook, away from Charlotte's green one, which was over the heated rail. Her sponge bag was on the windowsill, with her wet pink and white striped flannel folded on top of it. She hadn't even hung it on the side of the bath. This was the behaviour of a well-trained schoolgirl, and Charlotte felt tears stinging her eyes. What was going on in Imogen's head?

When Lorna telephoned half an hour later to see how things were, Charlotte reported that Imogen had slept well, was being no trouble, and had just gone out for a walk. She did not add that the girl had had no breakfast, but since she had eaten a large meal during the night, Charlotte thought that was of no consequence.

Imogen had to find the church. She was going to meet Nicholas, but he would not come to the house because of Charlotte's presence, so they had had to choose a meeting-place which both could easily find. Wherever you were, you could always find the church, he had said. Nicholas had a car – Imogen had not yet passed her test – and they could go off in that for a bit, decide what to do next.

She hadn't asked Charlotte for directions because that would have revealed where she was going, but if she didn't come within sight of the church as she walked along, anyone she met would know where it was. Imogen had seen nothing of Granbury when they arrived the previous evening, for by then it was getting dark. She had never been there before; it was about twenty miles from White Lodge, her grandparents' house, which she had often visited, particularly before the death of her grandmother and several times after her grandfather had married Charlotte. His death had been a great shock to her; Imogen had loved him, and he had always indulged her. With him, she had never felt herself to be ugly, as she did with everyone else, and especially her brother, who had all the looks, as she had often heard people comment when she was younger. She turned right out of Vicarage Fields into the High Street, walking past several houses, a post office with a telephone box outside it, and, set back from a small parking area, a butcher's and a general store. After passing a row of terraced houses, she came to a side road. Meadow Lane, said a sign, and she decided to go that way. She had walked only a short distance down it – there was no footpath – when a police car overtook her; it slowed down, stopping just ahead of her, and a uniformed officer got out of it, walking towards her, putting his cap on.

Imogen halted. He couldn't be after her; her brief vanishing trick was over. Going missing wasn't a crime.

'Excuse me, miss,' said the officer, very politely. He was young and fair-headed. 'Do you live in Granbury?'

'I'm visiting,' said Imogen cautiously.

'There was a break-in at a house down this road last night,' said the officer. 'We caught the offender but we think he had an accomplice. Did you see or hear anything suspicious?'

'No,' said Imogen. 'I went to bed early and slept all night,' she declared, not altogether truthfully, since she had woken feeling hungry and had raided the fridge during the night. 'I'm staying with my step-grandmother,' she added. 'In Vicarage Fields.' It sounded very respectable.

The officer seemed satisfied.

Did he think she might be the accomplice? Imogen felt affronted at the mere notion of being a suspect and she would not stoop low enough to ask the policeman where the church was. She wondered which house the thief had chosen. In the dull grey light of a chilly morning she glanced at the trim façades, the tidy gardens and spruce boundary fences. Some bore names painted on decorative pottery plaques. She saw Apple Cottage and Candlemakers. One gate-post had Rose Cottage etched in Roman capitals on a dark brown varnished board, and as she paused to glance at it, a man came round the side of the house and walked towards the gate. Embarrassed at being caught staring, she moved on, but he called out, 'Good morning,' and she hesitated.

'Good morning,' she replied, uncertainly.

'Not that it is,' he said. 'It may rain.'

He was very tall and very old, Imogen observed as he came towards his open gateway. He would know where the church was. She asked him.

'I'm going there,' he said. 'It's down this way – not far.' She saw then that he was carrying a small bunch of tiny daffodils. 'I'm taking these to my wife. She's buried in the graveyard. Aren't they lovely? These small ones come out before the main crop, you know.'

Imogen didn't, but she nodded, and the old man walked round behind her so that he was on the traffic side of the road. Her grandfather had done that, she remembered. When he died, he wasn't nearly as old as this man.

'I met a policeman,' she said. 'He told me someone's house was broken into during the night.'

'It was mine,' said the old man. 'But no one was hurt and the thief didn't manage to get away with anything. That's something to be thankful for. Wouldn't you agree?'

'Yes,' said Imogen. 'Certainly. The policeman said he'd been arrested. He thought there might have been an accomplice.'

'I don't think so,' said Howard Smythe. 'If there had been, he'd have tried to help his friend.' A second youth, entering the house and using force, might have been too much for him.

'Would he? Wouldn't he have just run off and saved himself? People let each other down all the time,' said Imogen. 'But it was smart of the police to catch him.'

'Yes,' said Howard Smythe, not revealing what had really happened. 'There's the church,' he added, pointing with the hand that held the flowers. 'It's very old,' he told her. 'Parts of it date back to the thirteenth century.'

They walked the rest of the way together, and once through the church gates, he raised his hat to her.

'I go this way,' he said, stepping off the path and on to the damp grass. 'The church isn't locked,' he added. 'Goodbye.'

'Goodbye,' said Imogen, and walked on, oddly moved by this encounter. What a nice old man, and he seemed quite calm even though his house had been broken into.

Imogen did not realise how unusual it was for the church to be unlocked; most churches were no longer open to passers-by because of theft and vandalism, but St Mary's, Granbury, was an exception; experimentally, under a new vicar, it was accessible for most of every day. Imogen lifted the latch on the heavy old oak door and opened it, expecting it to creak, but it moved silently. She stepped inside, closing the door behind her. The damp interior felt chilly, and she shivered, looking round her. A worn blue carpet stretched along the aisle, and the original pews had been replaced with chairs. Nicholas hadn't arrived; she knew that, for if he had, his Peugeot would have been outside. Restless, she prowled around, peering at the memorial slabs set into the wall. There were several generations of one family, starting with Sir Alfred Rowan and his lady; their descendants and their siblings were remembered, some killed in various wars. How dreadful, but that wouldn't happen now, Imogen thought vaguely, and then she saw a small tablet recording the death of another Rowan, lost in the Gulf War. She blinked and looked away, wandering between the choir stalls to the altar, which was draped in a purple frontal. There were no flowers. It was Lent, but that did not register with Imogen, although she quite enjoyed the services in the school chapel which she was obliged to attend during term-time. She liked singing hymns and sitting quietly, with no one hassling her. Thinking of this, she slumped into a choir stall and gazed at a restored painting on the wall, a coat of arms, wondering what its symbols signified. She was still sitting there when the church door opened and Nicholas came in.

He did not see her at first as he looked around. His bright presence seemed to light up the whole building. Nicholas had dark golden wavy hair, worn slightly long to just below his ears; he had deep blue eyes and was over six feet tall. Imogen sat still for a few moments, watching him as he glanced around impatiently. He paid no heed to the memorial tablets that had caught her attention, walking halfway down the aisle and then stopping in frustration, gazing about him.

She moved then, and he saw her, and she ran towards him so that they met at the chancel where they hugged.

'Hmm – you smell nice,' she said, inhaling his aftershave.

She smelled faintly of Charlotte's Crabtree and Evelyn soap and the shampoo she had used that morning, a clean and unseductive smell.

They sat down together in the front row of chairs, and Imogen began to cry.

'What are we going to do?' she wailed.

'Same as everyone else. Get on with it,' said Nicholas robustly. 'Lots of people's parents split up and they survive.'

'You must mind. You disappeared,' Imogen said. She pulled a crumpled tissue from her pocket and feebly blew her nose.

'Ugh – that's disgusting. Haven't you got a clean one?' Nicholas asked her. Imogen was usually fastidious, which made her current predicament all the more disturbing.

She shook her head.

'I'll get some more at Charlotte's,' she said. 'She's got loads. Where have you been, Nick?'

'I holed up with a friend,' Nicholas replied. He'd been with Phoebe.

'But why? Why did you vanish?'

'I wanted to give them something to think about that wasn't you, silly,' he answered. 'What did they think I'd done?' he added, curious.

'Granny thought you'd gone abroad, like blokes ran away to sea in her young days,' said Imogen, and she giggled. 'She's got a thing about the sea – she's off on another cruise.'

'Got a thing about a sailor, more likely,' Nicholas said. 'Harking back to her navy days.' Their grandmother had been a cypher officer in the WRNS during the war. 'Did it work?'

'Did what work?'

'My diversionary tactics.'

'Not really. Dad's just furious with both of us,' she said.

'Well – can you wonder? What a pair we are,' he said, and they both began laughing.

Imogen was feeling better. When Nick was around, things were never quite as bad as she had thought at first.

'We haven't brought Mum back,' she said, speaking sadly. 'And Granny's fed up with Mum – her own daughter. She won't talk about it. Just says it's most regrettable and it's lucky we're not little children.' She mimicked their grandmother's clipped tones, making him laugh again. 'Wouldn't you think she'd want to stand by me?' she added. 'Mum, I mean.'

'Not really,' said her brother. 'She'd probably tell you what an idiot you'd been, not to take more care. Can you imagine Mum getting caught like that? What did she say, anyway?'

'Just what you've said,' Imogen told him, and burst into

tears once more. 'It was on the phone,' she said. 'It was horrible.'

Nicholas produced a spotless white linen handkerchief from his pocket. It was perfectly pressed and laundered. He gave it to her, and she mopped her face, then glared at him.

'You've got that slag doing your washing,' she accused. 'Phoebe. What a name.'

'It's a very nice name and she's not a slag, she's a good woman,' Nicholas declared. 'She knows I like things nice.'

Phoebe lived in Oxford; she was twenty-three and a single mother with two small children. Nicholas had met her some months ago when the wheel came off her pushchair in Tesco's. He hadn't been able to fix it on the spot, so he'd driven her and her children back to their flat, which turned out to be not far from where he shared a house with five other students. He'd managed to mend the pushchair, and a few evenings later, bored, he'd called round to see whether the repair had lasted. He'd stayed overnight. Phoebe had wanted him to move in, but he had enough wit to see where that might lead; she received occasional maintenance from the father of her children – they had not married – and she had support from social security, which could have been jeopardised if anyone suspected that she had a permanent lodger. Besides, he liked his freedom.

'I'll bet she's not the only one you're on with,' Imogen said, sulkily.

'You're wrong, but that's not what we're here to talk about,' said Nicholas. 'Who's got you into this pickle? I'll sort him out in no time.'

But she wouldn't tell him, nor would she tell him what she planned to do.

'You can't have meant it to happen,' he said, challenging her.

'Maybe I did,' she said.

They were still sitting there when the church door opened and the old man who had walked to it with Imogen entered. He removed his hat, closed the door, then came slowly down the aisle towards them.

Howard Smythe had heard the young man's car draw up outside the church, and had seen him walk rapidly up the path and enter the building. When, after an interval, no one reappeared, he decided to make sure all was well before he went home. Now he saw that the girl had been crying.

'Is everything all right?' he asked, looking from one of them to the other.

'He's my brother,' Imogen said.

'Oh – I see.' Could it be true? They were not the least bit alike.

Nicholas stood up and held out his hand.

'Nicholas Frost,' he said. 'Imogen and I are twins, but, as you see, dissimilar.'

'But close, no doubt,' said Captain Smythe. 'You don't live in Granbury, do you? Howard Smythe,' he added, shaking the young man's hand.

He hadn't seen either of them before today, and he had lived in Granbury for thirty years, since retiring there with Helen, who had died ten years ago. Even so, the pair could be residents, for the population had grown and its composition had altered profoundly. The girl, however, had not known where the church was; that must mean they were strangers.

'No, we don't, but Imogen is staying with our step-grandmother,' said Nicholas. 'I'm at Oxford,' he added, hoping Howard would imagine him to be a member of one of the older colleges.

'Who is your step-grandmother?' he asked. 'Perhaps I know her?'

But he didn't. They told him that she had been living in Granbury for only a few months, since soon after their grandfather's death, but they did not mention their own parents' troubles. Howard Smythe nodded.

'I'll get on home, then,' he said. 'Goodbye,' and he left them to it.

They drove past him as he reached his own gate. Nicholas tooted the horn, and Imogen waved. Howard hoped she had cheered up so that this Charlotte Frost, of whom he'd never heard, would not have to deal with tears.

'Don't let's go back to Charlotte's,' Imogen begged, as Nicholas paused at the High Street junction.

'You've got to, some time,' Nicholas said. 'Until something better turns up, that is.'

'Like what? Can't I come to your place?'

'And crash out in a sleeping bag on my floor?' he said. 'It's a house of blokes, Immy. You wouldn't go for it, not in your condition. Besides, they'd set the police on us, for all we know. Charlotte would. She's quite prim.'

'We could just take off.'

'That won't put things right,' he said. 'You've got to have a plan. Which way's her house? It's all right – I won't dump you there now.'

'You go to the left here,' said Imogen.

'We'll go the other way, then,' he said. 'Let's suss out Nettington.'

He pulled into the main road and set off to the market

town six miles away, accelerating as soon as he passed the decontrolled sign. The car was quite lively; he could get up a good speed. He'd bought it with money his grandfather had left him. Imogen's legacy was in a National Savings account. Driving along, he put on a tape, so that they could listen to music and not be forced to talk or think.

Nettington's main street had a number of shops interspersed with estate agents' and solicitors' offices; they went into a shoe shop and Imogen tried on some boots, but neither had enough money to pay for them. Imogen had not brought her purse, and Nicholas, who had his bank card, knew his balance was low. He'd need petrol, and they'd better get something to eat; he'd had no breakfast. They decided to go on to Becktham, where Imogen had arrived on the train the previous day; it might be larger, with perhaps a cinema where they could spend the afternoon.

In the outskirts, Nicholas saw a chip shop, and he stopped.

'Let's get some fish and chips,' he said. 'We can ask if there's a cinema or anything interesting to do. It seems a bit of a dump.'

'I didn't see much of it last night,' said Imogen. 'I don't know where the station is.'

'Well, we don't need it – we're not catching a train today,' Nicholas said. He pulled in to the kerb and parked behind a lorry outside the chip shop. 'You stay there and mind the car,' he instructed.

In the chip shop, a youth much his own age was behind the counter, and a middle-aged woman was tipping sliced potatoes into the frier. A burly man with a shaved head and an elderly woman in a long brown raincoat were ahead of Nicholas, and he waited patiently for his turn. The youth was efficient, packing up the orders and taking the money with a smile.

'Where are you off to now?' he asked the man.

'Manchester,' said the man. 'Want to come, Jerry?'

'I might do, one day,' Jerry answered. 'I might just take you at your word,' and he handed the man his bundle. 'Cheers.'

'Cheers,' said the man, and left the shop, climbing into the lorry.

Jerry was now serving the woman. She wanted a small portion of cod and chips.

'How's your mum?' she asked him.

'She's good,' said Jerry.

'Likes that job, does she?'

'Seems to. Sounds a bit dull to me. Making out accounts all day.'

'Has to be done,' said the woman who was frying the chips. She turned away from the frier to the counter. 'Can I help you?' she asked Nicholas.

When he came out of the shop, the lorry had gone and there was no other vehicle near them.

'Let's eat here,' he said. He had seen a litter-bin attached to a wall nearby. They could get rid of the rubbish after they'd eaten and then decide what to do. He didn't like mess in his car.

It occurred to neither of them that Imogen should telephone Charlotte to say she would not be back for a while, and, in Granbury, Charlotte, annoyed by Imogen's prolonged and silent absence, but not yet worried, and needing to cater for her guest, pinned a note on the door saying that she would be home in half an hour. It was an invitation to burglars, she knew, but Imogen had left without a key to the house, and if she returned before Charlotte, would not be able to get in.

Do her good to have to wait outside in the cold, Charlotte thought sourly. It wasn't raining, but it was distinctly raw and chilly. She would not be long; the village shops could provide enough for the next twenty-four hours, and tomorrow she would go into Nettington for a proper stock-up. Imogen might be persuaded to come too. On the other hand, if she continued to sulk, it might be better to leave her behind.

First things first. Wrapped up well in her dark green padded jacket, she set off into the High Street, turning right towards the general store which Imogen had passed earlier. Two women with pushchairs came towards her, not moving into single file to let her pass, but Charlotte had already stepped into the road, for she knew they had not seen her. A man with a border collie was not far behind them, and once again she moved off the path. He did not look at her. People avoided eye contact these days, even in Granbury. The shop sold newspapers – Charlotte's was delivered every day by a schoolboy – sweets, and basic groceries. Charlotte bought butter, Flora – for all she knew, Imogen eschewed butter, though she had used some in her nocturnal fry-up – eggs, a sliced loaf – the shop sold no other kind – and biscuits. She might make a cake. During her brief marriage to Rupert, he had enjoyed her baking, and a chocolate cake might sweeten Imogen. Invisibly, she moved past the shelves, stocking up her basket, and was surprised when a tall old man, who had entered the shop behind her, stood aside to let her pass. So she was not invisible to him.

'Thank you,' she said.

The old man had come to pay his paper bill.

'You shouldn't have bothered today, Captain Smythe, after what happened,' said Beatrice Evans, who ran the shop with her husband. 'It could have waited.'

'News travels fast, Mrs Evans,' Howard Smythe replied. 'As a matter of fact, I wanted to get out.' Calm though he thought he was after the incident, and used to far worse experiences during the war, among them having twice had his ship torpedoed, Howard Smythe felt restless, and he had been further disturbed by the distress of the young woman in the church. It was not being a good day and the walk had tired him.

'You were tied up and robbed, I heard,' she said. 'Surely you should be taking things quietly?'

'I wasn't robbed and I wasn't tied up,' Captain Smythe replied. 'The thief was caught before anything like that could happen.'

He paid and left the shop, pausing to lift his hat to Charlotte, who was now waiting near the counter.

Mrs Evans seldom looked at Charlotte when she bought things at the shop, merely focusing on the items, the money and the till, but today she did.

'Captain Smythe's house was broken into in the night,' she said. 'I'd heard he was hurt and all his war medals were taken.'

'How dreadful,' said Charlotte. 'But he said it wasn't like that,' she pointed out. Mrs Evans had sounded almost disappointed. 'Where does he live?' She had seen the old man before. There was a track across some fields to the river, and Charlotte sometimes walked down there. The tall old man had walked there a few weeks ago, and he had been in church on Christmas Day. Charlotte went to church only then, and for funerals and weddings.

'In Rose Cottage. That's in Meadow Lane,' said Mrs Evans. 'He's lived here for ever such a long time – before we came here.'

Charlotte had assumed that the Evanses were incomers, like herself and a good percentage of Granbury's residents. Mr Evans had a real Welsh lilt to his voice, and he took notice of her in the shop, but she bought very little there, going once a week to the supermarket in Nettington where there was so much choice and delicious bread. If it hadn't been for want of time, because Imogen might return, she would have gone there today, but it was wrong not to use the general store more; village shops deserved to be supported.

She resisted the temptation to question Mrs Evans about the robbery. Gossip should not be encouraged, and, in any case, Mrs Evans had not known the true story. Charlotte left the shop and went on up the road to the butcher, who also sold vegetables and fruit. Captain Smythe was just leaving as she arrived, emerging with a single chop. He nodded and lifted his hat, and Charlotte smiled. Then she plunged.

'I'm sorry to hear what happened,' she said. 'Mrs Evans told me, after you'd gone.'

'She exaggerates,' he said.

'Well, even so, it must have been—' Charlotte had been going to say terrifying, but that might seem extreme to an old man who no doubt had a distinguished war record. Mrs Evans had mentioned medals. 'Alarming,' she decided on.

'I was angry,' Captain Smythe told her. 'The wretched little youth has probably never done an honest day's work in his life. I didn't see why he should help himself to my possessions.'

'You caught him,' Charlotte realised. 'Well done!'

'Luckily I woke and heard him,' Howard said. To his surprise, although he had turned down the offer of a visit from Victim Support, it was quite a relief to talk about it.

'I threatened him with a golf club,' and he laughed, a croaky sound, as though he did not laugh a lot.

'Did you? Did you clobber him?' Charlotte asked.

'No. He surrendered fairly quickly,' said Howard Smythe. 'He didn't seem to be armed,' he added.

'Well, you didn't know that, did you?' she said. 'He might have had a knife.'

'True.'

'Which way do you go home?' An awkward thought had come to Charlotte: she remembered the young offender who had called at her door a few nights ago. Could he have been responsible for this? 'I wondered if you'd like a cup of coffee,' she went on. If he accepted, she could ask him to describe his burglar. Surely that nice young man hadn't been responsible for the break-in? 'I live just round the corner, in Vicarage Fields,' she added.

Captain Smythe thought it would be rather agreeable to be given a cup of coffee by this pleasant woman.

'Thank you. How kind,' he said.

'I've just got to buy a chicken and some vegetables,' she said. 'I won't be long.'

He waited for her, and they walked to Vicarage Fields together. There was no sign of Imogen. She unpinned the note from the door.

'My step-granddaughter is staying with me,' she explained. 'She went out today without a key. I left this message in case she returned before I did.'

Captain Smythe peered at her. There couldn't be two wandering step-granddaughters in Granbury today.

'Has she a twin brother?' he asked.

*   *   *

Charlotte made proper coffee in a pot. Once he was settled in a large armchair in her sitting-room, Captain Smythe had turned rather pale. He must be at least eighty, Charlotte thought, and however lightly he chose to regard it, he had had a shocking experience during the night and doubtless not much sleep afterwards. While he drank his first cup, he told her about meeting Imogen that morning, and of her brother's arrival at the church.

'I didn't know the young man was her brother,' he said. 'I felt I must ensure she was safe before I came away.' He did not mention the tears.

'I'm so glad you did,' Charlotte answered. 'And I'm relieved to know they're together, because however late she decides to return, or even if she doesn't, he'll look after her, now he's appeared on the scene. They're both rather upset,' she felt obliged to explain. 'Their parents have just separated.' There was no need to enlarge.

'I'm so sorry,' Captain Smythe replied. 'Such things are very sad.'

'Have you a family?' Charlotte asked.

Sitting there, facing her, Howard Smythe felt strangely soothed. In Granbury there had been several women whom he had known for years, who had known Helen, and whose dead husbands he had known, and they all had concern for him, left on his own. After her death they had invited him round to meals and popped in with cakes, flowers, and invitations at Christmas. But all were dead now, or had moved away to live near their families, or were so frail that it was he, though older than all of them, who made duty visits to them. Now he was in the company of a woman young enough to be his daughter and one who, unlike his own daughter, maintained a comfortable house and was neat in her ways. Howard's daughter was an academic; she taught economics at a university in the north of England and had six children whom she had neglected while she pursued her career. It hadn't seemed to harm them, though they were often unwashed, unfed, according to Helen, and frequently left to fend for themselves with the older ones minding the younger. All had turned out well, and all led conventional lives, two becoming teachers, one an engineer, one a chef, and the other two were accountants. All had found work overseas. 'To get away from their mother,' Helen had said, sad not to see her grandchildren. Their father, a history tutor, had been bludgeoned by his wife into entering politics, but had abandoned the struggle at fifty, worn out, struck down by a heart attack.

Howard delivered a brief sanitised account of all this to Charlotte. He explained that he had a computer, and communicated by e-mail with his grandchildren. If in England, they visited him, and he had stayed with a grandson in New Zealand and a granddaughter in Canada.

'And your daughter?' Charlotte asked.

'She comes sometimes.' When prodded by one of her children, or by her conscience, or if she wanted to pose as a caring child. 'My aim is to cause no trouble,' he declared.

'Mine, too,' said Charlotte, and filled him in briefly on her own background. 'About your burglary,' she said. 'You saw the thief? You said you captured him, in fact?'

'I certainly saw him,' said Howard. 'A miserable little runt of a fellow,' he added.

'Oh!' No one could have described Charlotte's caller in those terms. 'I was afraid it might have been a young offender who called selling dusters,' she explained. 'He was such an engaging lad. I was hoping he'd learned his lesson.'

'I know the lad you mean,' said Howard. 'He called on me, too.'

They worked out that they had probably both received visits on the same evening, about three weeks ago, with Howard's an hour after Charlotte's. So the youth had paid no heed to her advice not to call so late. Howard revealed that the police suspected his burglar had had an accomplice.

'The nice lad,' Charlotte said.

'I think my thief was alone,' Howard said. 'An accomplice would have come to his aid.'

'Not necessarily. He might have preferred to save his own skin,' said Charlotte.

As it was now one o'clock, she insisted on making some sandwiches. It was after three when he left, and even then, handing him his chop, which she had kept in the refrigerator during his visit, she was anxious, watching him walk away, tall, thin, and upright, one of the last of his kind.

4

Felix listened to Charlotte's clear voice on the telephone as she told him that Nicholas and Imogen had met in the village earlier that day, and they had gone off somewhere together. She expected them back at any time. This was a euphemistic description of her opinion, yet it was true; she had no idea when they would turn up, if ever, so to say 'any time' was fair enough.

Charlotte was always so controlled and courteous; she was totally unlike Felix's mother, who had been an amateur painter, thin and beautiful, and a brilliant hostess. She must have found his father dull; Felix knew she had had lovers, and this consoled him when he did the same, but just as his father had never known about them, he was confident that neither had Zoe learned about his. When she took off with Daniel, her latest, he could not believe that she was serious; none of his affairs, not even his current one, had, as he saw it, threatened the stability of their marriage. Surely she could have got over the fever in the blood and continued with a life in which she had her independence. His fury at the behaviour of his children was a reaction to his anger against her; Charlotte,

'The Wise One', as he and Zoe had referred to her behind her back, was, he suspected, aware of this. Charlotte had brought a new dimension into his father's life, and even knowing that the short time they had spent together had been happy, Felix continued to resent her, and he resented the financial drain on his father's estate. It was base to feel like this; he knew it. She could have claimed much more than the free tenancy of the modest house.

'You'll keep me up to date,' he said now. 'Make Imogen see sense,' and, having done his duty by telephoning, with the bonus of being spared a conversation with his daughter, he rang off before she could suggest that he should come and remove her. How had things come to this, he thought, despairingly: how could so much hope and trust end in bitterness and hatred?

What did he mean by sense? A termination? Charlotte did not know what would be the best decision; in any case, it was Imogen's to make, not hers, but she would point out the options, including having the baby adopted, a solution which rarely seemed to be considered nowadays. With more babies available for adoption, draconian fertility treatment, with its limited success rate, might, in many cases, be avoided. Charlotte fretted about children not knowing who their fathers were, or even their mothers, thinking of donor eggs. Such choices had not been available in her day. She had become pregnant with Tim soon after marriage, but there had been a gap of several years before Jane was born, with two miscarriages after that. It hadn't all been plain sailing.

After their sandwich lunch, she had left Captain Smythe in the sitting-room while she cleared away, and when she returned he was sound asleep, his mouth a little open, a gentle snore escaping now and then. She'd sat down with her book, and, sure that he would be embarrassed at dropping off in the presence of a stranger, as soon as she noticed that he was stirring, she had gone to make some tea, returning with a pot and cups and saucers on a tray.

'I believe I had a little nap,' he confessed.

'Did you? Well, I'm sure you needed it after the disturbed night you had,' she said. 'Milk and sugar?'

Departing, he had said, 'If you're worried about those twins, do telephone.'

He had discovered that she was scarcely on nodding terms with the neighbours on both sides; the couples were out at work all day, and some children she had noticed were young teenagers, all at school. Uprooted from her past, she had no friends.

Imogen and Nicholas sat in the car listening to tapes while they ate their fish and chips. Imogen savoured hers, finishing every last morsel.

'Course, you're eating for two, now, aren't you?' Nicholas said. 'What are you going to do about the brat? Have it?'

'Why not? I'd cope,' she said. 'Dad and Mum would have to help, if it was a fact in front of them.'

'And yelling its head off,' said Nicholas. 'Do you think Mum will go all cooey and granny-like?'

'Not really. She wasn't all that maternal,' said Imogen.

Nicholas had to agree.

'Only when we were sweet little things, being admired,' he said. 'It was really always Mum and Dad, exclusive.'

They remembered their parents, young and handsome, dashing out to parties, or the theatre.

'Dad wanted to move to White Lodge after Granddad died,' Nicholas said. 'He fancied being a country squire. That was why he was so keen for Charlotte to clear out straight away. I think he hoped Mum would like all the county bit. Being important. All that status stuff.'

'But we've got a lovely house already,' Imogen said. 'And she loves her job. It makes her independent.'

'She'd retire one day. Maybe Dad thought he'd persuade her to do charity stuff instead, like Granny and Charlotte.'

'They didn't do it in a fine lady sort of way,' said Imogen. 'Granny grew into it, you could say, over the years, and Charlotte just did her best to carry on, but low key, sort of.'

'You like Charlotte, don't you?' he asked.

'Mm. She's always been nice. She's being nice to me now, and I've been being a pain,' said Imogen.

'She knew Dad wanted her out of White Lodge. He was miffed at having to pay for her new house.'

'They sold White Lodge. They could have sold The Elms,' said Imogen.

'But they were splitting up. Maybe Dad thought moving would save their marriage, only it was too late. Mum had decided to bunk off.'

'What's Daniel got that Dad hasn't?' Imogen asked.

'Perhaps he's better in bed,' said Nicholas.

Imogen ignored this.

'Dad's got more money,' she said.

'Maybe, but the business hasn't been going so well,' said Nicholas. 'Some merger hasn't been a success. And he's going to have to give Mum a mega settlement. He used some of the money from White Lodge to pay off the mortgage on The

Elms. He told me that. He's going to need the money from Charlotte's house before he's through.'

'But Mum dumped him.'

'That's how it works,' said Nicholas.

'It's not fair.'

'What is? It's not fair that you're in this mess,' said Nicholas. 'But anyway, Dad was screwing around first, so you can't blame Mum.'

'Was he?' Imogen sounded shocked.

'He's been having it off with Amanda for years,' said Nicholas. Amanda was Felix's personal assistant. 'Anyway, what about you?'

'I don't want to talk about it,' said Imogen.

'Well – you'll have to some time, but you needn't now,' said Nicholas. He began gathering up the paper trays and the wrapping from their meal. 'I'll chuck these,' he said. 'Then we'll get moving.'

He walked the short distance down the road to the bin, and had just thrown away their rubbish when the young man from the chip shop emerged on to the pavement.

Nicholas gave him a friendly grin and said, 'Hi.'

'Hi,' said Jerry, recognising him. 'You still here, then? Too late for more chips – we're closed till five o'clock.'

'No – we're just leaving,' said Nicholas. 'We ate them in the car. What's there to do in this place, anyway?'

'Not a lot,' said Jerry. 'I'm going home to my mum's. Might watch a video. She's at work. You can come if you like,' he offered. 'That your bird?' he added, glancing at Imogen, who was watching them.

'My sister,' said Nicholas, startled by this sudden invitation.

'Oh, right. Well, do you want to?'

'Why not? Yes, thanks. We're visiting our step-grandmother and it's best if we don't go home just yet. Is it far?'

'No,' said Jerry. 'Less than a mile. Shall I get in the back? I walked here.'

'Help yourself.'

Nicholas tipped the driver's seat forward and Jerry climbed in.

'Hi,' he said to Imogen, and put on the smile that had charmed Charlotte and a great many more people of all ages. It was working already on this pair.

'Hi,' said Imogen, smiling back.

Nicholas was relieved at having a plan for the afternoon, one which would enable him to postpone returning Imogen to Charlotte; and Jerry, who had not been with Pete the previous night but who had heard of his arrest, was happy to have company to take his mind off what his friend had done.

Pete had come into the chip shop just before it closed yesterday. He'd bought some chips, then said he was going out that night. He wanted Jerry to come along when he finished his evening shift. Jerry had given up the door-to-door selling, breaking up their partnership. He said he'd met a householder who had smiled at him, and it had made him feel bad about conning her. Besides, now he'd got the chip shop job, he wanted to keep out of trouble. One term in prison was enough for him; his mother had been ashamed of him and he intended to make it up to her. Pete had said he had gone soft. He'd marked down several targets in Granbury, houses where entry looked easy, and he meant to try them. He needed wheels; Jerry's mother had a car and he could borrow it, if he talked her up enough.

But Jerry wouldn't do it. Pete waited for him to finish work and walked home with him, trying to make him change his mind, but Jerry was firm. He'd passed his test before he went to prison, but his mother's car was insured so that only she could drive it; she'd said if he kept out of trouble for three months, she might consider getting cover for him and letting him use it so that he could get practice. Then he might get a driving job.

At the chip shop they knew about his record but were giving him a chance. If no one would employ him, how could he reform, they reasoned. Jerry didn't mind the work; he was getting to know the regular customers and he enjoyed chatting to them, but between shifts, it was boring. He had been arrested after going on a spree to London with some friends; they'd been round several stores and got away with some good stuff, in Jerry's case a wool jacket, worn under his big anorak, a Walkman, trainers. Then, on the tube, Jerry, euphoric with success, had lifted a purse from a woman's unzipped shoulder-bag.

Not an experienced pickpocket, he'd been seen by an off-duty police officer who was on the train. Jerry, wearing the concealed wool jacket and without a receipt, with the other items in his pockets, and the purse, was desperate to escape. He had punched the policeman and broken his nose, but the arrest was made with the help of another passenger who had been called as a witness to Jerry's violence. There were no mitigating circumstances, and Jerry received a two-year sentence, getting out after a year because of his good behaviour. Pete, whom he knew from school, was also in the young offenders' centre, serving a sentence for robbery.

Last night, Jerry's mother's car had been stolen. As usual, she'd parked it in the road outside their small semi-detached house. His mother worked at several jobs; her main one was with a lighting equipment firm which had just moved from Becktham to Denfield, two stops up the line by rail, and this week the firm was doing short days because building work in the new premises was not complete; she also put in three nights a week as barmaid at a pub close to where they lived, and on Fridays she did night duty at an old people's residential home. When she found her car had gone, she was hysterical. She ran to the station, telling Jerry to report it; she'd miss her train today, for sure.

He hadn't reported it. He'd known who'd taken it. The spare key, kept on a hook in the kitchen, had gone. Pete had helped himself the day before and when Jerry went round to his house to demand the return of the car, he learned on the way there that Pete had been arrested in Granbury. If Pete hadn't got himself nicked, he'd have brought the car back and no one would have been any the wiser. And if Jerry had gone with him, he might not have been caught and the car would have been there this morning. Because of that, it could be Jerry's fault that the car was missing. It was probably parked in Granbury. He'd go and look for it when the chip shop closed after his evening shift; he'd get there somehow, hitch a lift, even walk.

If he could persuade them to stay long enough, his new friends might save his mum a taxi fare by giving her a lift to the residential home tonight. She'd be impressed because they were a classy pair – students, probably – and she'd be glad he'd got such respectable friends. He led them into his house, quickly shoving some magazines under a cushion in the living-room, which wasn't too untidy considering his mum had rushed off in such a state this morning.

Hospitably, he offered them drinks – there was a can of lager in the old, slightly rusty fridge in the kitchen, and some orange juice. Nicholas asked for orange juice but Imogen said she'd like the lager, if Jerry – he had told them his name – didn't want it. Nicholas frowned at her.

'Should you be drinking?' he asked her.

'Should I be living, you mean,' Imogen growled. 'One lager's not going to hurt it, surely.'

Jerry caught on quickly.

'You expecting? That's nice,' he said.

'You're the first person who's said that,' said Imogen.

'Kids are all right,' said Jerry. 'Specially little kids, before they start turning into monsters. How about we split the lager? It might cheer you up.' He found a glass and poured her half the tin, poured Nicholas some juice from the cardboard carton into another, and prepared to drink the rest of the lager from the tin. Then he gestured to his guests to sit down on the large, comfortable sofa, and turned on the television. There was a gardening programme on one channel and horse-racing on another. Jerry found a *Star Wars* video and put it on, then sank into an armchair with his drink. Easy together, spared the need to talk, they were content. Nicholas and Jerry concentrated on the film, while Imogen glanced curiously around. The three-piece suite looked almost new but the room was shabby, needing doing up; however, that wasn't what was odd about it. She realised that she couldn't see a single book, nor a photograph; there were several china ornaments on the mantelpiece, and some flower prints on the walls, which were a dirty, washed-out blue. A rubber plant stood in a pot in a corner, and there was a pot of yellow chrysanthemums on the windowsill. Although dingy and characterless, it was a cosy room. She returned her attention to the film, but soon their peace was broken by the telephone. It was Jerry's mother, ringing from her office to find out if her car had been recovered.

Nicholas and Imogen heard his side of the conversation.

'No, Mum. Nothing yet,' he said. 'You'll have to take a taxi tonight, and get one back. I know, but tomorrow's Saturday. Something may turn up,' he encouraged her. 'Cheers. See you,' and he replaced the handset. Then, turning to the others, he told them that his mother's car had been stolen during the night.

'She's at work,' he said. 'In Denfield. When she gets back, she'll be off in an hour to do night duty at an old people's home. It's ten miles away. There isn't a bus. She'll have to get a taxi.'

He had turned the sound down on the television while he was on the telephone; *Star Wars* was continuing to unfold in silence.

'How did she get to work today, if she couldn't drive?' asked Nicholas.

'She goes by train. There's not much parking at the other end, and her office is right by the station. She's been doing short hours this week as they're not properly open yet at this new place. She's not fixed up with a season ticket in case she decides to drive but she's nervous about the rush hour. She's a very nervous person,' he said.

'That's awful about her car,' said Imogen. 'I suppose a taxi would be quite expensive. We could give her a lift, Nick, and then go and face Charlotte.'

'That your gran?'

'Yes.'

'Mine died,' said Jerry.

'So did ours,' said Imogen. 'Charlotte married our grand-father after that. Now he's dead, too.'

'Don't you like this new gran of yours?' asked Jerry.

'She's all right,' said Imogen. 'But where she lives is a dump. There's nothing to do, and I'm stuck there for ever.'

'You're not. I'll rescue you somehow,' said Nicholas.

'Where is this place?' asked Jerry.

'Granbury. Do you know it?' said Nicholas.

'Granbury?' Jerry could hardly believe it. 'You mean she lives in Granbury?'

'Yes. She's been there since just before Christmas,' said Imogen.

She had felt it was wrong that Charlotte had had to move so soon, but her father had said it was her own wish. If she'd stayed at White Lodge for Christmas, which she could have done as the new people – it had sold instantly – didn't move in until the middle of January, they could all have spent it with her, had a real family time as they'd done before, and maybe Dad and Mum would have made up and stayed together.

'Could you take me there now?' Jerry demanded.

'What? To Granbury?' Nicholas was startled.

'Yes. You've got to go there anyway, haven't you, back to your gran?'

'Yes, but what about your mother?'

'I've had an idea about her car,' said Jerry. 'If I'm right, she won't need a lift and I'll be able to get back for opening time at the chip shop.'

'You mean you might know who'd taken it? Someone from Granbury?' asked Nicholas.

'Someone with no wheels who wanted to visit a friend in Granbury,' said Jerry.

Brother and sister exchanged glances.

'It's a friend of yours, isn't it?' said Nicholas.

'Maybe,' said Jerry, poker-faced.

'It'd be good if you're right,' said Imogen. 'I mean, not about your friend taking the car, but if you could get it back.'

'Let's find out, then,' said Nicholas. 'If the car's not there, we can bring you back and decide what to do about your mother.'

It was a long shot that if Pete had taken the car and left it somewhere in Granbury, it was still there, but if the police had found it abandoned, Jerry guessed they'd have traced the owner by this time and come knocking at his mother's door. If that happened, they might even connect him with the burglary. He and Pete had borrowed his mother's car more than once, unknown to her, when she was working in the bar at The Bugle, which was just a short walk from the house; she never took the car there. It meant she could have a few drinks during the evening, which she needed to keep her going.

'Right,' said Jerry. 'Let's go.'

They put on their jackets – the boys had flung theirs down on the floor in a corner of the room but Imogen's was neatly draped over the banisters in the hall – and piled out into Nicholas's car. Setting off down the road, they began to sing along with the tape he put on, Imogen joining in, briefly happy, but as they approached Granbury, Jerry fell silent and began to look about him.

'Where does this guy live?' asked Nicholas.

'I'm not sure,' Jerry prevaricated. They had called at so many houses in Granbury and neighbouring villages, sometimes finding people out, sometimes with Jerry gaining entry doing his patter and Pete often successful in getting in at the back and grabbing loot. 'It may be near the church,' he tried. That was a quiet area, and there were several houses in the narrow lanes which were surrounded by shrubs and bushes offering concealment to the approaching thief. Pete had thought it promising territory. It was where the tall old man lived who'd advised Jerry to get a job.

'Well, let's start down there,' said Nicholas. 'What sort of car is it?'

'It's a Metro. Red,' said Jerry, peering out.

But he saw it before they reached the church. It was among other cars in a small parking area outside the butcher's. Pete must have left it centrally so that he could leg it back from several possible targets. He shivered, unnoticed by the pair in the front.

Imogen had also seen it.

'There's a red Metro,' she called out.

Nicholas jammed on his brakes, almost causing a following car to crash into him.

'Sorry, sorry,' he said, moving on. 'I'll stop in a tick.' He went up the road, turned and came back, indicating as he turned into the small bay outside the butcher's. 'Is it the right car?'

It was.

'Have you got the key?'

Jerry hadn't, for Pete had the spare and his mother had the other, on a ring with her doorkey.

'Yes,' he said quickly. Once, in Nettington, they'd been in a hurry to get away, after a householder had given chase; Pete had reached the car first and had to wait while Jerry, with the key, had caught up with him. After that, they'd left it tucked into the exhaust pipe for the first one back to seize. Would Pete have done that last night? Though he was alone, he might not have kept it on him in case he was caught and linked with car theft. If the key wasn't there, Jerry would have to hot-wire it. 'Just drop me,' he said. 'And thanks a lot.' He hopped out of the car and went round the back of it, stooping down and fumbling. The key was in the pipe. 'Just checking,' he called out, and gave a thumbs-up sign to Nicholas and Imogen as he unlocked the Metro. What luck that no one else had nicked the car after Pete's escapade, but it was probably pretty late when he left it. Jerry's heart was high as he drove away. He wasn't covered by insurance, but he had a valid licence. He must concentrate on getting back to Becktham safely.

Nicholas and Imogen waved as he left. The butcher, who had noticed the car outside, was busy serving someone and never saw it go.

5

'You'll come in with me, won't you, Nick?'

Nicholas had no desire to face Charlotte, but he couldn't leave his twin to meet her possible wrath unsupported.

'You can rely on me,' he said bracingly, parking outside Charlotte's house, which he had never seen before. 'I'll take the blame for whisking you away.'

Belatedly, it had dawned on the pair that Imogen's unexplained absence for the entire day might have caused Charlotte some inconvenience, even worried her, but Nicholas had always managed to deflect trouble by the use of charm; he was confident it would work now, and anyway, if Charlotte had been worried, she would be too relieved at Imogen's return to be angry.

He was, to some extent, correct in this assumption. She was in her sitting-room trying to do the crossword in the paper when she heard the car arrive. Concentration had been difficult for months, ever since Rupert's death, but she had been through bereavement before and knew it was a reaction which, in time, would ease. As well as grief, however, she felt that she had lost her identity. The last few years had brought so many changes:

unexpected happiness, but the need for swift adjustment to fit in with Rupert's ways had involved the suppression of her own. Then, abruptly, he was gone and she was transplanted to a place where she had no roots or associations, and no friends. If, when she married, she had let her own house instead of selling it, she could have returned there and resumed her previous existence, but at the time it had made sense to sell, pay off her outstanding mortgage and have the rest to draw upon, so that she was not wholly dependent on Rupert; however the same result could have been achieved by letting. It was easy to be wise afterwards; she had an income from the pension Rupert's arrangements had included, and, with no rent to pay, there were financial advantages in her present situation. It couldn't continue, though, for it meant she had obligations to his family and they would call on her, as now with Imogen, to help them out. She ought to want to help them, she supposed, and as Rupert's widow it was, to some extent, her duty, but not to be manipulated and made to feel beholden. Once this business with Imogen was over, she must structure her life more effectively, take up a hobby, join an educational class, improve her garden, but most important, she must insist on paying a fair rent. Also, she could try to make a friend of Captain Smythe. He was so old that he would not misconstrue her motives, and he might be lonely. She would like to hear about his life, his war experiences; old men like him had endured all sorts of rigours, survived perils undreamt of by a modern generation. They were the sort of men who should be role models for the young, not pop stars and footballers.

She had been half-listening for Imogen's return, or for the telephone to ring. Now, with the twins approaching up the path, she refrained from rushing to the door to let them in.

She must conceal anger and anxiety, though she was feeling both. She was standing in the hall behind the door by the time the bell rang, but she did not open it at once. When she did, Nicholas was smiling warmly – ingratiatingly, was how she later thought of it – while Imogen looked defiant.

'Ah, there you are,' she said calmly. 'Nicholas, how nice to see you. Come along in.'

There was no scolding, no recriminations. She held the door wide and, like recalcitrant ten-year-olds, they trooped across the threshold.

Imogen had been ready to withstand reproofs; now she did not know how to react, but Nicholas slid into his performance. He bent to kiss Charlotte on both cheeks.

'I hope you weren't worried when Imogen was out for so long,' he said. 'But she was with me all the time.'

'I wasn't to know that, though, was I, Nicholas?' she said sharply. The fact that she did, thanks to Captain Smythe, need not be disclosed, or not yet. 'It would have been thoughtful to have telephoned. You had the number, after all. I had no idea if you would be in for lunch, Imogen,' she said. 'Are you staying to supper, Nicholas?'

His sister sent him an imploring look; she did not want to be left alone with Charlotte, facing a possible dressing-down or at least an inquisition.

'Yes, please,' he said, without enthusiasm. 'If there's enough.'

There would be; Charlotte was an excellent cook and provider; but he didn't need a ticking-off for irresponsibility, nor did he wish to take part in a discussion about Imogen's situation, which he feared would be inevitable.

But he underestimated Charlotte.

'You'll want a wash,' she told them both. 'I've made a chicken casserole and we can eat at any time. And you're welcome to stay the night, Nicholas, if you'd like to.'

'Thanks, but I must get back,' he said, though he was almost tempted. Charlotte had a way of making you feel welcome, warm and soothed, even in this boring house, not much bigger than Jerry's, where they had spent the afternoon, though in better shape and furnished with more taste.

Charlotte's casserole was ready and was keeping hot in a low oven. She had only to cook some rice and the frozen peas. The brother and sister went meekly upstairs to freshen up; they took their time, consulting together, or plotting, Charlotte supposed. When they reappeared, she offered them elderflower cordial or fruit juice; Nicholas was driving, and Imogen was pregnant, so, as she reminded them, rather meanly she thought, they could not share the bottle of wine she had opened.

They both drank orange juice and asked if they could dilute it with tonic water to give it zip.

'I met an interesting man today,' she said, making conversation during the meal, and described her encounter with Captain Smythe. 'I think you met him, too, Imogen, on your way to the church.'

'Yes – yes, I did.' Imogen addressed her plate.

'I don't suppose he told you his house was burgled during the night,' said Charlotte. 'Nothing was taken, because he heard the burglar and caught him.'

Now she had caught the attention of her audience.

'He did say something about it,' mumbled Imogen. 'He said his wife was in the churchyard. He seemed pretty old,' she added.

'He was lucky the burglar didn't beat him up,' said Nicholas.

'Yes, he was, but he's very tall and he said the burglar was quite small,' said Charlotte. 'Besides, Captain Smythe is a brave man, and the burglar was a coward. The police told Captain Smythe that there have been a series of burglaries around the district recently with people calling at doors, selling things, while their accomplices go round the back and, if they can get in quickly, take anything they can find while the householder has been occupied at the door.' They preyed upon the old and solitary, it seemed, which implied that they were watching target houses. She decided not to tell them that both she and Captain Smythe had had a young offender calling after dark. Captain Smythe had also had a well-dressed woman purporting to be from the county council at his door, but he had insisted on telephoning her office to confirm that she was genuine, and when he asked for her identification, she had made an excuse and gone away. At the time, he had reported this to the police, and they had taken details over the telephone, but he had heard no more.

'They caught this guy? The one who broke into the old man's house?' Nicholas wanted to be sure. 'They didn't let him out on bail?' A very uncomfortable thought had struck him as he remembered Jerry's accurate deduction about where his mother's stolen car might be. But Jerry couldn't have been the burglar; Charlotte had said he was small. Could he have been some mate of Jerry's, though? Had Jerry even lent him the car without his mother's knowledge? It was possible.

'No, he hasn't been released. Or not yet, anyway,' Charlotte answered. 'At least, I don't think so. I suppose he could be out by now, if he was in the magistrate's court today. But he might have been remanded in custody.' Rupert had been a magistrate, so she knew something about how such things worked; strictly speaking, the thief hadn't been violent, so he might get bail.

'Better be careful, Charlotte. Don't let anyone in who you don't know,' Nicholas warned.

'I won't,' she promised.

He left when the meal was over. Imogen walked out to the car with him, but he did not mention his theory about Jerry's mother's car to her. She had enough to worry about, and it wasn't as if Jerry lived in Granbury.

Imogen, after he had gone, was trying not to cry as she went to help Charlotte with the washing-up. Poor girl, thought Charlotte. She needs her mother, not me. She'd gladly hug her and try to comfort her, but Imogen had constructed a barricade of invisible prickly barbed wire around herself. How could Charlotte break through it? She must try.

'Nicholas looks well,' she said, as she put the glasses away.

'He's all right,' said Imogen.

'I know you're both very upset about your parents,' said Charlotte, deciding that Imogen would probably dash up to bed if she didn't tackle her now. She might run off anyway. 'It happens, though,' she went on. 'People do separate and it's always sad, but it's sad for the couple, too. They don't make such decisions lightly.'

'Mum met this guy. She took off. It's as simple as that,' said Imogen. 'She can't care about me at all.' Her voice became a wail.

Charlotte had her chance. She put an arm round Imogen's shoulder and tried to draw her close, but Imogen resisted. Tears began to flow, however, which had to be a good sign.

'She didn't know you were pregnant when she left,' said Charlotte. 'You hadn't told her, had you?' Perhaps Imogen herself hadn't known then.

'She knows now, and she hasn't come back,' sobbed Imogen.

'But she will, in time,' said Charlotte. 'If you have the baby, then she'll come when it's born, I'm sure.' But would she? Zoe, in the grip of either a steamy sexual passion or a burst of romantic love, even both, might be as insane and selfish as many lovers were.

'And if I don't have it, will she come then?' demanded Imogen.

'I don't know, Imogen. How can I tell?'

'None of this would have happened if Granddad hadn't died,' wailed Imogen, still sobbing. She took a tissue from the box on the worktop and blew her nose.

'You don't know that,' said Charlotte gently. 'He wasn't Zoe's father, after all. He couldn't have prevented her.'

'Everything went wrong after that, though,' said Imogen. 'Dad got cross and he wanted you to leave White Lodge, and then you did, and it was cruel to you, and then Mum was always angry and so was he. It was horrid.'

'Let's go and sit down,' said Charlotte, leading Imogen out of the kitchen and across the hall to the sitting-room; she seized the box of tissues as they went. 'Now,' she said, guiding Imogen to the sofa and gently pushing her down so that she folded up in the place where Captain Smythe had had his nap. 'When someone you love dies, it's always very sad, and they leave a big gap in your life. But your grandfather wasn't young, and he died very suddenly. He didn't suffer. That's a comfort.' She was touched at the sympathy for her which Imogen, in her outburst, had revealed. 'Your grandfather was very fond of you,' she went on. 'He was proud of you. You're a clever girl.' Imogen had gained ten GCSEs, all As except for a B for history, at the girls' day school she had attended, but then, in a move Rupert had not approved of, Zoe had a whim to send her to a boys' public school which took girls for A levels. It would develop her, Zoe had said, broaden her horizons. It seemed that she had been only too right about that. If the boy's identity was known – for surely the baby's father must also be at the school – he would be expelled, and Imogen's permanent departure must be assumed, one way or another. For all Charlotte knew, though she had run away from the place, she might already have been expelled.

It was no good scolding her. They were all supposed to know so much about safe sex, the morning-after pill, and the mechanics of the act, but was love mentioned in the talks they heard, or, more important, lust? What about loneliness and the need for human contact, an embrace, some sympathy? A few steps along such paths and basic physical desire could banish any shreds of self-control, just as alcohol could overcome inhibition. The inexperienced were not aware of this.

'It's possible that your mother and father haven't been getting along for quite a while,' she suggested. Lorna had declared that their separation was an accident waiting to happen, with Felix using money to stave off a final break.

'They haven't,' Imogen admitted. 'They had some awful fights. It scared me.'

'I expect it did,' said Charlotte. 'They may be happier apart. Zoe will be coming back after this job she's doing ends.'

'She won't. She's going to leave the magazine. Daniel – that's her bloke – is transferring to some outfit over there and she'll either do the same or find another job in California,' said Imogen.

It was the longest speech she had uttered since they met the day before, and surely that was progress, but Lorna had not seemed to know these details, so how had Imogen learned them? Or were they guesses? It didn't matter now; that could be discovered later.

'I see,' she said. 'Well, you'll be able to visit them in America. That would be rather fun.' But would the baby be a welcome guest? Zoe couldn't have expected to become a grandmother quite so early in her life.

Imogen didn't answer this.

'You're going to have to see a doctor fairly soon, Imogen. You know that, don't you? There's a very nice woman doctor in the practice here. What you discuss is entirely confidential. You can talk things through with her – and with me, too, if it will help.'

'You mean, get rid of it,' said Imogen bluntly. 'That's what everyone will want. Then go on as if nothing's happened.'

'It wouldn't be as easy as that, but after a while it would fade,' said Charlotte. 'It's not your only choice. You could have it adopted, or you could keep it. But you can't put off a decision for very long. I suggest I make an appointment for you with the doctor for Monday or Tuesday. Will you keep it, if I do?'

Imogen had still not looked Charlotte squarely in the eye. Now, gazing at her own jean-clad knees, she grunted an agreement.

That was something accomplished, Charlotte thought. It was enough for now. There was a wildlife programme on the television, and she proposed that they should watch it. After it was over, Imogen went up to bed.

'Goodnight, Charlotte. Thanks,' she managed, as she left the room.

In Becktham, Jerry's mother, Angela Hunt, had returned from Denfield to find her car in its usual place outside her house.

She walked all round it and could see no sign of damage. Almost dizzy with relief, she fumbled in her handbag for her keys, found them, and got in. Her memory of the mileage on the clock was vague, but as far as she could recall, it hadn't altered all that much. She turned on the ignition and saw the petrol gauge rise to show almost full; the day before it had been nearly empty. The thief, or the police, must have put some in the tank. Thoroughly cheered, she locked the car again and went into the house, throwing her bulky shoulder-bag down on the sofa and going through to the kitchen to put the kettle on.

That morning, seeing from her window that the car was missing, she'd left without breakfast or even a cup of tea, running up the road to try to catch her train. Luckily for her, it was ten minutes late, a legitimate excuse the other end, but next week, when the office would be running normally, she would have to catch the ten past eight. Because her office was so central, and taking into account the rush hour – particularly bad, she knew, in school terms – the train was quicker, but she hadn't yet compared the costs. If she were to go by car, there would be the problem of finding somewhere to park in Denfield, and she might not find a residential street with unrestricted parking space close enough to the office. Leaving it in a pay area would be too expensive. She'd have to do some calculations, and she should walk to Becktham station; parking there was adding to her outgoings. One of her problems was that she never worked things out enough in advance, muddling through, finding out her misjudgements after the event. She'd discussed some of this with Heather, the stock controller at the office, whose own routine had been helped by the move, for she lived in Denfield and now caught a bus to the office. Angela could park at her house and do the same, she had suggested. It was worth investigating, Angela decided, putting a tea bag in a mug and adding boiling water.

Because there were no breakfast things waiting to be washed, she noticed the glass, rinsed and upended on the drainer, where Imogen had left it, but gave no thought to it, though she frowned when, on the coffee table in the sitting-room, she saw an empty lager tin and a second glass, which, on inspection, had held orange juice. Maybe Jerry had given the police drinks when they brought the car back.

She changed quickly into the black trousers and tank top she wore at The Gables and stuffed her blue overall into her large bag. She was thankful that Jerry was holding down the chip shop job, and because he was there in the evenings, had given up the door-to-door selling he'd been doing with that other lad, Pete Dixon. Angela knew it was supposed to be authentic employment for those trying to go straight, but she wanted him to drop his old associates for fear of being tempted to further wrong-doing. It had been so dreadful when he was arrested, and worse when he was sentenced; it was a sentence for her, too – a single mother who had failed, a stereotype who'd fitted the pattern spelled out to her when, pregnant at the age of seventeen, she'd elected to keep the baby.

It had been very hard. She'd intended, when Jerry was old enough, to study – get a degree and a high-powered career – but all she'd managed was a business course, and her computer skills were limited. With her different jobs, she paid the rent, fed them, and ran the car, and now Jerry was contributing a little.

'You need a love life. Someone rich,' Heather had told her.

'Chance would be a fine thing,' Angela had replied.

'Maybe one of the old dears at The Gables will leave you a fortune,' Heather had suggested optimistically.

'I wish,' said Angela, laughing.

Over the years there'd been a few men – none rich, but some she'd been really fond of, and apart from the sex, which had varied as a pleasure, the closeness, someone to cuddle up to, had been such a comfort. She'd been very careful not to fall pregnant again, and that had upset Mike, who'd been around for three years, though not all the time, and who was wonderful with Jerry. He'd wanted to have a child with her.

'And then you'd go off and leave me with it,' she had said.

None of them would commit, not even Mike. Soon after that discussion they had broken up. He'd found someone else and married her, and that really hurt.

She'd gone to singles clubs and had a few one-night stands while Jerry was in prison, but she hadn't brought anyone home for a long time. Now it was just her and Jerry, and she had to keep him straight. He'd got the job at the chip shop because she knew Val and Bobby Redmond, who owned it. They were customers at The Bugle on Sunday nights when the chip shop wasn't open. They knew about his record, but they'd lost a son of their own in a road accident when he was twelve; he would have been nineteen now, like Jerry, and they wanted to give another lad an opportunity.

'Just one chance,' they had warned.

It had been enough for Angela to weave a fantasy about Jerry doing so well that Val and Bobby opened another shop and made him manager.

Why not? If you didn't keep on hoping, you might as well give up.

She drove past the chip shop on her way to The Gables but she didn't stop. For one thing, she hadn't time, and for another, she didn't want Jerry, or his employers, to think that she was checking up on him.

She'd left a note on his bed.

'Great about the car. Well done, the fuzz,' she'd written.

It never crossed her mind to wonder how the thief had stolen it without breaking the lock.

6

Charlotte had had a troubled dream, in which she was running across a field chasing Imogen, who was carrying a bundle and heading for the river. It was a relief to discover that it was a nightmare, and infanticide was not on today's programme. It was still early, but she had been waking at five or half-past ever since Rupert died. During the dark winter days she had usually gone downstairs and made a cup of tea, taking it back to bed and sometimes dozing off, listening to the World Service on the radio or trying to read. Often she would think back over the last few years and months, wondering how so much could have happened in so short a time, when before she married Rupert her life had been comparatively uneventful. She had been a widow for twenty-six years. After David died, she had returned to teaching – her career when they met and during the first part of their marriage. David was a research scientist, working for a pharmaceutical firm. She had returned, part-time, to her profession when Tom and Jane were both at grammar school, and had settled to longer hours when David's short but harrowing illness had struck. She had compassionate leave during those dreadful months; afterwards, she went back to teaching, quietly, as was her way, making no fuss. She took early retirement when it was forcibly suggested to her because younger, less experienced teachers could be employed more cheaply. Implicit was the fact, also, that her successful methods of teaching children to read were out of date. The fact that all the children in her care could read by the age of seven, often earlier, was not thought relevant.

Disenchanted, she had found the position with the charity and this had led to her brief second marriage. It wasn't like her first; she hadn't expected that it would be; there were no fireworks and no excitement, but she had loved Rupert warmly, and he was reliably there, unlike David, who had so often worked long hours, and, as his career progressed, had had to attend conferences in places as remote as New Zealand and Panama. They'd talked of how she would go with him when the children were old enough to be left. That day had never come. Now, it seemed as though all this had happened to another person.

Who am I? Where do I belong, thought Charlotte, and, unable to find a consoling answer, got out of bed.

She'd have to shop properly today. Unless Imogen refused point blank, she'd take her into Nettington, round Waitrose, where she might reveal what food she'd favour for the next part of her visit. And Charlotte decided to ring Felix up; she would invite him to lunch tomorrow.

When Angela returned from The Gables, she always went straight to bed. Jerry was usually still asleep. Even before he started at the chip shop, he seldom rose before eleven, and now, most days, he got up just in time for work. There was nothing to get up for, he reasoned, unless there was work to be done in the garden; he enjoyed that. He could listen to the radio or his Walkman in bed, and sometimes he would read – Tom Clancy, Stephen King – exciting books. He lived from day to day, rarely looking further ahead; what was the point?

He'd met up again with some former school friends. A few of them thought it cool that he'd been inside, but Jerry didn't want to repeat the experience, and he told them so. When he was out with Pete, he couldn't go drinking with them in the evenings, and now he'd got the job, he wasn't free until the chip shop shut and sometimes, then, he went to visit Tracy. Two lads he knew played football at weekends, and Jerry had briefly thought he might take it up. He'd played a lot in the young offenders' unit; he'd enjoyed it, but back at home, it was easy to slip into idleness.

This Saturday, waking late, he thought about the brother and sister he'd met the day before. Twins, though you'd never think it. Fancy the girl expecting! She didn't seem too thrilled about it, but maybe she was having a hard time from her family, and the grandmother. The brother was all right – lucky guy, with that car, able to get around. Jerry reflected that it would be years before he'd be able to have one. He liked cars; he'd quite like to be a mechanic and it would be useful to be able to fix cars that broke down, like his mum's did sometimes. He mused about it, wondering how you found a job like that, without any training. Then he began thinking about Pete. Would he have been bailed?

He might go and find out, ask his mum. There'd be time before work. Pete was a mate; it'd been bad luck that he'd got caught, and even with a good brief he'd go down because there was no doubt about his guilt. Jerry, though reformed, gave no thought to the victims of Pete's thefts. However, with a mission planned, he rose. He went off to shower, although, as usual, he'd showered when he came home from work last night. In spite of wearing a starched white cap and overall, he always felt he smelled of fat and fish. He'd grown accustomed to prison smells while he was inside, and to the noise, but already, three months after his release, he'd got used to fresh air, being able to shower when he liked, and to his privacy, although sometimes that palled. He'd liked the company, yesterday, when those two came back with him. He should have asked them where their gran lived, then they could have met up again. Never having had a grandmother himself, Jerry like the idea of someone else's; he pictured a bent old lady, maybe with a zimmer, white hair framing a wrinkled face, like those old souls at The Gables – though some of them were lively enough, and a few still drove. Jerry wouldn't mind working there himself, in a handyman sort of way, maybe, but he guessed, with his record, they wouldn't think of giving him a job. He'd have to stay at the chip shop for the moment, and it wasn't bad, though it was hard work at busy times, and the cleaning up had to be meticulously done. He liked chatting to the customers.

Jerry took trouble over shaving, and slicked down his brown hair. He'd let it grow a bit since leaving prison, but Val at the chip shop had said he mustn't let it get too long or else he'd have to put it in a net, like hers; now each strand was about an inch long, brushed forward over his forehead. He smiled at himself in the mirror. A nice smile could get you almost anywhere, as he had proved, but it was surprising how few people had the habit. Lots of folk went round looking as miserable as sin – Imogen, for instance. What sort of name was that, for goodness' sake? She'd a reason, though; she wasn't exactly jumping for joy about the baby. Jerry wondered about its father, just as he wondered about his own. He had asked his mother about him a few times, but she never wanted to discuss it. She'd snap at him and say there was no need to puzzle his head over such things. Sometimes he wondered if his mother even knew who it was, but she must have done, unless she'd been a proper slag, and he didn't want to believe that, or unless she'd been raped. It would be terrible to be the result of such a thing. If he had a grandmother, she might tell him. It said *father unknown* on his birth certificate. He looked quite like his mother, except that he had brown eyes and hers were blue. Her hair wasn't really blonde; it was naturally much the same colour as his.

He was glad he looked like her. He'd caused her a lot of worry and he regretted that. It was thanks to the smiling woman in Granbury that, just in time, he'd pulled out of the scam with Pete. Otherwise he might also be on remand today. He hoped Pete wouldn't grass him up for previous things they'd done. Though it was always Pete who did the entering and actual nicking, Jerry had been an accomplice and they had got a lot of useful stuff – mainly cash and credit cards, but also radios, bits of jewellery and watches, which they sold around the pubs.

He made his mother a cup of tea before he left the house, and took it in to her. She was still asleep, but she stirred slightly, one bare arm emerging from under the dark blue duvet, which was patterned with stars. She turned her head and peered up at him, muttering his name drowsily.

'Brought you some tea, Mum. Then you can go back to sleep,' he said, and heard her murmured thanks as he went out. She might be asleep again before she had time to drink it, but she did like a cup any time she hadn't to get up early.

Whistling, virtuous, Jerry strode off down the road and walked for nearly a mile before he came to Pete's house, where he rang the doorbell.

It was a different sort of place from his, a pebble-dashed post-war former council house. Pete's was also semi-detached, but it was much bigger and had a garage; there was a lawn at the front with neat flower beds round the edge and beneath the bay window. At the back there was another patch of grass with more flower beds and a small pond, and two apple trees. Jerry thought both house and garden wonderful, but Pete spent as little time there as he could. He found his parents boring. Pete stole for excitement as much as for profit.

It was a neighbour of the Dixons who had told Jerry about Pete's arrest; now his mother came to the door and Jerry saw at once that she had been crying.

'I'm surprised you dare show your face here, Jerry,' she said, wearily. She didn't sound angry; simply sad.

'I came to ask if Pete got sent down, Mrs Dixon,' Jerry said, awkwardly, embarrassed by her distress. 'I'm sorry about what happened.'

'You were there, too, weren't you? But you ran off and got away,' she accused.

'No,' said Jerry, put out by this unjust allegation. 'I've got a job at the chippy. I was there till ten and then I went straight home.'

'And your mother can confirm it, I suppose,' said Mrs Dixon, in a tone he didn't like.

'Yes,' said Jerry. 'Anyway I've given all that up.'

Pete's mother gave a sniff of disbelief.

'Is Pete here? Did he get bail?' asked Jerry.

'No. He's remanded in custody for a week. He might get bail then,' she said. 'But if he does, you'll keep away from him if you know what's good for you, Jerry Hunt.'

'He did ought to have bail,' said Jerry. 'Didn't hurt anyone, did he?'

'Of course not. He's not violent, not our Pete,' said Mrs Dixon.

That's all you know, Jerry thought. In prison Pete had been handy with his fists and it wasn't because he was little and people went for him. He had a vicious temper when he was roused. That was what frightened Jerry now; he might drop Jerry in it, and so might Mrs Dixon. But Pete might be expecting the police to find the car; that would connect Jerry with the crime without his grassing.

'Where did he go? Where did he get caught?' he asked. He meant, at whose house.

'As if you didn't know,' said Mrs Dixon.

He'd better not push his luck.

'I don't,' he said. 'I wasn't there. I'm sorry he got nicked. Goodbye, Mrs Dixon,' he said, and this time did not risk his smile.

He walked back into town and to the chip shop leaving Mrs Dixon wondering if his denial could possibly be the truth.

Imogen refused to go to Waitrose with Charlotte. She wasn't rude, just slightly surly, and Charlotte decided that it was probably better to leave her at home than try to persuade her to change her mind. In any case, she could not insist; Imogen could scarcely be dragged screaming into the car.

'I won't be long,' she said. 'What will you do?'

Imogen had appeared downstairs at eight o'clock, asking if she could take some coffee up to her room and Charlotte had told her what she intended, explaining that she must go into Nettington early as Waitrose's car park soon filled up on Saturdays.

'I don't know,' said Imogen. 'Nothing much. I expect I'll still be in bed when you get back.'

'Is Nick coming over? Do you plan to meet him?'

'We didn't fix anything,' said Imogen.

'Well, if you go out, please leave me a note saying when you expect to be back,' said Charlotte. Judging by yesterday's events, impulse could dictate the day. 'And please telephone if you'll be late. Have you any money?'

She had two pounds.

Charlotte gave her a twenty-pound note.

'It'll cover a taxi if you wander off somewhere and get lost,' she said. 'And I'll find you a front door key.' She had a spare one.

'Oh, thanks,' said Imogen, and at last she smiled. What a change, thought Charlotte, as the pale, discontented face lightened up.

'I'll leave the key on the kitchen table,' Charlotte said.

'Right,' said Imogen. She definitely looked brighter at this prospect of some freedom and fixed herself a tray with cereal and coffee, which she took upstairs.

When she had gone, Charlotte, convinced that Felix ought to come and see his daughter, telephoned him, but all she got was his answerphone. Bleakly, she left a message inviting him to lunch the next day, but she was sure that he wouldn't reply till too late to accept, even if he received the message in time to do so. He was acting irresponsibly; he hadn't even made sure that Imogen had some cash.

Charlotte sighed, recalling her own years of bringing up Tim and Jane alone, her financial worries when they were growing up, her fears for their safety. They'd done well; Jane, in New York, had a successful career which she enjoyed, and Tim's naval promotions seemed to be following upon one another in a satisfactory way. Captain Smythe might be interested in hearing about this. If Felix wouldn't come to Sunday lunch, perhaps he would like to come instead.

She set off on her shopping trip, determined not to hurry. While she was in Nettington, she'd buy a lottery ticket; she'd done this before, fantasising that if she won, she'd wave goodbye to Felix as her benefactor and buy a house of her own, but where? Not in the Plymouth area, where Tim's was; Victoria wouldn't want her mother-in-law on the doorstep, even if she were to be a useful babysitter. Her own parents lived only thirty miles away and were very supportive during Tim's absences at sea. Charlotte could go back to the market town where she had lived throughout her first widowhood, but even during her brief absence, things had changed there; people she had known had moved, and some had died. She might slot back into her former niche; at least some of the tradespeople would be the same, but they wouldn't know her as Charlotte Frost; to them, she was Mrs Paterson, and she had taught some of them, and their children, at school.

She could revert to her previous name.

Such an idea was startling. In a sense it would mean the abandonment of her second marriage, a rejection of Rupert and his calm but genuine love. The idea, however, once acknowledged, was intriguing.

But she wouldn't win the lottery: that was certain; and both her husbands would have teased her for even trying. All the same, she'd take a ticket. She put on her crimson cashmere-lined jacket; perhaps, if she wore it more, she would be less invisible to other people, but she hadn't felt like wearing anything brighter than her dark green padded jacket or her grey overcoat since Rupert's death. He had given her the jacket for her birthday in November, saying he liked to see her in rich colours. A little cheered, because it suited her, she went off, glad to escape from the house and her new responsibility. Imogen, if she decided to get up, must amuse herself, but starting on Monday, a more disciplined regime must begin.

It was a raw day; the spring-like weather of the week before, when people had joked that here was summer, had ended. In the supermarket, Charlotte tried to plan ahead and think of what might tempt Imogen's appetite; in the early stages of pregnancy, she could be feeling queasy. Inspecting the fresh fruit, choosing apples, Charlotte thought that she should be encouraged to study; surely the school would forward her work? Charlotte did not know if the school was aware of her predicament; maybe that was a bomb yet to explode and when it did, she would certainly be expelled. She had been due to take A levels in the summer and, depending on when her baby was due, she could do them, if necessary from a sixth-form college like her brother. It must be arranged and Felix should have thought of it already, even if Zoe was in such a state of besottedness that it precluded her considering the interests of her daughter. Charlotte, who had taught young children, might not be able to help her with her work, but, if Imogen were to stay on in Granbury, there would be other retired teachers in the area, or even working ones, who might be prepared to coach her privately. But she wasn't staying on; this was a temporary solution.

Cheered by such positive thinking, Charlotte extravagantly put some imported peaches into her trolley and two bunches of daffodils which were still in bud but would come out in a day or two. In the newsagent's, where she went to buy her lottery ticket and had to wait in line to pay, she glanced at the tabloid newspapers. On the front page, international news was ignored in favour of a celebrity sexual scandal that had been exposed, but on the front of the *Nettington News*, stacked nearby, in a boxed picture at the side, Charlotte recognised Captain Smythe. PENSIONER FIGHTS OFF ATTACKER appeared in bold script beside it. Charlotte bought the paper.

When she returned home, the house was empty. Imogen had left a note on the kitchen table saying she had gone to meet a friend and would be back around six o'clock.

Friend? What friend? This was the first Charlotte had heard of Imogen having friends in the area. But perhaps the friend wasn't local: perhaps it was the father of her baby, come to seek her out, even to stand by her. However tragic the whole business was, that, at least, would be some comfort to the wretched girl, Charlotte told herself as she put away her shopping. She arranged the daffodils, some in a vase in the sitting-room and the rest in another on the kitchen windowsill; then she went out to survey her small garden. She'd been here so short a time, too late to put in any bulbs; there was just a patch of grass, much scuffed, from where the previous owners' small children had played. Felix had told her, bracingly, that she was such a good gardener, she would soon sort it out and that she would enjoy doing it.

'We should have got someone to come and plant it up for her,' Lorna had said.

'Why waste more money on her?' Felix said. 'She's not old, she likes gardening, and she's got nothing else to do. It'll be therapeutic.'

This attitude would have horrified their father, but Lorna did not argue. Felix and Zoe's lives were in a mess and he could think of little else, convinced that Zoe would take him for his last penny if she could. Anyway, Charlotte wasn't destitute; she could afford to pay a gardener for a few hours.

Unaware of this discussion, Charlotte sighed, looking at the bare wooden fencing, up which no single climber – no rose, no clematis, no jasmine – had been trained. The patch of grass had too many bare patches to be called a lawn; it needed to be sown or laid with turf. Laying turf would mean a swift improvement, but she must make it interesting by breaking it up with flower beds and perhaps a winding path. Standing there, she wondered about shape: where would roses look good? Should she have an arch and trellis? Would Imogen be interested in such a project? It was unlikely, but Charlotte would mention it; it would be something impersonal that they could talk about. She went back into the house and made herself a cup of coffee. She'd forgotten about the paper, which lay unread on the kitchen table. Picking it up, she took it and her coffee into the sitting-room where she put on her spectacles and began to read what it had to say about Captain Smythe's experience.

Late on Thursday night, she read, *pensioner Howard Smythe, 86, was roused by a noise downstairs. Armed only with a golf club, the former sailor bravely tackled an intruder who was ransacking his desk, and took him captive until the police arrived to make an arrest. As a result of this incident, a man aged 19 is now in*

*custody. Howard Smythe, a former Royal Navy captain, brushed
off suggestions that he was a hero.*

At least it stated that he had been in the navy; why start
by labelling him a pensioner? It wasn't an occupation, yet that
was how retired people were described whenever they were the
subject of media reports. Charlotte would be so defined, she
supposed, if some mischance – or even a lottery win – befell
her – twice widowed pensioner, probably, or even invisible
pensioner widow, Mrs Frost, not retired teacher. And Imogen
would be a pregnant teenager, not a student.

Angered by the report, which seemed to diminish Captain
Smythe, Charlotte put on an old anorak and her boots and
went into the garden once again, where she began arranging
clothes pegs to mark out possible future flower beds. She was
on the point of digging out trial edges when Captain Smythe
himself appeared round the side of the house.

'I rang the bell. Perhaps you didn't hear,' he said. 'I came
to thank you for your kindness yesterday. Your neighbour said
you were in the garden.'

'Oh—' Charlotte was surprised, unaware that either neighbour had noticed her existence.

'A helpful young man,' said Howard Smythe. 'He'd just come
back from shopping.'

Charlotte had occasionally seen a couple leaving early in
the morning and returning, the man at about seven and the
woman some time later. The man drove a large black car and
the woman a small blue one. She'd seen no children there,
though there were some on her other side.

'I don't really know them, I'm afraid,' she said. 'I haven't
been here long.'

But it was long enough to have exchanged casual greetings

with the couple. She could have taken the initative, but she wouldn't have recognised them if either of them had been in Waitrose earlier, as probably they were, if the man had just been shopping.

'Things have changed in Granbury,' said Howard Smythe. 'These young people come and go – they move into larger houses – they get to know one another through having children at the school, or they meet in one of the pubs. It was very different when my wife and I first came here, thirty years ago. Then a lot of the people living in the older cottages, like ours, were retired; all those folk, except myself, have died off and now city slickers and whiz kids have bought them on enormous mortgages and modernised them into gems.'

At this, Charlotte laughed.

'You've seen a lot of changes,' she observed.

'Too many,' he replied. 'I've lived too long.'

She wouldn't contradict him. Perhaps he had, but he seemed reasonably fit and little the worse for his experience with the burglar.

'Come in and have some sherry,' she said. 'Imogen is out, heaven knows where, so we won't be setting her a decadent example.'

'I don't think sherry at noon is decadent,' he answered, following her into the house through the back door. 'I think it's civilised.'

Again, she laughed, kicking off her boots. She took off her old coat and hung it on a hook nearby, and Howard hung his beside it. It had been good to hear her laugh. She washed her hands at the sink and then took two sherry glasses from a cupboard, putting them on a tray with a bottle of Gonzalez Byass Fino.

'Young people don't drink sherry,' he remarked. 'Or very seldom. Had you noticed?'

'Not really, but you're right, now that I think about it,' she replied, leading the way to the sitting-room.

Howard instantly noticed the local paper. He picked it up and began to read the piece about the break-in.

'I've been to Nettington. I saw the photograph and felt I had to buy it,' Charlotte said. 'I'm sorry.'

'Don't apologise,' he answered. 'I hadn't seen it. Best to be warned. Some young fellow with a camera came sniffing round yesterday.'

Charlotte told him how she felt about his being described as a pensioner.

'At least it did say you'd been in the navy,' she added.

'Yes. When you retire, you lose your identity as well as a slice of your income,' he commented. 'Why not say retired bus driver, retired clerk – whatever it may be.'

'Why not?' agreed Charlotte, pouring out the sherry.

Captain Smythe, however, would never be invisible. He was too tall, and he looked much too distinguished.

Imogen had gone to Becktham.

Not long after Charlotte went off on her shopping trip, she'd got up, resolved to leave the house herself before Charlotte's return. She couldn't face their being alone together; Charlotte was being kind to her, and she was behaving like a prat, but she couldn't bring herself to break the chain of graceless conduct which she had constructed. Yesterday, in Jerry's house, it had been good. He knew nothing of her and Nicholas's history, so he took them both at face value, as they did him. He was just an ordinary bloke with a duff job at the moment – he couldn't want to spend his entire life frying fish and chips – but it was work for now; obviously he hadn't had the comfortable upbringing that she and Nicholas had shared until everything had fallen apart.

Imogen had been glad to leave her girls' day school, but she hadn't wanted to be sent away; that was how she'd seen it, when packed off to what she considered was a remote spot in the country. She'd hoped to go with Nick to his sixth-form college, but their mother believed in separating them; they couldn't always be together, so after primary school, they were sent in different directions, but, like mercury, when near enough they coalesced. Imogen had known none of the other girls at her new school, and she found the boys an alien tribe. She embarked upon her two years there in a spirit of having to endure. No one was unkind to her, but no one was particularly friendly. Imogen knew that much of the problem was her own fault; she was shy and awkward, which, when she tried to be more forthcoming, made her snap at people, sounding harsh and hostile. She was good at maths and physics, and had thought about becoming a doctor, but her mother had laughed and said she'd never stick the training. Nick had said her best plan was to get good A levels and take it from there, prove Mum wrong; academically she'd done well until this present term, and she'd even performed in the school play, as Lady Capulet in a curtailed version of *Romeo and Juliet*. She'd enjoyed that, forgetting herself while pretending to be the distraught mother of Juliet, who was played by a very pretty girl. Imogen's grandfather had died a few days after the final performance. He hadn't been there; at the funeral, Charlotte had said they would have liked to come, but they hadn't known about it. In other words, Mum hadn't given them the chance, but she hadn't come, either, nor Dad. They both wanted to be rid of her. Even now, at this crisis in her life, they didn't want to know, farming her out on Charlotte, who, when you thought about it, had no responsibility for her.

So far, Imogen had managed to avoid a serious talk with her, but she wouldn't be able to do it indefinitely. Today, though, she could dodge it by going out. She'd tell Charlotte that she had gone to see a friend. It would be the truth. Jerry was a friend. She didn't know his surname, so she couldn't find his telephone number in the directory to ring and ask him if it was all right, but she knew where he lived and where the chip shop was. He'd probably be working this morning. She'd go on the bus, or if there was no bus, hitch a lift.

7

It was after twelve o'clock when Imogen reached Becktham. The bus left Granbury from opposite the butcher's, where last night Jerry had found his mother's car, and went through Nettington, where it stopped in the market square. Imogen shrank into her seat, head down, while it paused, in case Charlotte passed and saw her. The journey took forty minutes, and the route did not pass the chip shop, so Imogen had to ask the way; however, when she reached it, there was Jerry behind the counter, busy serving. The shop was full; Imogen joined the queue and watched him joking with the customers in an easy, friendly way, which she envied. He wasn't cheeky or familiar, but he seemed to know some of them, regulars, she supposed, and asked one man about his dog, which was tied up outside and had an ear infection. Football prospects were discussed with someone else. None of this chat slowed up his preparation of the orders. By the time she reached the counter, Imogen was smiling; she could see that he was having a benign effect on everyone.

'Oh, hi,' he said, recognising her.

Imogen didn't want to get him into trouble by interrupting him while he was at work, so she bought some chips.

'I've escaped,' she said.

'So I see.'

'I thought we might meet when you finish,' she said, while he was wrapping them.

'Nick's not here?'

'No.'

'You can't be hanging about waiting. Can you find your way to my place?'

'Yes.'

'Mum's out.' She did a stint at The Bugle alternate Saturdays and some Sundays. 'There's a spare front door key under a little stone owl in the back garden. Go in and make yourself at home. Make some tea – whatever.'

She beamed at him, paying for her chips. Not everyone was an enemy.

'Right,' she said. 'Thanks. See you.'

'Cheers,' he answered, and turned to the next customer.

His employers, Val and Bobby, busy too, had barely noticed this exchange.

Imogen left the chip shop with her package, stopping at a newsagent's on the corner to buy a tin of Coca-Cola and a KitKat. Then she went on up the street, crossed over, turned up the wrong road but realised her mistake and worked her way back until she came to the house where she had spent the previous afternoon. She walked confidently round to the rear garden, not wanting to arouse suspicions in any watching neighbour by seeming hesitant. The plot was much longer than Charlotte's; this former council house was built when all such estates had space for tenants to grow vegetables to feed the family. Here, there was a lot of grass, but it had been cut, and there were several mature apple trees at the end, set in a patch of freshly-dug soil. Twigs stuck in the ground indicated that seed had been sown in rows, and flower beds, with wallflowers and polyanthus in bloom, punctuated the part nearer the house. Jerry's mother clearly loved her garden.

Imogen soon saw the owl, not far from a rotary washing line on which hung two pairs of jeans – Jerry's, presumably – a pink nightdress, three tee-shirts and some other washing. Imogen lifted the owl and found the key, then went round to the front door and let herself in. It was quite exciting, and it was great that Jerry trusted her.

She took her chips into the kitchen and ate them there, to avoid filling the sitting-room with their smell. Then she made herself a cup of coffee; the jar of instant was standing on the worktop so she did not have to search his mother's cupboards. There was a mug on the drainer, and milk in the fridge. With her drink and her KitKat, Imogen settled down to watch television. It would be a little while till Jerry came.

Angela Hunt left The Bugle early. She enjoyed her stints at the bar; Heather at work had asked her why she took on so many jobs, and Angela never gave her the true answer, which was that while Jerry was inside she had to keep busy or, she feared, lose her reason, and also it was difficult to make ends meet on her wages. Travelling to the young offenders' institution where he had served most of his sentence was expensive; she had to run the car to make the journey, which otherwise would have taken much longer and cost a lot in rail and bus or taxi fares, but because the Metro was old, it needed constant repairs and would soon require a new set of tyres. Before his arrest, Jerry had learned to drive unofficially, with other boys who borrowed their parents' cars with or without permission, and at a garage where he sometimes did odd jobs, cleaning cars and the premises. She'd paid for him to have lessons after his release, and he'd passed his test; if he were to be caught driving some car he wasn't entitled to, at least she could make sure he was licensed. She'd thought he'd kept straight so far, though he'd been mysterious about the evening work he'd been doing until recently. It was just casual, he'd said, a bit of this and that. He'd given her money towards his keep, and a nice little clock radio which she'd got by her bed. When he produced a video recorder, she had been worried, but he said it was one he'd bought cheap in a pub. Then Bobby and Val said they needed help in the chip shop, as their last regular assistant had walked out, and Angela had been eager to volunteer him for the post, but she told them of his past; she didn't want to mislead them, though no one at her office knew about his sentence.

Today she'd got a bad headache and was feeling dreadful, so Norman, the landlord at The Bugle, had sent her home. Angela had protested; she wanted to finish her shift; absenteeism was not in her nature. Norman knew this, but he was a good employer who appreciated her; she was reliable, was friendly enough with customers but never overstepped the mark, and if other staff failed to turn up, or were off sick, she would always fill in if she could. She was glad of the extra money. Friday night, when she went to The Gables, was the only time she could never come.

Now, seeing her white face, Norman wondered if working alternate Saturdays, after her night on duty, was too much for her. Perhaps she should phase them out, or give up The Gables, but she seemed to like that job. Last night one of the residents had died suddenly and her shift had been more demanding than usual; she confessed this when he noticed how unwell she looked and saw her swallowing paracetamol.

'Off you go,' he told her. 'Get your head down. Get some sleep.'

She'd given in, relieved to do as he said, putting on her coat and walking up the road, back to her house.

When she opened the door, she heard the television straight away. Jerry must be home, but he wasn't due till some time after two, when the shop shut. He'd lost the job, got the sack. Her heart sank, and bile rose in her throat as she moved towards the living-room, still in her smart black coat.

'Jerry, what's happened?' she demanded, entering, then stared, amazed, as an unknown, pale, plump girl sprang to her feet and stood at bay, like a frightened animal, backing away from her.

'Jerry's not here. He said I could wait for him,' she gabbled. 'I'm Imogen.'

As she stood up, the television remote control had fallen to the floor; a sports programme was in progress on the screen. Angela bent down, picked up the handset and clicked it off. Her head and stomach reeled. It was a migraine; she got them sometimes, particularly after periods of stress.

'Oh,' she said, and then, seeing the sheer terror on the girl's face, 'It's all right, I'm not going to eat you. You're a friend of Jerry's, I suppose.'

'Yes,' said Imogen, whose heart was pounding. 'He said he'd be back before you. He told me where to find the key, and to make myself at home, so I did.'

'That's OK,' Angela said. 'I had a shock, that's all. I didn't expect anyone to be here. Let's calm down.' She took a breath. 'I came home early, I've got a headache,' she explained. Fright was giving way to relief, because Jerry hadn't got the sack after all, and, moreover, he seemed to have acquired a new girlfriend.

'Oh, I'm sorry,' Imogen was saying. 'Can I get you anything? Shall I make you some tea?'

A cup of tea might chase down the paracetamol, or it might make her sick, but either way, it would be worth trying.

'Tea might be good,' she said.

'You sit down, and I'll make it,' Imogen urged her, and she smiled at Angela, who was not so far gone that she failed to notice how the girl's face lit up, giving her a charm that until now she had appeared to lack.

'That would be wonderful,' she said. 'Thanks.'

'Let me take your coat,' said Imogen, turning into a nurse, and she helped Angela remove it. Seeing no handy hook in the hall, she draped it carefully over the banisters at the foot of the stairs as she passed on her way to the kitchen.

Angela sank down on the sofa, her head throbbing, grateful to submit. She shut her eyes, opening them only when she sensed Imogen approaching with a tray. She had not just dunked a tea bag in a mug but had found a small teapot and made proper tea, with a cup and saucer, and milk in a small jug. She'd put some sugar in an eggcup.

'Oh, that looks good,' said Angela, as Imogen put the tray down, finding space for it among the magazines on the coffee table. She had already tidied them from their normal scattered state into two neat piles, Angela vaguely noticed. 'Aren't you going to have a cup?' she asked.

'No, thanks,' said Imogen. 'I had some coffee earlier. Jerry said to help myself,' she added.

'That's all right,' said Angela. 'Good.'

'Shall I pour it for you?' Imogen offered.

'Please,' said Angela.

Imogen did so, without spilling any.

'How much milk?' she asked, jug poised over the filled cup.

'Just a splash,' said Angela, immediately putting Imogen into a different social slot than her own. She sipped some tea.

'Have you anything to take? Paracetamol, or something? Can I fetch them for you?'

'It's all right – I took a couple before I came home. This'll wash them down,' said Angela. 'How long have you known Jerry?'

'We only met yesterday,' said Imogen. 'Me and my brother. We bought some chips and then Jerry asked us back here. He was very upset because your car had been stolen.'

'Yes – but the police were wonderful. They got it back for me – no damage had been done to it,' said Angela. 'And they'd even put some petrol in the tank. Wasn't that good of them? A nice surprise.'

Imogen was just about to say that it was Jerry who had returned it, when she stopped herself. He must have had a reason for keeping quiet about his part in its recovery but that was strange. And how had he known where to look for it? Perhaps he had some dodgy friends, and guessed they might have borrowed it. What for, though? To get home? Or to do a robbery? Much later than her brother, Imogen made the possible connection with Captain Smythe's burglary, but decided that these must be two separate incidents. Crime happened. The world was a cruel place.

'It must have been,' she said, and swiftly changed the subject. 'Your garden's lovely,' she volunteered. 'I noticed it when I picked the key up from under the owl.'

'Jerry does it,' Angela told her. 'He's got it all into shape. I'd let it go, rather, while he was away. He was working in another part of the country,' she explained, before the girl could ask awkward questions. 'What did you say your name was?'

'Imogen.'

'That's pretty,' said Angela. 'Unusual.'

'It's OK,' said Imogen, who didn't like it. Why couldn't she have been called Sarah or Catherine?

They had run out of conversation. Angela felt too fragile to make an effort.

'I think I'll go up to bed,' she said. 'You wait for Jerry. He shouldn't be too long now.'

'Shall I tell him not to disturb you? You might go to sleep.'

'Yes – yes, please,' said Angela. 'Thank you, Imogen.' She put the cup and saucer back on the tray.

'I'll clear that up,' said Imogen. 'You go along, Mrs – er – I'm sorry, I don't know your surname.'

'It's Hunt,' said Angela, and something stopped her from telling this very well-mannered young woman to call her by her first name.

'I put your coat over the banisters,' said Imogen. 'I didn't know where you kept it.'

'I'll take it up with me,' said Angela.

The girl was very quiet, moving about downstairs. Angela, as she drew her bedroom curtains, could not hear a sound from below. She took off most of her clothes and slid into bed. She'd kept the painkillers down; a few hours' sleep and she would recover.

Apart from the money, she enjoyed the social side of her job at The Bugle, the banter with the customers and the sense of being part of a team behind the bar. With staggered weekend shifts, there had been time to visit Jerry, and she had stayed with this routine since his release. She wanted to keep the structure of her own life secure, for there was no guarantee that he would keep out of trouble; alone at home, she brooded, blaming herself and her deficiencies for his misdeeds, and worrying about the future.

The girl, Imogen, was good news; she was well spoken and neat. So many youngsters were decent enough, though they were painted as potential troublemakers in the papers and on television. Plenty that she met were bright and civil, though there were a good few of the other sort, of course. That friend of Jerry's, Pete Dixon, had been in and out of trouble for even longer than Jerry, she'd heard, and now he'd been arrested for an offence in Granbury, breaking and entering a house and attacking some old man who'd turned the tables and nicked him. Well, at least Jerry hadn't been there. She'd been watching television when he returned from the chip shop on Thursday evening and they'd both gone up to bed around half-past ten; she'd have heard him if he had gone out again.

Having such a nice girlfriend would help to settle him down. She hoped this thing, whatever it was, with Imogen – very new, obviously – would last; she'd enjoy having the girl around the place. Comforted by these reflections, and tired out, Angela fell asleep.

Jerry returned to find Imogen reading one of his mother's magazines. She hadn't put the television on again for fear of disturbing Mrs Hunt, and she hastened to intercept him, finger to lips.

'Your mother's back. She's in bed – she's got a headache. We mustn't wake her,' she said.

'Oh!' Jerry looked startled, and Imogen gave a sudden giggle.

'It's all right. She was cool about me being here,' she said. 'I explained. She said you did the garden. It's marvellous. So tidy.'

'I like gardening,' he confessed. 'It's satisfying.'

She wondered whether to challenge him about his mother's car, and decided not to at the moment. He'd have his reasons for bending the truth.

Imogen went back to Granbury on the bus.

Jerry walked her to the stop. His mother was still asleep, and he then confessed that he wasn't supposed to drive the car because he wasn't insured. His mother had a one-driver-only policy and hadn't yet included him as a named driver.

'She thinks because I'm under twenty-five it would cost a lot,' he said. 'But it wouldn't, because her car's not worth much. It's a way of keeping me down.'

'She thinks the police brought her car back,' Imogen said. 'I didn't tell her it was you.'

'Shit – thanks,' said Jerry. 'Mum thinks I reported it missing, but I had to sort it. I didn't want to drop a mate in it, did I? Not if I could fix it.'

'No, I suppose not,' said Imogen, but doubtfully.

'He'd just borrowed it,' said Jerry. 'He won't do it again. My mate.'

'I hope not,' said Imogen. 'It must have been awkward for her, though.'

'Not as awkward as if a real villain had taken it and smashed it up,' said Jerry.

She could not think of what to say to that, so she made no comment. Jerry waited till the bus came, then, as he gave her a quick light kiss on the lips, her heart seemed suddenly to lift. It wasn't like the heavy, thrusting snogging which hitherto had been her experience, to be endured because this was LIFE.

'I'll ask Charlotte if you can come to lunch tomorrow,' she said. She'd given him her telephone number at Charlotte's, and she had his. 'I'm sure it will be all right. We could go for a walk or something, after. If you'd like to, that is.' She knew the chip shop didn't open on a Sunday.

'That'd be great,' he said, and meant it.

Charlotte, determined that Imogen should have a proper diet at least some of the time, had bought a leg of lamb on her shopping trip that morning. After Captain Smythe had gone, she made an apple pie in preparation for tomorrow's lunch, hoping Felix, if he were back in the country, would accept her invitation, and a sponge cake in case anyone arrived for tea. Imogen would eventually return, and it was good to be feeding someone other than herself. She prepared a fish pie for supper; it would heat up quickly when required. Perhaps it would be possible to persuade Imogen to talk about the future after they had eaten, unless she went out again with her mysterious friend. If it wasn't whoever was responsible for her condition, who was it?

Still hoping that Felix might be coaxed to come over, Charlotte left another message on his answerphone; he couldn't duck his responsibilities for ever. She didn't know how to get hold of Zoe; a transatlantic call to her might at least relieve Charlotte's feelings, if it achieved nothing else. A further talk with Lorna was indicated, but she should try to get somewhere with Imogen first.

Imogen arrived back soon after five; she let herself in and came straight through to the kitchen. Charlotte had just taken her apple pie, and some jam tarts made with the pastry remains, out of the oven. The sponge cake halves sat on wire trays, cooling.

'What a lovely smell!' cried Imogen, inhaling the warm aroma of Charlotte's baking. 'Mm. Can I have one?' and she reached out for a jam tart.

'Careful, they're very hot. You'll burn yourself,' warned Charlotte, carried back to when her own children were small – not young adults like Imogen – wanting to lick the bowl, as they called it, spooning out the scrapings. She prised a tart out of its tin with a knife and put it on a plate. 'There,' she said. 'Give it a minute or two. Would you like some tea?'

'Yes, please,' said Imogen, sitting down at the table, still in her fleece jacket.

Charlotte did not spoil her mood by suggesting she should take it off. The girl looked entirely different; she was bubbly and glowing. This change confirmed Charlotte's suspicion that she had met the father of her child – her boyfriend. Perhaps he had not wanted to know about it earlier, hence her misery, and now he was facing up to what had happened. It was hardly likely that they would plan a wedding; shotgun marriages had gone out of vogue. The outcome might depend on who he was, and on his background; he must be a pupil at the school. He couldn't be a member of the staff, surely?

Charlotte shut her mind to the problem. Live for the

moment, she told herself; Imogen is happy now; let's have
a good evening together, if we can.

Felix Frost had picked up Charlotte's messages. Surely she
could cope with Imogen for a few days without support, he
said to his sister Lorna on the telephone.

'For Christ's sake, she's got nothing else to do,' he com-
plained.

'You should listen to yourself,' said Lorna, who had six
people coming to dinner that night. 'This is your daughter
we're discussing.'

But she was not his daughter, and knowing nothing about
the man who was her father had become harder to endure with
every year.

'Zoe should be dealing with this,' he said.

'You mean it's women's work? She's ratted on it, certainly, but we didn't know about it till she'd left the country,'
answered Lorna.

'I can't think why the damn school couldn't keep her till the
end of term. It's not as if the brat's due next week,' Felix said.

'They didn't chuck her out. She left,' his sister reminded him.
'But once they do hear about it, they'll refuse to have her back.
And there's the boy concerned. This could be a major scandal
for the school if the press get on to it.'

Felix, wrapped up in his own concerns, which included
the possible bankruptcy of his company, hadn't thought of
this.

'I suppose we must be thankful for small mercies,' he
said.

'They may not be so small. She's a twin. They run in families.

What if she has twins?' said Lorna ruthlessly. 'Why don't you go down to Granbury and have a showdown?'

'Maybe I will,' he said. 'If she gets rid of it, she could go back to school and no harm done.' If he could find the fees for another term. He might have to pay anyway, as she'd left without warning.

'Oh, Felix,' sighed his sister, hanging up.

Felix had not yet commited himself to any programme for Sunday. Some better way to spend it than going to Granbury might crop up, but he wasn't in the mood to take himself off to a gallery or museum. It might have to be bloody saintly Charlotte, but he wouldn't ring her now. He'd wait until the morning.

'Did you like helping your mother in the kitchen when you were a child?' Charlotte asked Imogen, after she had eaten a second jam tart and drunk two cups of tea.

'We never did. Mum isn't a great cook,' said Imogen. 'She scarcely gave up work after we were born, even though there were two of us. We had a daily nanny and then lots of au pairs. Some of them were all right,' she added. 'Mum's a good journalist, you know.'

Charlotte wasn't sure that she did know. By the time she and Rupert met, Zoe had been on the staff of a fashion magazine for several years and she knew very little about her step-daughter's previous career.

'It must be interesting work,' she said, carefully.

'I suppose. She's met all sorts of people,' Imogen said. 'That's how she met this Daniel she's gone off with. They've been on several shoots together.'

'Oh,' said Charlotte. 'And have you met him?'

'Yeah, once. He was at home when I came for half term,' she said. 'Mum had forgotten.'

'So you went home on your own and he was there?' guessed Charlotte.

'Yeah.' Imogen drew patterns among the crumbs on her plate with a finger. 'Dad was abroad,' she went on. 'They were quite surprised to see me.'

Charlotte found that easy to believe. Had the girl caught them *in flagrante*?

'I don't suppose Zoe had really forgotten it was your half term,' she said. 'Perhaps she got the dates confused.'

'She was confused all right,' said Imogen. 'Daniel was cool, though. He said she should have remembered. I quite liked him, after a bit.'

Clever Daniel, contriving to beguile her.

'Well, that's good, then, if he's going to be around,' said Charlotte.

'He won't be. He's got a contract in the States and Mum's staying there with him,' Imogen said. 'I told you that.'

'Are you sure? Surely she'll have to come back and see about things?'

Imogen shrugged, and Charlotte judged that it was time to change the subject.

'Why don't you go upstairs and have a wash, and then we'll think about supper,' she said.

Imogen meekly rose.

'I asked a friend to lunch tomorrow. I hope that's OK,' she said.

'Perfectly,' said Charlotte.

'Jerry's his name,' said Imogen, and Charlotte heard her whistling as she went upstairs.

*   *   *

It was some time before Imogen reappeared. In the interval, she had had a bath and she was arrayed in a spotless white polo top and well-pressed black trousers; her face, innocent of make-up, shone. She had very good skin.

'How nice you look, Imogen,' Charlotte said, meaning it, and Imogen blushed.

'No one's said that to me before,' she mumbled.

'I'm sure they have, dear. You've forgotten,' Charlotte said. What about this boy? The one who'd made her pregnant, this Jerry? Or was he someone else? Or had something really dreadful happened, rape in fact, to cause her pregnancy?

'You said Granddad liked me,' Imogen conceded. 'At least, I think so.'

'Yes, he did. He was very fond of you,' said Charlotte, grasping at this reassuring certainty. 'You can be sure of that.' She hesitated. 'Did you have anything of his – any special thing – as a keepsake, after he died?'

'No,' said Imogen. 'He left me some money, though. Nick bought his car with his.'

'What about you? What did you spend yours on?'

'It's in the bank,' said Imogen. 'I might get a car, too, when I've passed my test. I failed, the first time,' she confessed.

'Well, you'll have to take it again, won't you?' Charlotte said. 'Perhaps we could arrange some lessons, while you're here.' Being pregnant needn't stop her driving; it would give her something to do.

'That'd be great,' said Imogen, then, as Charlotte put the fish pie in the oven to cook through, she said, 'Fish pie – great. I love it.'

Did she know no other word of commendation?

'Your grandfather liked it, too,' said Charlotte. 'And he'd want you to have something special as a memento. I've got just the thing,' and she went out of the room.

Left alone, Imogen began to set the table. Her mind was comfortably unworried; she had had an interesting, unusual day, spending time in Jerry's house and meeting his mother. It was so unlike her own home, a five-bedroomed postwar house in Surrey, set in nearly an acre of garden, mostly lawn and woodland, among other houses of a similar nature, many of them larger, all well separated from one another by shrubs and trees. There was no village nearer than two miles away; the station from which her parents travelled up to London was a fifteen-minute drive. It was a comfortable house, furnished in the best of taste, and she had a lovely room, with, recently installed, her own shower and lavatory. Now it would be sold, the money split between her parents, and where would home be?

Still sanguine after her day, Imogen thought she might be able to live here with Charlotte, who was kind, and didn't ask too many questions, for the present, anyway.

At this point in her thoughts, Charlotte returned.

'Your grandfather gave me this,' she said. 'It had been his mother's. I think he'd like you to have it. He never gave it to your grandmother; perhaps he always meant it to come to you eventually.' He would have known that Lorna, his daughter, would not have worn it; she went in for chunky, dramatic, modern jewellery. She handed Imogen a small tooled leather box, faded with age.

Imogen took it from her silently, and opened it. Inside was a chased gold locket on a chain.

'There are two photographs in it. They're of your great-grandparents,' Charlotte said. 'It's quite difficult to open. See if you can do it.'

Still without speaking, Imogen tried to prise apart the two halves of the locket; then, seeing a slight indentation, she inserted a fingernail into the tiny hollow and the hinge moved. There were the two faces, the whiskered man with a lofty brow and large eyes, and the round-faced woman in her high-necked lacy dress.

'Your grandfather had meant to change the photographs inside,' she said. She'd dodged the issue; she hadn't wanted to put in theirs, as he had suggested. She had worn the locket, however.

Imogen looked up at Charlotte.

'It's lovely, thank you,' she said. 'But I'm not a bit like either of them, am I?'

'Not yet. They must have been in their sixties when those photographs were taken,' Charlotte said.

'You see, Felix isn't my father. We're test-tube babies, Nick and me. We don't know who our father is,' said Imogen.

'Oh, my dear child!' Charlotte exclaimed. She had no idea if this was true. 'How do you know?' she asked.

'Something I overheard. Mum and Dad were arguing. Mum said something about Dad being useless and not even being able to give her a child,' she said, and her large eyes began to fill with tears.

8

'They must have wanted you very much,' Charlotte said, deciding that it was no good contradicting Imogen when she did not know the facts herself. She'd read a certain amount about the subject; you couldn't miss it, these days, and she had noticed several pairs of twins and even one set of triplets on her trips to Nettington, when once seeing twins was a rarity. It was possible.

'Well, they don't now,' said Imogen. She had got it all worked out. 'Mum might have had a lover. It could be that,' she said. 'But anyway, it's put Dad off us – me more than Nick, because I'm a disappointment. And it's set Mum and Dad against one another.'

'I can't disprove what you're saying, Imogen, because I simply don't know the truth. You haven't asked your parents to tell you, have you?'

'No.'

'Well, I suggest you do, when you get a chance,' said Charlotte. Whatever the answer, Zoe must be the twins' mother, even if they were the result of an adulterous affair, but at the moment, saying so would be no comfort to Imogen.

'Your grandfather certainly regarded you as his granddaughter. You must believe that. And I'm extremely fond of you, Imogen. I'm just sad because you're going through a bad time at the moment.'

'I'd no right to take it out on you, and I've been doing that,' said Imogen. 'I'm sorry. Here you are, stuck with me.'

'And you with me, which can't be too much fun,' said Charlotte. 'Let's forget all that and have a truce.' Tentatively, for she had never been demonstrative, Charlotte put her arms out, and the girl embraced her in a bearlike hug, from which eventually Charlotte, touched but embarrassed, drew back. 'The fish pie's ready. I can smell it,' she declared.

After supper, Charlotte managed to get Imogen to play rummy. She kept cards and a few board games in preparation for visits from Tim's children, though so far they had been over only once, for a day, when Victoria brought them to see the house. Victoria's dismay at her changed situation had been patent; she remembered Charlotte's earlier house, before she married Rupert, where she had lived for years. It wasn't large, but it had character, and it contained a lifetime's acquisition of furniture and trappings, some of which were now to be seen in Number Five, Vicarage Fields. Charlotte had been determined that her daughter-in-law should send a good report to Tim; he must not be given cause to worry and she had been resolutely cheerful during the visit. Her brief marriage to Rupert had not alienated Tim and Victoria; she was never the grandmother first called on for support, as Victoria's own parents were nearly always available, but she had been a backstop, and she had seen quite a lot of the children when they were very small. While Tim was based in Portsmouth they had visited White Lodge several times, swimming in the pool and running free in the large garden, but, abruptly, everything had changed.

Victoria felt very sorry for her, facing such sudden changes; the years with Rupert had undeniably been happy, and she had moved up the social ladder. Victoria, a service wife and daughter – her father had been in the army – was very conscious of hierarchical significance and saw that her mother-in-law, because of where she lived, had now dropped lower down the scale. Several times she had invited Charlotte to stay, but Charlotte had only ever come down for a day – a long drive for a short visit.

On Saturday evening, Victoria telephoned; there was news of Tim, whose ship had been patrolling in the eastern Mediterranean, and she mentioned that the children's school holidays would soon begin. Perhaps Charlotte would like to come for Easter?

'I've got Imogen staying for the moment,' Charlotte said. 'Imogen Frost. Rupert's granddaughter,' she explained, in case Victoria were confused. 'Her mother's in America and she's here for a visit.' She glanced at Imogen, who was studying her cards, as she said this. 'No, I'm not sure for how long. Shall I ring you in a few days' time? It's very kind of you, Victoria.'

With more civil exchanges, they ended their conversation. Victoria, if she were to be in touch with Tim soon, could tell him that his mother had some company.

'That was my daughter-in-law,' said Charlotte.

Imogen remembered her from Rupert's funeral, a composed, quiet but confident woman; she was much younger than Zoe but she was the conventional sort of mother Imogen wished that she had. It was difficult to think of Victoria having lovers;

Zoe had had several before this last one, Nicholas asserted, and reminded Imogen of various men who had been about the place, particularly when Felix was overseas.

'She wanted you to visit, didn't she? And you said you couldn't because of me,' Imogen said now.

'She did invite me, yes,' Charlotte agreed.

'You could go. I'd be all right here on my own. I am eighteen,' said Imogen.

And pregnant, to boot, thought Charlotte, refusing even to contemplate what might happen if her back were turned.

'She asked me for Easter,' she said. 'If you're still here then, there will be other times.'

'But her children are your real grandchildren, and you haven't any others, have you?'

'We could both go to see them, for a day, if you're still here in a week or two,' said Charlotte. 'Some sea air would be good for you. For both of us, perhaps.'

She felt suddenly immensely tired. It was part of bereavement; she knew that, a huge fatigue which seemed to linger so that you felt it would never ease, and then, very gradually, it lifted. This time, she hadn't yet reached that stage. They finished their game, and though it wasn't late, Charlotte said she was going up to bed.

'You can stay up and watch television, if you want to,' she said. 'But you won't go out again tonight, will you, Imogen?'

'No, of course not,' Imogen replied. 'Don't you trust me, Charlotte?'

'Of course I do, my dear,' said Charlotte, but it wasn't altogether true. What if this boyfriend Jerry suddenly turned up and swept her off to some nightclub? There must be clubs in the area, decadent places where the young took drugs. Or

Nicholas, who was probably no more reliable, might reappear and do the same.

She had to take a chance. Charlotte went upstairs.

Imogen did think of going out again, but where to? Her only friend was Jerry, and he lived miles away; there were probably no buses after ten o'clock, just as it was at home, and anyway, with the chip shop closed, he might be out clubbing or in a pub. Granbury was a dull sort of place, full of commuters leaving early in the morning and coming back at night, quite late. She'd seen the neighbours going off, and noticed how quiet it was when she went to meet Nicholas the day before. Any children in Vicarage Fields would be at school by then; she'd seen the primary school when driving round with Nick. What a dead and alive dump for Charlotte to end up in; there didn't even seem to be any oldies for her to socialise with, except for that really ancient man who'd escorted Imogen to the church and been burgled. Imogen banished a pang of anxiety about Jerry's possible indirect link to this incident and fell to contemplating her own situation. What a mess she had made of everything! She and Nick had gone to separate single-sex schools, but in the same area, and she hadn't wanted to change; her school had had its failings and she'd never been one of a group of girls all hanging out together, but most people had been decent enough and beyond some minor teasing, she'd got by. Besides, she had a huge asset in her good-looking brother whom her schoolmates clamoured to meet; invitations to The Elms had been prized, and were extended when it amused Zoe to offer them. Because of Nick, and because she was good at maths and physics, she had earned respect, and she was expected to do well academically. Then Mum had had this idea that she ought to mix around a bit and meet more boys. Imogen thought the truth was that she wanted to get her out of the house, and now she knew why: so that Mum could go ahead with her own little schemes, have it off with Daniel or anyone else she fancied without a schoolgirl coming home each night. Other girls who went to the same school as Imogen and lived in the neighbourhood had managed an outside social life, partly in each other's houses, or, as they grew older, meeting in the local town, but somehow Imogen didn't fit in with any of this. She and Nick both loved swimming, however, and went to the local pool in the winter when their own outdoor one was covered up against the weather. While Nick was around, Imogen's other problems didn't matter, but then, at sixteen, they were parted.

Imogen had hated the school to which she was sent as a boarder. She had a room to herself, which was something, but she knew no one. Never good at making friends, though more at ease if Nicholas was with her, she met overtures with suspicion, and her brusque response alienated both girls and boys, though she learned to get along, on a superficial level, with a few of them. There were new rules and mores to absorb, and she had to learn the layout of the building and the grounds. She had struggled through her first sixth-form year, working hard and revelling in the swimming; there was a huge indoor pool, available all year round, and in the water she was happy, but out of it, she felt herself to be a misfit. There were occasional taunts because she was overweight, but most of the other youngsters who enjoyed the pool admired her ability, though some envied it and were jealous when she won races and competitions.

Things had gone seriously wrong after Christmas. Mum had

taken off to New York, and Nicholas had come to see her at school only once in all the time she'd been there; if he had come more often, his visits would have improved her standing, as had been the case before. He should have found it easier now he had a car, but he'd met this Phoebe and become entrapped, as Imogen saw it. Well, he'd made the effort to get to Granbury, now that she was in a lot of trouble. That was something.

Her flight from the school had been hushed up. Pupils should not run away, but she had set the scene for her abrupt departure by scratching from a house swimming competition. She told the PE teacher that she felt unwell, but, defiantly, she told the other members of the team that she was pregnant.

'Why cancel? You could still swim,' said Daphne, also in the team, when she had recovered from the immediate shock of Imogen's revelation.

'It might not be good for the baby,' Imogen had said.

'It would solve your problem, then, wouldn't it?' said Daphne. Fancy getting caught like that, she'd said later to her friends. 'Probably thought it was safe the first time, or standing up, or some such crap.'

Daphne had a boyfriend at home; the boys at school were all too young and inexperienced to interest her, and she and her cronies spent some time wondering who had been Imogen's partner in folly. In the end they decided it must be the assistant groundsman, a drop-out from a local comprehensive who might fancy her as a bit of posh.

'Posh – Imogen?' said someone.

'To him,' qualified the speaker.

'He'll get the sack,' said someone else.

One girl, who in fact was having a furtive affair with the assistant groundsman, conducted in the shed where the tennis nets and other equipment were stored, kept silent to preserve herself. She thought it might be a boy from the town.

Imogen fled before she had to face further questions and exposure. Her safe arrival at her grandmother's was a relief to the staff; the girls who knew about her pregnancy kept quiet about it, except amongst themselves, but her grand-mother, arriving days later in a silver-grey Jaguar to collect her belongings, and angry, was less discreet. Imogen had refused to come with her, and the housemistress had had to organise the packing. Where, wondered the housemistress, were the fruits of all the talks on human biology, covering sexual mechanics and contraception? She had a difficult interview with Imogen's grandmother, a well-preserved seventy-year-old who looked as if she might have had a racy past, and advised that, with special arrangements, Imogen's A level exams might still be taken, a message Zoe's mother neglected to pass on.

Imogen, lying in bed in Charlotte's spare room, thought about the immature groping boys who, at discos in the school, had kissed her wetly, slobbering and thrusting their aggressive tongues down her throat as they tried to fumble her, and felt disgust, but she was not going to reveal the truth. Let them wonder.

The morning was again fine and sunny. Charlotte went into her garden and once again surveyed the dismal plot. In this continuing good weather, the faint urge of the day before to do something about it persisted. Roses, she thought; scented ones, climbers to hide the raw fencing on either side, and shrubs around the patch of so-called lawn.

Imogen, from her bedroom window, saw Charlotte out

there. Absorbed by her own troubles though she was, Imogen nevertheless recognised the despairing droop of Charlotte's shoulders.

A wave of sympathetic pity swamped Imogen. Charlotte was another of her father's victims, forced out of White Lodge at short notice and parked in this dump – well, it wasn't a dump by most people's standards and the house was a palace compared with Jerry's, but after White Lodge it was a positive hovel, and it wasn't even hers. She was there by Dad and Lorna's gracious favour. Granddad would have been furious. Why hadn't he taken better care of her in his will? Imogen wondered what he'd actually said; Dad was capable of having turned it around to suit himself. She'd thought wives had the right to stay in the family house after the husband died. Unaware that Charlotte had contributed to the haste of her own departure, Imogen condemned her father utterly, and thought that Lorna might have done more to see that Charlotte was treated properly.

She'd settle down here eventually and be all right, Imogen decided. What she needed was friends and outside interests. She hadn't had outside interests at White Lodge; running it and looking after Granddad had, as far as Imogen knew, kept her fully occupied, but maybe she'd done other things before they married; she'd been a widow for a very long time. It was rather a pity they'd married, really, since it had lasted such a short time and now she was a widow once again. Kindly planning for Charlotte's future, Imogen washed and dressed, and went down to find her still in the garden.

Charlotte did not comment on her early rising as they greeted one another.

'I was trying to decide what to do about all this,' she said, gesturing at the bleak scene around them. 'I've made some marks where beds might look good.'

'Won't you need some help?'

'Probably. I might be able to find a man – a jobbing gardener.' Captain Smythe might know of someone; perhaps he had help.

'You can get firms to come in and do it all, can't you?' said Imogen.

'Landscape gardeners, you mean? Yes, but I think they're very expensive,' said Charlotte.

'Jerry wouldn't be,' Imogen said. 'He'd need a fair wage, of course, but he wouldn't want to fleece you.'

'Jerry? He's a gardener? A horticulturist?'

'No, but he knows a lot about it and his mother's garden is as neat as anything,' Imogen declared.

'This same Jerry who's coming to lunch?' Charlotte needed to be sure.

'Yes. He works in a fish and chip shop, but he gets lots of time off when the shop's shut,' said Imogen, in her enthusiasm ignoring any difficulties about his travelling to Granbury when he had no transport. 'He doesn't work on Sundays, and the chip shop's shut on Mondays,' she continued.

'Well, let's see what he thinks about it,' Charlotte temporised. It was good to see Imogen looking animated, but this information about Jerry eliminated him as the father of her expected child. The fact that Imogen had met his mother was in his favour.

'He's nice. You'll like him,' Imogen assured her. 'He's not a frightening sort of bloke.'

'Do you find most – er – blokes frightening?' Charlotte asked.

'Some – yeah,' said Imogen. 'They're big and noisy and they want to make you drunk,' she said. 'I'll go and put the kettle on, shall I?' and she went into the house.

Charlotte would not probe further now. She followed slowly. Goodness knows what had happened to the girl, but this new friend, Jerry, could be welcomed without reservation. Plenty of students worked in fast-food shops; why not Jerry?

After breakfast she tried Felix again, but the only reply was from the answerphone.

'Imogen, I've tried to get hold of your father to ask him down to lunch,' she said. 'However, he seems to be away. I'm going to invite Captain Smythe.'

'Good idea,' said Imogen.

Charlotte thought he would be a help in the entertaining of Jerry from the chip shop, background otherwise unknown. She found his number in the telephone book and caught him just as he was setting off for church. He was happy to accept.

Imogen helped her to lay the table in the dining-room. Charlotte still had the cutlery and crockery from before her second marriage, and some Swedish glassware; these and other things not needed at White Lodge, but not sold, had been stored there in the loft. She had some good claret; Tim and Victoria had sent her a case of wine as a house-warming present. There was also Coca-Cola, which Charlotte had bought on her trip yesterday, but no lager, which Imogen, remembering the tin they had shared at his house, suggested Jerry might prefer.

'Too bad. We have none,' she observed.

'He won't mind,' Imogen said airily, and, sure that she could do no more to help, went upstairs to have a bath and wash her hair before the guests arrived.

She really likes this Jerry, Charlotte thought. That was good, but what about the father of her baby? What was to happen? Since Thursday, they had drifted along in a state of limbo, deferring looking to the future, not facing facts. It must stop tomorrow. Tomorrow an appointment with the doctor must be made, and a serious discussion must follow.

When Imogen returned, her hair still slightly damp, she was wearing a long black skirt and a clean red sweater reaching to her hips. Her pregnancy had not begun to show; it must still be in its very early stages. What a pity it had been discovered before the school term ended. Depending on the decision that she made, it might have all blown over with no fuss, but, of course, there was the boy involved.

Captain Smythe arrived before Jerry. He was carrying a Waitrose plastic bag; inside was a bottle of sherry.

'A contribution,' he said. He had wondered what to bring. If you took wine, the hostess might feel it should be used at once, but it needed to settle and it might be inappropriate for the chosen meal.

'Thank you,' she said. 'You've met Imogen,' she reminded him.

'How nice to see you again, Imogen,' he said, bowing slightly.

'How are you, Captain Smythe?' Imogen asked. 'I hope you've recovered from what happened.'

'I'm none the worse,' he said. A veteran of the Murmansk and Atlantic convoys in the war, Captain Smythe had many times met extreme peril, but then he had been in his youthful prime; now, the loss of physical strength and mobility was what he found hard to bear.

'What time did you tell Jerry to come?' Charlotte asked Imogen.

'I didn't. I just said lunch. He'll know one-ish,' said Imogen with confidence. After all, he worked in a chip shop which catered for that meal.

'Jerry is our other guest,' Charlotte explained. 'Imogen says he's a keen gardener. She thinks he might be able to help me.'

'Excellent,' said Howard Smythe.

'We were looking at the garden this morning,' Charlotte said. 'It's desperate. There's nothing there.'

'I can give you some slips and seedlings, and other plants,' said Howard. 'My garden is well stocked and it will do the perennials good to split them up.'

'Oh, thank you,' said Charlotte.

'You'll have to plan it first, of course,' said Howard. 'Shall we have another look at it now? It's such a fine day, it won't be cold out.'

They trooped out through the French window on to the rough patio outside and surveyed the scene.

'A blank canvas,' said Howard. 'It takes five years to make a garden, I always say, but there are these instant gardeners nowadays who do it in a trice.'

'Perhaps there can be a compromise,' said Charlotte.

They were discussing possibilities when the doorbell rang. Imogen sped to answer it.

'I don't know her friend Jerry,' Charlotte warned. 'Imogen's only just met him. He's working in a chip shop in Becktham.'

'That's in his favour,' Howard Smythe remarked. 'He's not a layabout.'

'I imagine he's a student,' Charlotte said.

Imogen, at this moment, was leading Jerry out into the garden, telling him it was a mess which needed making over.

Charlotte saw a youth dressed in well-pressed dark jeans and spotless trainers, and a dark green sweatshirt. She'd seen him somewhere before, but where? It took her a little while to remember, but Howard recognised him straight away.

'This is my step-grandmother, Mrs Frost,' Imogen was saying. 'And this is Captain Smythe,' she introduced, with pride.

'How do you do,' said Captain Smythe, holding out his hand.

Mesmerised, Jerry shook it. He had very nearly decided to turn back when he located Vicarage Fields and realised that he had been there with Pete, but it looked different in daylight and maybe this would be a house where no one was at home when they called. Imogen was a nice kid and down on her luck, and she was just a friend, no more. Besides, his mother liked her. Hitherto always ready to take a chance, he'd do so now; however, he was confronted simultaneously with the woman who had smiled so warmly and the old guy who had turned him away but who later Pete had robbed.

Not a coward, Jerry steeled himself.

'Pleased to meet you,' he said, returning the old man's steady gaze squarely, for after all, he had taken his advice and got a job, an honest one.

The grandmother was smiling once again.

'Come along in, Jerry,' she said, and offered him some sherry.

9

After this, Charlotte marvelled that the lunch went off so well.

Neither she nor Howard Smythe was aware that the other had met Jerry in different circumstances; each was determined to hide the knowledge from the other and from Imogen, until the time for disclosure was appropriate. Charlotte carved the lamb, Captain Smythe poured the wine, Jerry made sure that everyone was able to reach the vegetables, which were served in Denby dishes on the table. Howard automatically poured wine for the two young people; there were wine glasses set at each place, and they were adult; it was automatic.

He did not know Imogen was pregnant. She did not refuse the wine. Charlotte, in her own pregnancies, had not given up moderate social drinking except when suffering from sickness in the early months with Jane. In those days, people were less prescriptive and also much less hypochondriacal; the claret might be good for Imogen; wasn't it full of iron? Wine had not figured much in Jerry's life thus far, but he could see there was no beer so, in the spirit of adventure, he tried it, having accepted, also, the pre-lunch sherry he was offered. His mum liked sherry, but her choice was rich brown in colour and very sweet, not like cat's piss, which Jerry thought his glass of fino resembled.

'Are you driving, Jerry?' Charlotte had asked him before the wine was poured, and he said no, he'd hitched a ride over as the bus took for ever, and he'd hitch one back.

'Tell us about your job in the chip shop, Jerry,' Howard Smythe invited, when everyone was settled, with mint sauce or redcurrant jelly – both, in Jerry's case.

'This is so good,' said Jerry, before answering the question. 'Mrs Frost, you beat them television chefs, you really do.'

Imogen hastened to endorse this commendation.

'You are brilliant, Charlotte,' she said. 'When we went to White Lodge, you always put on a great meal. Better than Gran ever did. Even Mum agreed with that. Granddad was lucky to get you.'

Some explanation was needed.

'Rupert – Imogen's grandfather – and I were only married for two years before he died, very suddenly,' Charlotte said.

'What a bummer,' Jerry said.

'They were good years,' Charlotte stated quietly, and it was true. There had been several holidays abroad, and they had been friends as well as tender lovers – again, a new experience for her. But if they hadn't married, her life would not have been turned topsy-turvy twice in a short period of time. Pressing her to marry him, Rupert had thought he was conferring material benefits on her and raising her social status; so he was, but briefly, and she needed neither.

'Dad and Lorna made her feel she couldn't stay on at White Lodge – that was their house – a lovely old house in the country, with a swimming pool and all that – and so she's here,' said Imogen, her colour high, her eyes bright.

Perhaps the wine was a mistake, thought Charlotte.

'It doesn't matter, Imogen,' she said. 'I chose to go quickly and your father found this house for me.'

Both the men were listening intently to this story, but while Jerry couldn't hear enough of it, Howard was embarrassed for Charlotte; these revelations must be painful for her. He returned to the subject he had tried to introduce.

'The chip shop, Jerry,' he prompted. 'Please tell us how you found the job and what it's like.'

He fixed the young man with a blue gaze before which mightier men than Jerry would ever be had quailed, and Jerry, remembering that this was the old bloke who'd nicked Pete, did as he was told.

'My mum found it for me,' he artlessly explained, without disclosing why he was not in work already, which two members of his audience already knew. 'She's got lots of jobs herself,' he went on. 'Well – three. One's in a pub, The Bugle, in Becktham, and my bosses in the chip shop drink there sometimes. Not often, because they're working most nights, but they go in at weekends. They mentioned that they had a vacancy.'

'Their fish and chips are very good,' Imogen contributed. 'Nick and I had some on Friday. That's how we met Jerry. And I've met his mother,' she added, for though Charlotte knew this, Captain Smythe didn't.

It sounded admirable, even respectable.

'We get all sorts in the chip shop,' Jerry volunteered. 'On Tuesdays – that's pension day – we have special prices for pensioners. You should see the old dears lining up. It's great for them, means they get a square meal cheap. You get to know them after a bit – there's one with a dog that's in a right mess, he leaves it tied up outside because they aren't allowed in. Hygiene, you see. And then there's Nell, who's on the game – she has a regular on Wednesdays at twelve, and she comes in for chicken and chips at half-eleven. She keeps it hot and they have it after.' He paused in his narrative, not for dramatic effect but to get on with his meal.

Howard and Charlotte exchanged glances. The old man's mouth was twitching, and Charlotte dabbed at hers with her napkin, hiding her smile. Even Imogen gave a snort of laughter, quickly suppressed.

'Who else is a regular?' she asked, and Jerry told them about the schoolchildren who came in the evening, and the sales representatives, and the lorry drivers. He needed very little prompting to keep talking, and he seemed to know individually a great many of the regular customers and their stories.

'How have you found out so much about them, Jerry?' Charlotte enquired.

'I just ask them about themselves while I'm putting up the order,' Jerry said. 'People like to talk. Lots of them are lonely – and that's not just the old folk.'

He was being a success. Imogen listened, happy and proud. He might come from a different background but he fitted in. Howard wondered if he had genuinely reformed, and if so, whether it would last. If not, he had the makings of a prize con man – which, of course, he was already. Both Howard and Charlotte, well aware that thieves, and even those who had shown violence, often got little more than a reproof these days, were wondering what offence had led to his incarceration.

The apple pie was consumed completely; Jerry had a large

second helping and Imogen a smaller one. After Howard Smythe had finished with a tiny slice of cheese, Imogen announced that she and Jerry would clear away and do the washing-up.

'We'll bring you coffee,' she said. Charlotte had already left the tray prepared. 'If we can't find where things live, we'll stack them neatly.'

'Thank you, Imogen,' said Charlotte.

She and Howard moved into the sitting-room.

'Well,' he said, when the young people were out of earshot.

'Well, indeed,' said Charlotte. She was wondering what to tell him.

'That was an excellent meal. Thank you,' he said. 'A treat.'

'I had thought Imogen's father might come,' said Charlotte. 'He's been conspicuous by his absence, so far.'

'Is the girl in some sort of trouble?' Howard asked, and Charlotte nodded.

'The oldest kind,' she said.

'How very unfortunate,' the old man observed. 'She's only a child.'

'She's just eighteen,' said Charlotte. 'But immature.'

'And now she's taken up with this youth. Hm.' Howard hesitated. She had to know.

But she forestalled him.

'I've met him before,' she said. 'He's the one who rang my bell one evening.'

'Yes,' said Howard. 'Mine too. Perhaps we should discuss this later, privately.'

At this point Imogen arrived with the coffee. She set the tray on a small table in front of Charlotte, and went out. They heard the kitchen door close.

'He said he was a young offender,' Charlotte said. 'When he called, I mean. He seemed so nice. Did he admit it to you, too?'

'He did,' said Howard. 'He's clearly a lovable rogue, as the saying is.' He'd met a few in his time.

'Imogen doesn't know about it,' Charlotte said. 'I'm sure she doesn't. They met by chance on Friday. He could have reformed.'

'Yes. Perhaps he has,' said Howard. 'Some do.'

'He still came today. He must have recognised the house. And us. He didn't run away. He can't have had anything to do with your burglary,' said Charlotte.

'He could have known the culprit. They may have been together when Jerry called on us originally. Reconnoitring,' said Howard.

'But that was about three weeks ago. At least, that was when Jerry came here.'

'Two weeks, certainly,' said Howard. 'Perhaps it was longer. It doesn't let him off the hook of being implicated.'

'Oh dear,' sighed Charlotte. 'Do I warn Imogen?'

'Not immediately,' Howard advised. 'It might make him seem all the more appealing and in need of her friendship. And I doubt if he'll steal the silver from under her nose.'

'I could let him do the garden,' Charlotte said. 'It would give him a chance to prove he's genuinely trying to keep out of trouble, and it might make a difference to Imogen.'

'How long is she staying?'

'I don't know. Her parents – her father is my stepson, as you know – have parted and they seem to have washed their hands of her. Her mother is in America.'

'And her present predicament?'

'We haven't discussed it in any depth,' said Charlotte. 'Not yet.'

Sounds from the garden now indicated that the washing-up was done and the washers were outside, conferring about its condition.

'Why don't you all come back with me and look at my garden,' Howard suggested. 'I can show you various plants which can be split up to give you a start. We can see if Jerry really does know what he's talking about. You obviously think we should give him the benefit of the doubt about having turned over a new leaf until proved wrong.' Howard didn't sound convinced that this was a good idea.

'I do,' said Charlotte. She stood up. 'It's a lovely afternoon and it will do the young people good to have some exercise. I'd love to see your garden.'

Howard thought it a great pity that he was so old. If he were twenty years younger, he might have considered aiming to become her third husband; she was kind and restful, and extremely capable. But would he be offering her more than a post as an unpaid housekeeper, albeit with an affectionate employer?

Twenty years ago, probably. Not now. And thirty years ago, a widow in reduced circumstances could be offered a position as a resident housekeeper, but today, in such a case, all sorts of wrong assumptions could be made by outsiders, and tiresome legalities might be necessary.

They walked in pairs along the road, past where Jerry had found his mother's car, and turned down Meadow Lane towards the church. They met other people out enjoying the sudden warm spring weather, some with children, some with dogs, some with both. Each group seemed absorbed in its own affairs and no one greeted them. Howard Smythe told Charlotte that he recognised no one, not even from attending church.

Imogen and Jerry, walking faster, were ahead.

'Your gran's all right,' said Jerry. 'I expect she's sad, your granddad having died.'

'She must be, I suppose. I haven't seen her cry,' said Imogen. 'Not even at the funeral.' Imogen herself had wept copiously.

'That generation – her and the captain – they're brought up not to cry,' said Jerry. 'It's good. I don't like it when women cry.'

His mother's tears had overflowed when he got into trouble, and that had happened more than once before he went to prison, but on the earlier occasions he'd got off with community service, which was a doddle. Sweeping roads, he'd seen chances for opportunist theft and had taken them, sometimes even when still on the job, but usually returning at another time. He was wondering whether to tell Imogen about his earlier meeting with Mrs Frost, who seemed to have said nothing. Perhaps she hadn't recognised him. It was possible. He decided, for the present, to keep quiet.

He almost gave himself away by stopping at Captain Smythe's gate, but Imogen forestalled him.

'This is it,' she said. 'I asked him where the church was on Friday, when I was meeting Nick there. Churches are good places to meet because you can always find them. Captain Smythe said it's not kept locked.'

In his previous life, Jerry would have stored away this useful information. Churches contained valuables, even collecting boxes. Now he told himself to forget it. They waited for the other pair to catch them up. Captain Smythe opened the gate and ushered them through, then showed them round his rosebeds, all lightly pruned.

'I don't cut them back hard,' he said. 'It's not necessary with these continual flowering ones. I cut out the weak growth and the flower heads.'

Jerry marvelled at the long lawn, almost free of moss, and the trimmed shrubs. Early daffodils and crocuses bloomed, and under some trees there was a sheet of fading snowdrops.

'Do you do it all yourself?' he asked.

'A man comes once a year to trim the hedges,' said Howard. 'And I get someone in occasionally to help me tidy up. Otherwise I manage. It's an interest.' He led Jerry down the garden, intending to ask him what plants he could recognise but also, as he had arranged with Charlotte on the way here, to let him know that they had both recognised him. They would allow him time to tell Imogen about his past himself, and Mrs Frost might consider employing him to lay out her garden, but both of them would be keeping a careful eye on him.

'You'd be on probation,' he said sternly, after delivering this decision.

'I am already,' Jerry answered cheekily.

'You understand me,' Howard said.

'Yes – sorry, sir,' said Jerry, inspired to use this respectful term.

'And you will tell Imogen, in your own time,' Howard repeated.

'Yes. Poor kid, she's got troubles too,' said Jerry.

'She has. You'll respect her,' Howard said.

'Course,' said Jerry, adding, 'Sir.'

'The burglar who broke in here last Friday. Pete Dixon. Do you know him?'

The question took Jerry by surprise. His instinct was to deny it, but the old man might see through him.

'Yes, I do,' he said. 'And I did go round with him, on the sell, when I called on you and Mrs Frost. But she was nice, and smiled at me, and you were all right, too, sir. I never done the stealing, I just rang the doorbell and kept the person talking, while Pete went round the back. Often he couldn't get in,' he added, and went on, 'I decided to chuck it, because of you and Mrs Frost, and for my mum's sake, and then she got me the other job. You told me to get a job. Well, I did,' and he turned on his irresistible smile. 'Sir.'

'So you had nothing to do with the break-in here?'

'No, sir. Not at all,' said Jerry. 'Sir.'

'If you take advantage of Mrs Frost, or of Imogen, I'll see the police throw the book at you,' said Captain Smythe.

Jerry believed him.

Charlotte and Imogen had discovered the pond. They had walked through an archway in a clipped yew hedge into an enclosed area, and there it lay before them. It was about twenty feet across at its widest point and perhaps twice as long, irregularly shaped, and was fed by a spring which flowed from it into a rivulet joining a stream beyond Captain Smythe's boundary.

'How lovely,' Charlotte exclaimed. 'What a surprise!'

She spoke as Jerry and Howard Smythe came round a further corner of the hedge, arriving at the far side of the pond.

'We used to get a lot of flooding down here,' said Howard.

'I had the pond enlarged to prevent it. All's well unless the stream gets blocked. Eventually it connects up with the river. Sometimes it does overflow.'

The grass around the area was very lush, and water-garden plants – reeds and rushes, mainly, and clumps of iris – flourished round the edges. Water lilies covered part of the surface and a small wooden jetty on stout stakes jutted out into the water at one side.

Jerry stared, entranced. Charlotte, watching him, saw that he was genuinely spellbound by its tranquil charm.

'If you had a little bridge, it would be a miniature Monet,' she said. 'It's lovely. Are there any fish?' She moved on to the small jetty to peer into the depths.

'No,' said Howard. 'There were some carp. My daughter gave me a pair one year. She thought they might breed, but instead they vanished. They're quite valuable. Someone may have removed them.' A workman, he had thought at the time, not sorry to have lost the fish. 'I didn't like them much,' he confessed. 'I thought they had a baleful look.'

'How can fish look baleful?' asked Jerry.

'Oh, they do,' Charlotte confirmed. 'Not just carp. On fishmongers' slabs they do.'

'There were carp in the pond at White Lodge,' said Imogen. 'Granddad liked them. He used to feed them.'

'Well, all the fish I meet are dead fillets. Cod and haddock,' Jerry said. 'Would you like a water feature in your garden, Mrs Frost? You needn't have any fish in it, but a little fountain would be nice. We could do it.'

'Let's not be too ambitious, Jerry,' Charlotte said.

'I am going to help you, then?' he said eagerly. 'I can start tomorrow. The shop's shut on Mondays.'

'Is that all right?' Imogen looked equally enthusiastic.

Captain Smythe and Charlotte exchanged glances. It seemed to have been decided. The young people were going to seek each other out anyway; Imogen, when she heard about Jerry's record, would doubtless disregard it. At least, if he were working here, Charlotte would know where they were and that would spare her worry. Captain Smythe, on the other hand, thought she might be inviting trouble, and he determined, if this went ahead, to keep an eye on things.

He saw them off at his gate. The trio walked along together, talking animatedly. Jerry was gesturing, making plans for the garden and telling Charlotte that Captain Smythe could spare plenty of specimens.

'Not just cuttings,' he explained. 'Things that have self-seeded or that need splitting up, like phlox and Michaelmas daisies.'

'We must discuss rates of pay, Jerry,' Charlotte said. 'I shall consult Captain Smythe about what would be fair.'

'Yeah – right, Mrs Frost,' said Jerry.

'How will you get here?'

'I'll hitch,' said Jerry. 'It's OK – I'll get a lift eventually. The bus takes too long.' And costs, he thought.

It wouldn't be easy to come over during the week, when he had only a few hours off in the daytime. Still, he could do a lot in two whole days each week.

Charlotte hoped this would work out, but whatever happened, Imogen must see the doctor as soon as an appointment could be arranged. She must face up to her situation.

She was going to have to do it rather sooner than expected. As they walked along Vicarage Fields towards Number Five, Charlotte noticed a car outside her house. There were other cars parked in the road, but this was a large Mercedes. She and Imogen simultaneously recognised it.

'It's Dad,' said Imogen.

Charlotte took a deep breath.

'Yes.'

'He's a bit late for lunch,' said Imogen.

'I'll be off, then,' Jerry said, hastily. 'Thanks for the lunch, Mrs Frost, and I'll be over tomorrow about the garden, as early as I can get here. Cheers, Imogen,' and he hurried away.

'I'm delighted that your father's come,' said Charlotte firmly, walking towards the car.

There was no one in it.

'He'll have a key. He'll have let himself in,' said Imogen.

She was right.

10

Charlotte was outraged at Felix's effrontery, while acknowledging that perhaps he had some right to enter what was, in fact, his house. Trying to suppress her anger, she opened the door and beckoned Imogen inside.

Felix was sitting on the sofa reading the paper, a glass of wine beside him.

'Make yourself comfortable, why don't you?' Imogen almost snarled the words.

Felix slowly laid the paper down, took off his half-glasses and, without haste, rose to his feet. Not inconsequentially, Charlotte realised that neither of his children looked the least like him, though Nicholas was as tall, and as slimly built. Felix was much darker; he was, she noticed, very thin, surely much thinner than at their last meeting, when he had handed her the keys to this house. He wore a dark green shirt, tieless, under a darker green v-necked sweater, and black cord trousers with expensive-looking loafer shoes.

'Sorry I'm too late for lunch,' he said smoothly.

'Have you eaten?' Charlotte, too, spoke sharply. 'There's some lamb left. I see you found the wine.' They hadn't quite finished the bottle, but she knew he was capable of searching for and opening another if they had.

'I've had lunch, thank you, Charlotte,' Felix said, sitting down again. 'You seem to have had a full table without me.'

Charlotte realised that he had deduced this because Imogen and Jerry had not put the wine glasses away, and the coffee tray, though with only two cups and saucers on it, was still waiting to be dealt with.

'We had friends in, yes,' she said. 'As you hadn't said if you were coming and I couldn't get through to speak to you in person.' Because he had let himself in, he hadn't seen Jerry; at least he need not be explained.

'You look well, Charlotte. Been for a walk, have we?'

Charlotte and Imogen were both waiting for him to speak to his daughter, or even to notice that she was there.

'Imogen is here, standing beside me, Felix,' Charlotte said. 'A greeting would be in order, don't you think?'

'Oh, Christ. Are we going to be in a mood?' said Felix wearily, rubbing his hand across his forehead. He sank back upon the sofa.

'It's all right. You don't have to recognise me. I'm not your child. Father unknown, that's it, isn't it?' said Imogen, and rushed out of the room.

'Christ,' said Felix again. 'What have I done now?'

'It's what you haven't done,' said Charlotte. She was still standing, while he reclined, and now she gripped the back of a chair to give her support. 'You've just completely ignored her, and you've handed her and your parental responsibility over to me.'

'Now come, Charlotte. Haven't you a duty to us? Can't we expect you, as our father's widow, to fulfil your obligations?'

'Hasn't Imogen a right to your support? She thinks you're not her father. Could that possibly be true?' Charlotte demanded.

For the first time, relucantly, Felix saw what had made his father want to marry Charlotte; she wasn't just a capable woman who could rise to most occasions; she was passionate. He didn't like the thought, and banished it.

'What's given her that idea?' he asked, warily.

'She heard you say so, when you and Zoe were quarrelling.'

'Zoe had some affairs in the past,' said Felix.

'But no test tubes? That's what she suspects, because she's a twin. Fertility treatment sometimes results in multiple births,' said Charlotte.

'Twins are hardly multiple, are they?' Felix snapped.

Charlotte ignored this.

'You could have tests, if there's some doubt,' she said shortly. 'But anyway, to all intents and purposes you are her father and you have a duty towards her.'

'Well, I'm here, aren't I?' he snapped. 'Fetch her down and let's have it out with her.'

'I won't do that,' Charlotte said. 'I won't have you upsetting her.'

'What about her upsetting us? Me and Zoe?' he demanded.

'Zoe and me,' Charlotte, ever the pedant schoolteacher, corrected him, and then went on, 'Oh, never mind. You upset her first, breaking up and not telling her about it. You upset both of them, but Nicholas has always had more confidence than Imogen. It worried Rupert.'

'Granddad's pet, eh?'

'It's a good thing she was someone's pet,' said Charlotte. 'And for the moment, she's mine. She'll see a doctor next week and if necessary a counsellor, to help her decide what's best. That is, unless you've come to take her home.'

'I haven't, as you well know,' said Felix. 'What's best is that she gets rid of it, and sharpish.'

'She may not agree,' said Charlotte. 'I'll back her up, whatever choice she makes. If she does have a termination, there could be a huge emotional problem.'

'She'd get over it.' Felix was dismissive.

'She'd never totally forget it,' Charlotte said. 'And what about her mother? Where does Zoe stand in all this?'

'She can't think of anything except her big romance,' Felix said. 'This Daniel.'

'Imogen seems to like him,' Charlotte said. 'And Zoe must be worried about her.'

'She's confident that you'll sort it. Do what's best,' said Felix grudgingly. 'So's Lorna.'

'What about your business worries?'

'What about them?'

'You don't deny you've got them?'

'Lorna told you, I suppose.'

'I believe it's been reported in the business columns, but I rarely read them,' said Charlotte, who intended to do so in future if Felix's company were to be mentioned.

'It's bad. The receivers are coming in,' said Felix, dropping some of his aggression. 'We're just holding on.' He wouldn't tell her about the possibility, still uncertain, of a management buy-out. He needed every penny he could raise, and now Zoe was determined on a divorce which was an additional and superfluous complication.

'I'm sorry,' Charlotte said, realising that for Felix to admit it to her, the situation must be very serious.

'Yes – well, it's not your fault,' he managed to allow.

'It's not Imogen's either. Felix, whether you're her biological father or not, you are her legal father, as much as if you had adopted her, and you can't just walk away from her without discussing her problems.'

'Can't I, though?' he challenged her. 'Just you watch me,' and he stood up. 'Goodbye, Charlotte. I expect you to get in touch with me when the silly little bitch has come to her senses. And meanwhile –' he pulled his wallet from his pocket and plucked out several banknotes which he dropped, fluttering, to the ground. 'These will help towards her keep.'

Charlotte was too astonished to react before he marched from the house. He banged the door behind him, and she heard his car start up, leaving with much exaggerated acceleration. She bent to gather up the money. He hadn't counted it, simply pulling out a wad, in a gesture: there were four twenties and a fifty-pound note.

If he needed petrol on his homeward way, he'd always got his credit card, if it was still worth anything, she supposed.

Imogen entered the room while she stood there, holding the money.

'I think you ought to change the locks,' she said.

'How much of that did you hear?' Charlotte asked her.

'Enough,' said Imogen. 'You were great.' She flung her arms around Charlotte and hugged her. 'Thanks.' She had clearly been crying, but there were no tears now. 'I'm right, aren't I? There is something strange about us. Our birth. Nick and me.'

'There may not be,' Charlotte temporised. But Felix had not denied the possibility. 'Your mother could have had an affair. It happens. As it's worrying you, you should ask her, when you get a chance.' Imogen's need to understand her own heredity would increase, now that she was pregnant. Perhaps, if confronted with the problem, Zoe would be able to reassure her.

'And when will that be?'

Charlotte shrugged.

'Maybe sooner than you think,' she said. 'Eventually she'll have to come back and see to matters over here.' Then she added, slyly, 'At least you know who your baby's father is.'

Imogen turned away.

'If I have it,' she said.

The moment of intimacy had gone. Charlotte handed her the money.

'Felix left this for you,' she said. 'Put it somewhere safe, and let's make a plan about the garden so that we've got something positive to talk about to Jerry in the morning. And I think you're right about the locks. I'll ring a locksmith first thing.'

But she forgot.

Nicholas telephoned that evening. Charlotte sent Imogen upstairs to talk to him on the bedroom extension; she had no wish to catch even a fragment of their conversation.

Jerry took some time to get back to Becktham. He was unlucky over lifts, with a dearth of commercial vans, and he was ignored by suspicious Sunday motorists who wouldn't take a chance, but eventually a man driving a shabby transit stopped for him. He was going to a store he'd got in Becktham and asked Jerry, as a return for a free ride, if he'd help offload some stuff he'd got in the back. Jerry was agreeable, only wondering when they unloaded it – a job lot of china, bits of furniture and several television sets – if they were stolen goods. The man said he'd bought everything at a boot sale. More likely he'd tried to flog it, Jerry thought, but he lent a hand and then sloped off, remembering the address for possible future contact.

His mother was at home, much recovered. She'd had a lazy day, but she'd cleaned the house up a bit. She didn't want that nice Imogen to think her a slut, even if she was one. Jerry told her about the old guy's garden and the plans for Charlotte's.

'It'll be great, Mum. I can be there all day tomorrow, and then Sunday and Monday next weekend. If it stays fine and I stick at it, I'll get a lot done. Imogen can help with the light stuff.' That wouldn't hurt her; it would do her good to be in the fresh air.

'Why only the light stuff?' asked Angela. 'She's a fit, strong girl. She can dig as well as you.'

Of course, she didn't know about the baby. She'd better not, or not yet.

'Very true,' he said, and found a pad of paper.

He spent some time that evening sketching out possible designs for Charlotte's garden, not to scale, for he'd taken no measurements, but by guesswork.

'You did learn something in that prison, didn't you?' his mother said, with satisfaction.

'Found my vocation, maybe,' Jerry answered.

Nicholas's term was ending and he hadn't decided what to do in the vacation. The Elms, their family house in Surrey, was up for sale, but he could still go there, since even if it went quickly, which was likely, it would be some weeks before the sale was completed. However, his father was based there and Nicholas had no wish, just now, to spend time with him. He needed funds. Over the weekend he had combed advertisements in the local papers, and he had found a job as a waiter at one of the hotels. He would stay on in his house, where the rent had been paid in advance; even though hand-to-mouth, he would manage. He had offers from two universities, depending on his A level results. He must do well in those exams; after that, there were other choices. If necessary he could take a year out and earn some serious money; maybe he should, to stand by Imogen if she went ahead and had the kid. What a mess she'd made of things.

Felix had rung him up on Sunday night. He'd gone to Granbury, only to find Charlotte and Imogen were out and he had to wait for their return.

'Did they know you were coming?' asked Nicholas.

'Charlotte invited me for lunch,' said Felix.

'Did you accept?'

'I hadn't spoken to her. I imagined the invitation stood,' said Felix.

'Well, what time did you get there?'

'Around half-past three. Maybe nearer four.'

'Four o'clock! Dad, you know Charlotte and Granddad always had lunch at one, or, at the latest, one-fifteen.'

'And that's another thing,' said Felix, refusing to be wrong-footed. 'Has Imogen spoken to you about this whim she's got, questioning your birth?' If she hadn't, she or Charlotte soon would. He'd better get in first.

'Our birth? What do you mean?'

'She thinks you might be test-tube babies, just because you're twins, and not identical.'

'Shit – does she?'

'She does,' said Felix, in a weary tone.

'Well, are we?' Nicholas demanded. 'All you have to do is say no, if we're not.'

'There was no reasoning with her,' Felix said. 'She ran out of the room before I could reply. Talk to her, Nick. Try to make her see sense about an abortion, there's a good chap. Must go. Talk to you soon.'

He rang off, and Nicholas, replacing his receiver, realised that Felix had dodged the question. And what a question! Nicholas didn't like Imogen's theory one bit. He thought about it, feeling rather sick. Surely it couldn't be true? All that stuff about test tubes was creepy, and weren't he and Imogen too old for it to have been possible in their case? Hadn't it got fashionable quite recently? He didn't know a lot about it. Certainly neither he nor Imogen resembled Felix, or their mother, come to that. Perhaps they were adopted, but wouldn't they have discovered this from their birth certificates? Nicholas couldn't remember ever needing his; he'd had a passport all his life, renewed without providing one. Perhaps he should ask for it, confront their father. If they weren't the products of straightforward sex, they had been deceived. He'd always got on well enough with Felix, for Nicholas, whilst not excelling in any particular direction, was an achiever, playing in school football teams and doing well academically. But so was Imogen; she had always had better results at school than Nicholas, and she was an outstanding swimmer, though not good at games, but their parents had never given her credit for her successes. In fairness to herself, and for the future, she ought to do her A level exams next term. He'd have to speak to Charlotte about it, and about this test-tube business.

Meanwhile, though, he was going round to Phoebe's place. She might know a bit about test-tube babies.

*　　*　　*

Phoebe knew about blue and brown eyes, the Mendelian theory. She explained it to him, and gave him a run-down on fertility treatment. Nicholas hadn't bothered much about her IQ. Their relationship had been intensely physical, and he had genuinely tried to help her, even getting quite fond of her little kids, a boy of two and another of four months. He felt pleased when he managed to shut them up when they were bawling, but they were messy. He tried to avoid all that, but Phoebe as a person was so clean; she washed herself, her children, and their clothes remorselessly. Nicholas, a bit of a dandy, appreciated that; it contrasted agreeably with the sluttishness of some other girls he knew. But Phoebe wasn't a girl; she was a woman. He liked that. Hearing her talk knowledgeably, he thought he could do worse than stick with her for a while.

In bed with her in her flat in a drab council building, he wondered if she'd thought of taking in ironing as a way of adding to her meagre income. His mother used an ironing service, had done for years. There might be money in it in Oxford.

Charlotte rang Granbury's Health Centre as soon as it opened on Monday morning. There was a slot when Imogen could see the woman doctor at half-past twelve. This was lucky; Charlotte had expected her to be booked up all day, and possibly on Tuesday, too.

She told Imogen that she must keep the appointment, and, sulky again, the girl agreed. She had been very cheerful when Jerry arrived. He'd got a lift from a neighbour, a plumber, who was a customer at the chip shop and went out of his way to drop him off half a mile from the village. Charlotte had been up for some time; Imogen was woken by their voices.

Charlotte had decided, overnight, that the scrubby patch of grass she had inherited must be replaced. Cut regularly, it would look good; taking up the old turf and levelling the ground would keep Jerry occupied while she faced up to things with Imogen, and Imogen might be reasonably content while he was there; he was young company for her. If she hadn't known about his past, Charlotte would have taken him for what he seemed, a pleasant lad, but she would be careful; she wouldn't leave money or valuables, such as her watch, lying around, though he must know that if anything were to disappear, he would be the immediate suspect.

She had a spade and a rake, and some other basic tools which Felix had permitted her to take from White Lodge, remarking that their value at the auction he was planning for the better things from the house would be negligible. Jerry set to work. He'd brought a spirit level, anticipating the need for one. He began stacking up the turf to be discarded; it would rot down and form topsoil. Imogen had come downstairs as soon as she heard his voice; she was dressed in what she slept in, a long tee-shirt with a flower motif across her chest.

'Hi,' she said.

Jerry said, 'If you're coming out, you'll catch your death like that. Put some clothes on.'

'Right – I'll be out later,' Imogen promised, and meekly went upstairs.

One up to Jerry, Charlotte thought. She walked down the garden to ask him not to stop Imogen keeping her doctor's appointment.

'She has told you she's pregnant?' She needed to be sure.

'Yes. Poor kid,' said Jerry in paternal tones.

'She won't talk about it at all,' said Charlotte.

'She hasn't told me who the bloke is, if that's what you're getting at,' said Jerry. 'Maybe she doesn't know.'

Charlotte looked at him, shocked.

'It's possible, but I don't like to think of such a situation,' she said.

'There's that drug now. I forget its name – begins with R,' said Jerry. 'The girl doesn't remember anything about it. The rape drug, they call it. It's slipped into a drink. Dead easy.'

That was an answer Charlotte hadn't thought of; it might be the right one, and would explain a lot about Imogen's attitude.

'She must see the doctor, anyhow,' she said. 'She may tell her what happened.'

'Doesn't make much difference, does it? She's still going to have a kid, whoever the guy is.'

Charlotte would not discuss with him the possibility of another choice.

'The father has a responsibility,' she said primly.

'Ah – but girls like babies, don't they?' Jerry said. 'Gives them something of their own, someone to love, who loves them back.'

'Someone who gives them sleepless nights and exhausts them,' Charlotte replied tartly.

'Yeah – well – worth it in the end, innit?' Jerry said. 'I never had no dad. Don't know who he was. My mum won't tell me. She managed, and she didn't have a gran like you to help her.' She'd died before he was born.

But Charlotte wasn't Imogen's grandmother and she didn't

want to help her with the baby. However, if Jerry's mother had had a family to help her, he might have kept out of trouble, she reflected.

She left him to his labours and went indoors.

Imogen brought an armful of clothing with her when she came downstairs again, dressed, and asked if she might wash it.

'Put it in the machine and I'll turn it on later, when you've finished your breakfast,' said Charlotte, and she reminded Imogen about the appointment.

Imogen went silent.

'You must go, Imogen. You must be medically checked. There are dates to calculate – matters to discuss.'

'I don't see why. I'm perfectly well. I'm not even being sick,' said Imogen.

That might be a treat in store.

'I'm responsible for you, Imogen. You have to see the doctor,' Charlotte said.

'Typical teacher,' Imogen said rudely. 'Bossy,' and, with a piece of toast in her hand, she went into the garden to help Jerry. He soon had her raking the revealed subsoil, levelling it by eye as best she could.

If Imogen mentioned the appointment to Jerry, he might make her see the sense of it. Jailbird though he was, he appeared to have a good effect on her.

Charlotte drove Imogen to the surgery, which was at the further end of the village, down a turning on the road to Nettington. Imogen had protested that she would walk there.

'You don't trust me,' she said.

'I think you might have trouble finding the way, and I'm giving you my support, Imogen,' Charlotte replied.

'Well, I can walk back,' Imogen said.

'I'll see you in, and then I'll wait for you in the car,' said Charlotte. 'I'll bring the paper and do the crossword.'

The surgery was in a modern block added to an older complex where there was a community hall and library. Charlotte had not consulted a doctor since she moved into the village, but she had registered with the practice. She had some sleeping pills which were prescribed after Rupert's death, but, fearful of dependency, she seldom took one; when they were gone, she might ask for more, as a precaution, but a new doctor might not want to give them to her. That could wait, however.

As it was such a lovely day, it was no penalty to abandon the warm waiting-room with its upright chairs and old magazines, and sit in the car with the window down. The receptionist had taken Imogen's details, and the fact that she was a visitor, smiling at her kindly. Even so, this must be intimidating for her, Charlotte thought. Worse was to come, whichever way she decided.

She had not locked the house up when she left, though she had considered it. At eleven, she had made a mug of instant coffee for herself and offered one to Jerry, who had chosen tea, and so had Imogen. The two of them had sat on cushions on the so-called patio – a few paving slabs outside the French window – while they drank it. They were chatting and Charlotte wondered what they found to talk about together. In fact, Imogen had asked Jerry how he came to be so keen on gardening, and he had taken the plunge; before Charlotte could ask him if he'd done it, as agreed, he told her about his prison sentence.

Imogen didn't react with shock, and she didn't ask him what he'd done, so he told her it was a bit of thieving, not mentioning his earlier conviction when he was with a group of youths who had beaten up a shopkeeper when they raided a small grocery store in a Midlands village. Jerry had been on other raids with this group, but because he was only fifteen he had got off with probation that time, though the ringleaders had been sent to prison; however, he was tainted by association and he had a record. His mother, aware that he had fallen into bad company, had resolved that they must move to a new area, and so they came to Becktham where he had done two years at school, scraping a few undistinguished GCSE passes. After that he had worked in a supermarket, stacking shelves, until, bored, he got into more trouble. This time, after his arrest, he had been sent down.

Imogen emerged from the surgery after little more than half an hour. She was smiling.

'Everything's fine,' she told Charlotte. 'The doctor was very nice. I'm to go back when I've thought about things a bit.'

'And when is the baby due?' asked Charlotte, knowing that if there was to be a termination, delay was not a good idea.

'October some time,' Imogen said airily. 'I don't want to think about it now.'

Charlotte could not force her to speak. They drove home in silence, to find that Jerry had finished lifting the turf. He'd marked out prospective beds and a curving path.

'We'll need to order that new lawn, Mrs F.,' he said, when they returned. 'I've measured up what we'll need, and I took the liberty of ringing up a couple of places listed in the Yellow Pages, to get quotes. One guy could deliver today.'

'Oh, Jerry!' One of these youngsters, but unfortunately the wrong one, had a sense of urgency. 'Explain it to me. Then we'll order them.'

11

Charlotte felt she was being rushed. She telephoned the turf supplier Jerry had mentioned, and some others, but in the end she settled for the original one which he had found; Jerry would be there when the load arrived and could stack it, ready to start laying it the following Sunday.

By the time all this was accomplished, dusk was falling, but Jerry toiled on, starting to roll out the new grass. Charlotte paid him at a rate of six pounds an hour, which was a pound more than Howard Smythe had advised when she telephoned to consult him.

'I'm sure the chip shop doesn't pay as much,' he told her. 'The boy's unskilled, and only nineteen. He'd be lucky to get four pounds stacking shelves in a supermarket.'

'What do you pay the man you employ?' Charlotte challenged.

'Ten pounds an hour,' confessed Howard. 'But he's a mature man, a knowledgeable gardener.'

'Jerry has been working hard,' Charlotte replied. 'He's done an amazing amount in a day.'

'And you've fed him, I expect,' Howard guessed.

She had, of course. She and Imogen had enjoyed his company as they ate cold roast lamb and baked potatoes. Imogen had raked up stones and marked out the edges of future flower beds, and when Jerry began laying the grass, she helped, crawling about on hands and knees, copying how he did it. Jerry asked for the lights to be on at the back of the house so that he could continue working; one of Imogen's tasks was to move within range of the external halogen light's sensor each time it went out, making it come on again.

When Charlotte went to tell him he must stop, all the turf was down.

'I'll fill in the joins and design the beds next time,' he promised. 'It would be good if you could water it, though, unless it rains. There may be some rough bits, but I'll soon neaten those up.'

Charlotte believed him as she agreed to carry out his instructions. She'd buy some plants, too, a few shrubs to begin with, as he'd otherwise have little left to do the next weekend.

While he washed at the kitchen sink, Imogen said, 'Do you think we could drive him home? It may take him ages to get a lift.'

'Oh!' Charlotte hadn't thought of that. Equally, even though the area was small, she had never expected him to remove the old grass and lay the new turf in a day. It had been achieved because he had found a firm able to deliver promptly and by the time it arrived, he had prepared the ground. He certainly did not lack initiative. 'You're right,' she said. 'We must.'

Jerry protested. Someone would pick him up in the end, he said. Then he had another thought. If he accepted, Mrs Frost could meet his mother who was sure to be impressed, and she might agree to arrange car insurance for him so that he could drive over at the weekend. It was worth a try. After a further amount of protesting, he gave in and they all piled into the car.

Jerry sat in the back. He had thoroughly enjoyed the day's work; transforming what had been a tip into a presentable plot was satisfying, and Mrs Frost had been grateful. A reference from her, in due course, would help him on his newfound upward path. The money, too, was good; if he offered to pay for the extra car insurance, his mother would find it difficult to refuse.

When they reached Becktham, Jerry directed Charlotte into his road and as she stopped, he said, 'Please come in and meet my mum, Mrs Frost.'

'No, Jerry, we must get back,' Charlotte said.

'Oh, please, Charlotte,' Imogen implored, already getting out of the car.

'It's late – your mother won't want visitors now,' Charlotte said.

'It's not a night for her evening job,' Jerry insisted. 'She'll be glad to see you.'

And he was right, she was. Angela had not drawn her sitting-room curtains and she had seen the car draw up outside, behind her Metro. By the light of the streetlamp, she saw Imogen emerge, and was out of the door in seconds, hurrying down the path.

Charlotte had to comply. As soon as they were in the house, she realised she had seen Jerry's mother before, but it was a little while before she remembered where.

For her part, Angela had never looked at her benefactor at Becktham station's ticket office; she had no connection to make.

*   *   *

There was no point in reminding her of the incident; one should not draw attention to one's good deeds. Charlotte remembered how she had thought the woman a troubled soul, and no wonder, with Jerry's record.

Angela was offering coffee. Imogen was astonished when Charlotte, intrigued now, accepted, thinking that it would be as well to learn what she could about this family as Imogen had already made friends with them.

'I'm Angela Hunt,' she had said, greeting them and holding out a warm, dry hand.

'Charlotte Frost,' said Charlotte. 'I think you know my step-granddaughter.'

'Indeed I do,' said Angela. 'She looked after me so nicely on Saturday when I wasn't feeling very well. Made me tea and bundled me off to bed. She's lovely,' and she smiled at Imogen who had turned pink with pleasure.

Imogen helped her now with the coffee, while Jerry took Charlotte into the sitting-room and guided her towards an armchair. Noticing the pristine large sofa and its matching chairs, she recalled the television advertisements which advised that you could buy now and pay nothing for a year, or even longer. What happened when the money was required? Perhaps you undertook another job.

Jerry drew the curtains.

'Mum ought to pull them when it gets dark,' he said. 'I'm always telling her. People can see in, and that. Gives them ideas. Or can.'

Charlotte refrained from commenting that he, if anyone, should know. He perched on the edge of the other chair and strove for something to say.

'Mum and Imogen got on brilliantly the other day,' he said.

'But she doesn't know about Imogen's trouble. That's for Immy to tell, isn't it?'

Immy. Charlotte had never heard her called that; the diminutive indicated that he really liked her.

'Yes,' she said.

'My mum works in Denfield. She goes on the train,' he said.

'Oh,' said Charlotte, who already knew this.

'Her firm's just moved from Becktham so she has a bit of a journey to make now,' he said. 'But she goes by train because of the parking.'

'I see,' said Charlotte.

'She's a great mum and I don't want to worry her no more,' said Jerry, fixing Charlotte with his most sincere expression.

'I'm sure you don't, Jerry,' she said. 'And if you go on working as hard as you did today, I'm sure she'll be proud of you.' How sanctimonious I sound, she thought, but what can I say to the boy? It's up to him, after all.

Angela and Imogen soon appeared, Imogen carrying the tray and Angela a plate of biscuits. Charlotte banished thoughts about supper, accepting a cup of excellent freshly brewed coffee and a Rich Tea biscuit.

'Jerry tells me your firm has moved,' she prompted, and Angela launched into an explanation of the various journey choices before her. Charlotte, seeing her less harassed now than at their earlier encounter, realised that she was a pretty woman, in a rather faded way, and probably still under forty.

'Jerry worked miracles today,' she said, when Angela ran out of steam. 'He took up a patch of so-called lawn and almost finished laying a new one. It just needs a bit of tidying up, doesn't it, Jerry?'

'Yeah – then a few shrubs and stuff around the place. We'll have it looking good in a few weeks,' Jerry said.

'Jerry's got green fingers,' said Angela. 'He only has to look at a plant and it grows.'

'Perhaps you should take it up professionally, Jerry,' said Charlotte. 'Do a horticultural course.'

'That's a brilliant idea. You could enquire,' Angela said. There were all sorts of courses you could do. She beamed. Things were looking up.

Going home, Imogen said that it had been a good suggestion, but wouldn't it cost? Even if Jerry were accepted, he might have to pay, and he wouldn't be earning.

'There could be a solution,' Charlotte said. 'We could find out what the possibilities are.' Thoughts of Kew, or the gardens on Tresco, ran through her mind. 'His mother must have had a hard time,' she said.

'And she's still having it. All those jobs,' said Imogen. 'She looked dire the other day. Greenish-grey.'

'She likes you,' said Charlotte.

'I like her, too,' said Imogen.

'There's enough chicken casserole for supper,' Charlotte said. 'I wonder what those two will have.'

In Angela's view the chip shop ought to open on a Monday, but Bobby and Val liked to have a proper break.

'We could have had some nice fish and chips tonight,' Angela was grumbling. Fully recovered, and having had a cheese sandwich for lunch, she was hungry.

'Let's have pizzas,' Jerry said. 'I'll pay.' He'd been at Charlotte's for ten hours and she had paid him sixty pounds, not docking time taken for lunch.

After this it was easy to ask his mother about the car insurance; she capitulated swiftly.

'I was going to walk to the station anyway,' she admitted. 'It'd save the car park fee. So you could go over to Granbury for a couple of hours in the afternoon. Only don't be late for the chip shop. That's a solid job – once the garden's done, the one with Mrs Frost will finish. I'll fix it up tomorrow, Jerry.'

'You won't forget? With work, and that?'

'No,' she promised. 'I'll do it first thing when I get to the office.'

'So I know it'll be OK to take the car in the afternoon?'

Sighing, she agreed.

Their pizzas soon arrived, brought by a youth on a motorbike, a boy Jerry knew. There was some badinage on the doorstep as he paid; then the courier sped off with much revving of his exhaust.

'She's a nice lady, Mrs Frost,' said Angela. 'Widow, is she?'

'Yeah.' Jerry related what he knew about Charlotte's history. 'Immy's sorry for her – said her dad – Immy's dad – more or less turned her out of the house because he wanted to sell it. He turned up yesterday in a bloody great Mercedes.'

'Why's Imogen staying with her gran?'

'Oh – some family trouble,' Jerry said airily.

'What's the father like?'

'I didn't stay to find out,' said Jerry. 'His car was parked outside when we got back from a walk in the afternoon.'

A walk, he said. But Imogen had told Angela that they had gone to look at Captain Smythe's garden, and she had revealed that Captain Smythe had caught a burglar in his house on Thursday night. Angela had not heard about this incident, and Imogen did not name the offender. Well, it wasn't Jerry; he had been safely in bed on Thursday night.

'Seen Pete lately?' Angela asked, and Jerry, cheese stringing from his mouth, shook his head.

She was not sure if that was true; later, in bed, she thought about her son and worried, eventually managing to console herself with the reflection that he had made friends with a nice respectable girl, and she'd now met the girl's grandmother. While Jerry worked in Mrs Frost's garden, and also in the chip shop, he was with people who could only influence him for good. She wondered if he fancied Imogen; that Imogen might fancy him went without saying, for he was a lovely-looking boy with that warm smile, and nice ways when he chose to use them. He was a good son who had fallen into bad company; that Pete, she thought, brushing aside Jerry's earlier misdemeanours committed without Pete's aid. A short film strip ran through her mind as she grew drowsy: Imogen, slimmed down a little and with her hair arranged in a flattering top-knot, wearing gleaming white satin and a shower of tulle, and Jerry in a morning suit, outside Becktham parish church. She was beside them, dressed to kill, and holding the arm of a handsome middle-aged man with greying hair: Imogen's father, owner of the Merc.

Basking in this vivid fantasy, Angela slept.

Jerry turned up in Granbury the next day, soon after half-past two. There was no one at home, and Mrs Frost's car was not in the garage. That was a disappointment, but Jerry spent his two hours neatening up the turf. The garden tools were kept in the garage and, though closed, it was unlocked – sheer folly, Jerry thought as he wheeled out the hose and connected it up. After he had carved out two new flower beds and forked them over, he gave the new turf a good watering. Then it was time to go. He couldn't leave a note; he had neither pen nor paper. They'd see what he'd done and would understand, and he'd telephone. He was, after all, due another twelve pounds, and Mrs Frost wasn't one to cheat.

Imogen came home just as he was leaving.

Charlotte had wasted no time in planning for her, and she had been out for a driving lesson, returning in the driving school's dual-control car to be dropped at the door by her instructor.

'Can I come back with you, Jerry?' she asked, when she saw he had the car.

'I've got to go to work,' he said. 'I'll be there till nearly ten o'clock. You'd be better here. Mrs F. will be back soon, won't she? Where's she gone?'

'Shopping. We ate everything yesterday,' said Imogen.

'Mum fixed the car insurance for me, so I did a couple of hours,' said Jerry. 'I'll be over tomorrow. Cheers,' and he leaped into the Metro, driving off with a flourish that impressed Imogen but not her instructor, who had been making a few notes before he, too, left the close.

She'd see Jerry the next day. It wasn't long to wait.

Charlotte, when she returned with washing powder and further food supplies, was pleased to find more work done in the garden, and Imogen with pink cheeks, looking happy. The driving lesson had gone quite well, too.

Jerry came over again the next day. He was eager to start planting. All three of them spent time standing on boards he had rescued from a skip and brought with him to lay across the new turf for them to stand on as they discussed what should go where. Charlotte could see that if she let him have his head, costs might become exorbitant.

'Why don't I ring up Captain Smythe and ask him if you can go down there and collect whatever he can spare; then we can buy other things later?' she suggested.

Jerry accepted this proposal, and she telephoned Captain Smythe who said they were welcome to come round straight away. Jerry whisked Imogen off with him in the red Metro; there wasn't much time before he must go back to Becktham but he could make a start.

In the end, he left Imogen at Rose Cottage with Captain Smythe, the two of them digging up various plants, keeping damp soil around their roots and putting them in plastic bags in boxes. They would be all right for several days.

His enthusiasm was infectious. After he left, Imogen and Captain Smythe spent a pleasant, peaceful hour together, jointly digging up and dividing irises and rooted shoots of jasmine and other shrubs, none of it strenuous, and Captain Smythe thought Imogen too fit and strong a girl to be at risk of a miscarriage from a bit of digging. That, if it were to happen, would be a solution to her problem, but not necessarily the right one.

They did not talk much, limiting their conversation to the work in hand.

Charlotte, meanwhile, with Imogen out of the house, and aware that the term was almost over, had telephoned her school to ask if there were any possibility of her work being sent to her. The house-mistress, eventually located, thought there would not be a problem. All her subjects could be worked on at home and references sought in libraries. A study plan might be set up; involved staff would certainly cooperate.

That was a big hurdle passed, Charlotte thought. Relieved, she decided to iron Imogen's washing, and took the pressed garments into her room to put away. She opened a drawer where Imogen had put underclothes and tights, and to her astonishment saw an opened pack of sanitary pads. Two or three were left, and there was an unopened pack beside them.

A pregnant girl would not be using pads.

Imogen had seen the doctor only yesterday.

She closed the drawer and put the freshly-ironed clothing on the bed.

As the afternoon passed, Charlotte realised that Jerry must have gone back to Becktham. Unless she had done another disappearing trick, Imogen might be still at Rose Cottage so Charlotte walked down there. What was she to make of her discovery? Imogen might have the pads in case she miscarried, or perhaps her period had come on late, and she had never been pregnant at all, the victim of a false alarm, but why not say so, if that were the case? Thoroughly confused, Charlotte arrived at Rose Cottage, walking round the house to the garden. Imogen's trainers were neatly placed by the back door, beside the captain's ancient, shining brogues, and alongside several wooden trays containing plants in plastic bags or pots. She continued down the garden and found the two of them standing on the little jetty surveying the pond. It seemed a pity to disturb them, though they appeared not to be talking; restful silence was a blessing. This part of the garden was well screened on all sides by trees and shrubs, a miniature forest glade. As if he sensed her presence, Howard Smythe turned and saw her; he said something to Imogen and came towards her. Imogen's jeans were tucked into a pair of old black wellingtons; later she told Charlotte that these had been Mrs Smythe's and the old man had kept them thinking they might come in handy. Charlotte wondered if he had retained other relics of his wife; people sometimes did, unable to bear the process of discarding once precious possessions. Felix had taken charge of Rupert's things; she neither knew nor cared if he would use the suits and shirts. She was the item that had been superfluous and she had been cast out promptly.

Left, however, with responsibilities which were not hers: this young woman now approaching, flushed and happy, apparently having banished all thought of her predicament. But was there a predicament at all? And if not, why had Imogen invented one? Whatever the answer, it looked as though the serious talk that must take place between her and the girl required a different script, and should not be undertaken in a hurry.

She called out to them. As Howard walked towards her, he stooped a little. Charlotte had never noticed that before; he had seemed to hold himself so straight and upright, as though on parade, but the experience of the break-in must exact some price; perhaps he was having a delayed reaction.

'We've boxed up lots of plants,' said Imogen.

'If I come down in the morning with the car, we could collect them and save time for Jerry when he arrives to do the planting,' Charlotte suggested.

'I wish I could bring them up for you, but I don't drive now,' said Captain Smythe. 'My sight's not what it was.' He had incipient glaucoma, but he was not going to tell them that.

Charlotte had wondered whether he still drove; loss of the car would have affected his independence. Now she knew, she could offer to give him a lift when she was going shopping. The thought warmed her; it would be good to have his company.

Back at the house, Imogen exchanged the boots for her trainers, and she and Charlotte set off home before it got too dark for them to see their way.

Imogen had devised a plan; it had occurred to her that afternoon, when Jerry had once again given her a soft, friendly, parting kiss before he drove away.

12

If Imogen isn't pregnant, there's no hurry to make plans, Charlotte thought, in bed that night. Even so, she must be tackled. No wonder there was no sign of morning sickness, not that every pregnant woman suffered from it. At least she'd seen the doctor, so if she had miscarried, there were no problems.

Circumstantial evidence doesn't prove a case; the presence of pads in Imogen's drawer was not conclusive. However, Charlotte was reluctant to reveal that she had found them, in case the girl, in a prickly mood, accused her of prying. Perhaps she should defer action until the next batch of ironing needed to be put away. However, she told Imogen that the school was going to send her work on.

'You must be occupied,' said Charlotte. 'You can still help Jerry when he's here. You've worked hard and done well at school; there's no reason why you shouldn't take your exams.' If she wasn't pregnant, perhaps she could return to school next term; there would be no grounds for her exclusion. However, that was looking too far ahead. Slyly, she added, 'If you're going to have a baby to look after, the more qualifications you can get, the better.'

'That's true,' Imogen said, almost meekly. 'I suppose there are crèches at some colleges.'

'I believe so,' Charlotte answered, somewhat unnerved.

I should have tackled her then, she thought later, challenged her, asked her for dates, for facts.

Another driving lesson took up time the next morning. While Imogen was out, Charlotte took the car down to Rose Cottage to collect the plants. Captain Smythe helped her load them into the Fiat. She felt an urge to tell him about her suspicions, but refrained; he was old, and a man, and she didn't know him very well. He might be embarrassed. There wasn't really anyone with whom she could discuss the theory; the doctor would respect patient confidentiality and disclose nothing. Charlotte realised that throughout most of her adult life she had walked away from confrontation; in her first marriage she had accepted her husband's preoccupation with his work and that her role was to manage an efficient household, not to worry him about trifles. He had not lived long enough to be in conflict with his children over their academic and professional choices; she had been involved with their decisions, discussing all their options, aware that their father might have opposed Tim's wish to join the navy and could have tried to direct them both towards careers of his selection. She'd even married Rupert rather than hold out for a part-time relationship which, these days, would have been appropriate for many in their situation and might, she thought now, with hindsight, have been just as happy and had a far less damaging aftermath.

She wouldn't have had this troubled, naughty girl to deal with, for naughty she was, if she had dreamed up a deception just to cause distress. Parents split up all too frequently these days but it wasn't as grim a fate as the death of either one, and it wasn't an abandonment. What had Imogen hoped to achieve? To draw attention to herself?

Was her real concern the question of her own heredity?

In the small hours, Charlotte fell into a troubled sleep and woke next morning feeling unrefreshed.

The break-in at Rose Cottage and the arrest of Pete Dixon was a satisfactory result for the police. Unfortunately they hadn't caught him in possession of stolen goods, to link him up with other burglaries; there were none at his address when it was searched, so no doubt he got rid immediately of what he stole, but with his record he was likely to go down for several months, if not a year or two, which would take him out of circulation for a while. Since his arrest no more similar crimes had been reported in the area where there had been a series, usually involving a distraction by a second youth selling makeshift articles at the door, so, although this incident had followed a different *modus operandi*, taking place during the night, there may have been a connection. Pete, however, had not mentioned an accomplice and no pointers towards one had occurred. With plenty of unsolved crimes to be resolved, and the paperwork for those and others piling up, no one was going to put in time looking for a second perpetrator unless there were strong indications of involvement.

Pete was likely to be remanded for a further week, though he might get bail. The case would be heard in full when the prosecution was prepared.

Jerry hadn't spent much time thinking about his former partner. Pete had been unlucky, getting caught; that was all.

Captain Smythe was a tough old guy and very far from helpless, as he had proved; Pete must have expected to be in and out in minutes, undetected. He'd not go down for long, Jerry decided optimistically, planning to ask Mrs Frost how he could find out about this garden training business.

Nicholas came over that morning. He turned up without warning, just as Imogen returned from her driving lesson. Two packages of her folders and books from school had already arrived, and Charlotte had said she could work in the dining-room. Nicholas's arrival was a distraction, but he approved as the big padded bags were undone and the contents stacked on the table.

He was full of new plans. He and Phoebe were setting up an ironing business; it was his idea, and he was buying her a fancy iron and ironing board. They would collect and deliver – that was Nicholas's role, and he would do the billing. Fliers would be run off on his computer.

'What about your exams?' said Charlotte, hearing this.

'I'll have plenty of time to work. Phoebe will be doing all the ironing,' Nicholas answered. 'I've got my job as a waiter, too. I'll be all right for money if it takes off, and it will, I'm sure. People hate ironing.'

Charlotte rather liked it; it was satisfying, and quite soothing, and you could listen to the radio.

'It sounds a good idea,' she said, wondering about Phoebe.

'You'll end up marrying that woman,' said Imogen darkly. 'She's got two kids,' she told Charlotte.

'Well, you'll have one, too, before long,' said Nicholas airily. 'I hope that won't wreck your chances.'

Here was Charlotte's opportunity to launch forth, saying, 'Oh, and by the way, are you really pregnant?' while she had a witness and possible support, but she let it go.

'Come and see the garden,' Imogen said, leading Nicholas out there. 'Jerry's done it.'

He was impressed.

'And all from a meeting in a chip shop,' was his comment.

He stayed to lunch, but he had gone by the time Jerry arrived.

Imogen had to get through the rest of the day and tomorrow before she could put her plan into action. To help time pass, she decided she might as well get on with some school work, and after Jerry left she settled down to revision. It was only two weeks since her abrupt departure from the school; she had not missed a great deal. Tomorrow she would have been in Granbury a week, yet it felt as if she had been there for ever.

Nicholas had determined to have a show-down with Felix and if necessary demand a blood test to determine their paternity. What worried him was that Imogen had blue eyes; his and Felix's, and their mother's, were brown. According to Phoebe's explanation, this supported Imogen's theory. The only other possibility seemed to be that he and she were not related, and that she was some foundling sharing the same birthday and taken in by Felix and Zoe; hardly likely.

Jerry was not due again until Saturday, when during his afternoon break he was to meet Charlotte and Imogen at the garden centre on the edge of Nettington, which was the best locally for shrubs and roses. He had prepared beds for what they would buy then, and for Captain Smythe's contributions, a few of which he had already planted; the rest could wait until Sunday, when he would put in everything.

Imogen's driving lesson went well on Thursday, and she did school work that afternoon. On Friday morning the instructor said she should put in for her test.

'But you won't be here, Imogen. Your grandmother will be home – you'll be with her again, or your father,' Charlotte said. 'You should apply in their area.'

'You want to get rid of me,' said Imogen, and the ugly, sulky look she had worn for the first few days of her visit returned.

'I don't, but this is a temporary arrangement,' Charlotte said, somewhat desperately, though really, if it were a faked pregnancy and she went back to school next term, she might as well spend the holidays, and Easter, in Granbury. 'Let's talk to the instructor on Monday,' she temporised. 'Let's see what he says about how long you'll have to wait.'

They left it. Imogen went upstairs to wash her hair and have a bath. After supper she settled in the dining-room with her revision, but at nine o'clock, saying she was tired, she went up to bed. Charlotte stayed in the sitting-room, with the television on. She did not hear Imogen leave the house.

Imogen had practised shutting the front door without a sound, using her key in the lock. She had rung the taxi on her mobile phone. At half-past nine, it was waiting for her at the corner of Vicarage Fields.

Jerry had enjoyed his evening at the chip shop. That afternoon, he'd given his mother's car a thorough wash and polish. It took him over an hour, and afterwards, noticing one of the tyres looked a little soft, he drove to the nearest service station to check them. Then he watched television until it was time to go back to the chip shop. Once the weekend was over, he'd have finished Mrs Frost's garden; it hadn't taken all that long to do. Someone less conscientious than he might have spun it out a bit, taken more time, and Imogen had helped, which had reduced the size of the task. She'd worked hard. What a funny girl she was, weird, not like other girls Jerry knew, kind of innocent, really. It was strange to think of her having a kid, but then again, plenty of girls her age or younger did, every day, and looked after them well, very often. Some had come visiting at the prison, bringing their little mites with them. The kids would be all spruced up and smart, the dads quite proud. It was good to have kids while you were young yourself.

He put out a tray for his mother's snack when she came in, with a salmon paste sandwich and a cup ready for her coffee. She'd get a proper supper at the residential home, but she'd need something to get her going after the office. She seemed to be managing to catch the train, though on Wednesday she'd been late and he'd driven her to the station. He always heard her moving about in the morning and sometimes got up to make tea, even when he later went back to bed himself. He wished she could meet some nice guy who'd look after her, make her life easier, but at the same time he'd resent an intruder; they were cosy, him and his mum, with never a cross word, and she'd been brilliant about his trouble. He was glad he'd met Mrs Frost with her smile, and her instruction that he must mend his ways, before he ended up in the nick again.

Fridays were always busy at the chip shop. During the day a brisk wind had sprung up, and the night was chilly. A group of lads, some of them known to Jerry, came in at nine on their way from one pub to another; they were rowdy and slightly drunk, but not too far gone. Val hoped the chips they bought would sober them up. Bobby hoped none of them was driving, and Jerry told him that all the lads were local, from Becktham; they'd have come on foot. Clearing up took some time; Jerry hurried home, eager to return to the warmth of the house.

His mother had cleared up her tray, which was quite a surprise. Jerry went into the sitting-room and put on the television, leaning back to enjoy the can of beer he'd bought on his way home.

Upstairs, in his bed, Imogen waited, shivering.

The taxi had dropped her on the corner of his road. On the way over, the driver, a middle-aged man with grey hair curling on to his collar, commented on the spell of fine weather they'd been having, and then the amount of traffic on the road – not a lot, for a Friday – to which Imogen replied in monosyllables; discouraged, he became silent, but he, a father of two teenaged daughters and a younger son, watched her in the mirror and saw that she was sitting perched forward as far as the seat-belt would allow, not at all relaxed. She didn't seem drunk, as girls needing cabs at night sometimes were, though rarely as early as this, nor was she visibly distressed; there were no tears. She leaped from his cab the moment it stopped, impatiently asking how much it was and thrusting a twenty-pound note into his hand, not waiting for her change. In her fleece jacket, her dark trousers and trainers, she ran up the road.

She had brought a small torch which she'd found in Charlotte's kitchen where it stood on a shelf beside a larger one. Using it sparingly, anxious again about curious neighbours, she went round to the back of the Hunts' house and found the owl. The key was there; her main fear had been that it would not have been replaced. She let herself in. A light was on in the hall. Going through to the kitchen, Imogen went into the garden through the back door, which she left ajar while she replaced the key, for suppose Jerry needed it when he got home? Then, seeing the tray used for Angela's snack, she quickly washed up the few things it had held. There was no time to waste; making sure the house was secure, carrying her trainers lest she leave marks on the carpet, she went swiftly upstairs. She knew which was Angela's room; there were two other bedrooms and Jerry's was easily identified. In the dark, Imogen drew the curtains; if he noticed, he might think his mother had drawn them before she went out. After that, unable to postpone the moment any longer, she undressed quickly, folded up her clothes and laid them neatly on top of her shoes in a corner where they would not be visible when he entered and turned on the light.

Taking a deep breath, Imogen got into Jerry's cold bed and pulled the duvet up round her neck. She lay there, gasping, while her heartbeat steadied; slowly she became aware of various smells, partly soap – Jerry always seemed very clean, except after hard work in the garden and then he smelled rather nice, if sweaty – and other strange, not unpleasant smells. She tried to breathe evenly. There was nothing to be afraid of, for Jerry wasn't like other boys she had encountered; he was friendly and kind. He wouldn't hurt her, or only as much as couldn't be helped. Imogen, though lacking experience, was not totally ignorant.

By the time she heard him come in, her uncontrollable nervous shuddering had settled into plain shivers. She thought he would come upstairs at once, but he didn't; she was aware of him moving around downstairs and she heard the television come on. It didn't matter, now, how long it was before he came up to bed, for Angela would be out all night at her job in the home. Imogen had thought no further ahead than this.

At last the television went off. Its faint sound had almost sent her into a doze, but now she began to shiver again as Jerry came upstairs. He didn't come into the room straight away, going into the bathroom first, where she heard him loudly urinating. He hadn't closed the door, and she heard the shower start. Jerry had shed his clothes on the bathroom floor, as he did every night, and stepped straight under it. He wouldn't smell fishy, Imogen thought, pleased; that might have been a bit of a turn-off. When he did come in, whistling, naked, she was right under the duvet, her face covered, and he did not see her when he switched on the bedside light. He only discovered her presence when he slid under the covers himself.

'Shit!' he cried, and he leaped from the bed, dragging most of the duvet off her to hold in front of himself.

This was not what Imogen had envisaged, though her planning had been unable to carry her far beyond the moment when he got into bed beside her. Warmth, and a cuddle, gentle kisses, and then something which he would know how to do and which she might not enjoy but which would, with luck, make her pregnant. She might be able to persuade him to do it again when the chance came along, to make sure. Blokes always wanted it; she knew that. You didn't have to be in love. Imogen, after telling the doctor she was worried about being overweight, which was true, had decided that the best way out of her false predicament was to make it genuine.

She crouched under what she could of the duvet, gazing

up at him, terrified, he began to realise, as his own first shock abated.

'Shit – what are you doing here?' he asked her.

'I thought you might like it,' she said. She was trembling uncontrollably.

'You're pregnant by some crap bloke, and you're missing it, and you thought I'd do? Is that it?' he demanded. In spite of his anger, or because of it, he felt a physical response which made him clutch the duvet more firmly against his wayward member.

'No – no, Jerry! I thought you liked me,' Imogen said, and she began to cry.

'Oh – shit. Tears,' Jerry muttered. 'I never came on to you,' he said. Would it be so wrong, though? Here she was, readily available, and he could always do with some sex, not that he fancied her. 'What if I'd brought someone back with me and we'd found you here?' he said, for he sometimes did bring a girl back on a Friday, knowing the coast was clear. There was Tracy, whom he knew from school, and Shirley, who frequented The Swan, where he sometimes went after work.

'Well, you haven't,' she pointed out.

His anger had frightened her, but now she relaxed a little.

'You're as cold as ice. How long have you been here?' he said.

'Not very long. I came in a taxi. I knew where the key was.'

'And you want sex?'

'Yes,' she mumbled.

'Well, then,' said Jerry. 'Why not?' and he slid in beside her, pulling the duvet over them both. A quick fuck and then he'd take her home.

He didn't kiss her. He tried to force her tightly clenched legs apart with his knee and at first met resistance, though she did not struggle nor try to push him away. Taking a deep breath, she separated her thighs, and in the light from the lamp Jerry saw that she was still crying, while her face was set in the same determined expression she wore when she was carting turf or rolling it out, though she didn't weep then.

'For Christ's sake, Imogen, do you want it or don't you?' he demanded, rolling off her, and then, suddenly, he understood. 'You haven't done it, have you? Not ever? You're a bloody virgin, aren't you, and you aren't pregnant at all.'

Downstairs, the telephone rang. Both of them ignored it.

13

They ended up cuddled together under the duvet.

Jerry, for safety, pulled on some boxer shorts and a tee-shirt, and he looked away while Imogen put on a blue shirt which he pulled from a drawer and threw to her.

'Now,' he said. 'What's this all about?'

So she told him that it had got out of hand. She was upset because her parents had split up, and she thought if she stirred things, they would unite in the crisis and be reconciled. Also, she hated her school where, she said, no one liked her and the boys either ignored her, or wanted to snog not her, particularly, just any willing girl. Jerry thought she had probably got things wrong about that.

'You were unhappy so you decided to make everyone else unhappy too,' he said sagely. 'But why add me to the list?'

'I didn't want to make you unhappy,' she said.

'Well, if I'd got you pregnant, you would have. Hadn't you thought of that?'

'But no one would have known it was yours. They'd have thought it was the other bloke.'

'What other bloke? The one who doesn't exist?'

'Yes.'

'But it would have been my kid,' said Jerry, who never had unprotected sex but who might have with Imogen, thinking her pregnant already. Whew! 'Don't they teach you nothing at your school?' he said, despairingly.

'I wouldn't have asked anything from you. You wouldn't have known,' she said.

'But if it's my kid, don't I have a right to know? To be a dad to it?' Jerry asked.

'Maybe. But I don't know about my dad,' she said, and, amid more tears, she revealed her doubts about her own paternity.

Jerry was out of his depth.

'You need to talk to Nicholas,' he said. 'He must sort you out.' He kissed her gently, as he had before; then, feeling her soft body, warm now, close against him, almost moved further; after all, he had condoms nearby and she had to start some day, so why not with him? But he thought of Mrs Frost. She would not approve; she would say he had taken advantage of Imogen, and it would have been true. Besides, once started, she might get keen and become clingy and demanding. It happened with girls.

'We must get you home before Mrs F. finds out you've gone,' he said. In the morning, he'd get hold of Nicholas. Imogen could tell him the telephone number and address. It wouldn't be right to discuss what had happened with Mrs Frost, but someone ought to know how mixed up Imogen was.

Charlotte had discovered that Imogen had left the house.

She was late going up to bed herself. When she woke after falling asleep in front of the television, she had shaken up the cushions and turned off the sitting-room light. In the hall, she paused. The cloakroom door was ajar, and she always kept it closed. Imogen could not have been in there after their meal; she had gone up to bed so early. Besides, she had never left it open during the week she had been in the house. Something made Charlotte not simply close it, but put on the light and look inside. Even then, she did not at first realise what else was wrong; then she saw that Imogen's fleece jacket was not on its peg.

That meant nothing; though normally it hung here, she could have taken it up to her room.

Charlotte went quickly upstairs and softly, so as not to disturb her, opened the door of Imogen's room. There was a shape in the bed, but it was the old trick. A pillow had been placed lengthwise to make it look as if the bed was occupied.

Charlotte sat down abruptly, her heart thumping. Where had she gone? All sorts of ideas ran through her mind. She couldn't be meeting her lover because he didn't exist; she wasn't pregnant – at least, it seemed unlikely. Had she left a note? Recovering herself enough to switch on the light, Charlotte looked round the room but saw no sign of a note. Everything was orderly; the girl was so neat. Her holdall was there; she had not packed her things.

Perhaps she had been unable to sleep and had gone for a walk. Maybe she had looked in on Charlotte to say she was going out, and, seeing her dozing, had decided not to disturb her. Briefly satisfied with this explanation, Charlotte looked about downstairs in case a note had been left there, or even in Charlotte's room, but there was nothing.

The cloakroom door might have been left open so that any possible noise it could make being closed was avoided.

The best course was to remain calm and hope she would soon reappear. Charlotte made some coffee and drank it, watching the clock. Imogen might have gone to a club, or even a pub. Perhaps she hadn't mentioned it lest Charlotte forbid her to go. Young people were often unpredictable. Wherever she had gone, it was nearly midnight and surely she would come home before long?

But she didn't.

Could she have planned to meet Jerry? They got on so well, and it seemed that there was no other boy in the background. She might have arranged to meet him after the chip shop closed, though if that were the case, why not say so? Because she, Charlotte, might disapprove?

At what point should she ring the police? Wouldn't they simply say it was too early to worry and to ring again if Imogen didn't turn up the next day? And she couldn't ring Felix so soon to say she was missing.

It was much too late to disturb Captain Smythe and ask his advice.

If she went to bed herself, Imogen would probably be safely back in her room in the morning.

Imogen was. It was Charlotte who was missing the following day.

Charlotte had undressed and made ready for bed. Then, propped up on pillows, she had tried to read, listening for Imogen's return, but she was unable to settle and sleep was impossible. Finally she gave up, deciding to look for Imogen around the village. Perhaps she had been sleepless too – there must be a lot on her conscience – and had gone for a walk.

As she'd arranged the pillow in her bed to resemble a sleeping form, she must have thought that Charlotte might look in, but there was no way of knowing when she had gone out. Before Charlotte left the house, she dialled the Hunts' number; they were Imogen's only friends, apart from herself and Captain Smythe. She just might be with them.

There was no reply. Mrs Hunt had several evening jobs; she must be at one of them and Jerry was probably out on the town, after his stint at the shop. It was possible that Imogen was with him, in some club or other. He might have picked her up, having arranged it with her earlier. Charlotte did not know if Mrs Hunt would need the car to get to whatever work she would be doing tonight.

Hoping that this was the answer, Charlotte, nevertheless, put on trousers and a thick sweater, her padded jacket, and strong shoes, then set off for the village areas where she had been with Imogen. If she had gone for a walk, she might have had an accident – fallen and hurt herself, even been hit by a car. If she did not find her, Charlotte would ring the hospitals, then the police, and try to contact Imogen's father.

Granbury seemed to have settled down for the night. No cars passed while Charlotte was on the main road, and the parking area outside the few shops was deserted. She hesitated, wondering whether to go straight on towards Nettleton; then she decided to go down Meadow Lane, a more likely route if Imogen were simply out for a walk. She had taken her big torch, not noticing that the smaller one was missing, and she used it as she walked down the narrow lane where there were no street lights. All the houses were dark. Imogen wouldn't have gone to Captain Smythe's for a sympathetic chat, but she might have gone into the church. Charlotte tried its door, which was locked now.

If Imogen had done the same, maybe guiltily wanting to sort out the confused tangle she must have in her head, and aware that it was open during the day, what would she have done next, finding it closed? Walked round the church to the east end? Tried other doors, if there were any? Charlotte followed this course. There was a side door, but it was locked. She shone her torch over the graves, some marked with flowers, and went carefully round them till she came to the wall at the end of the churchyard, where there was a stone stile. Charlotte climbed it, and followed the path on the further side as it crossed a field. This way led down to the river; she had been along it several times before and though she had not brought Imogen here, the girl, pursuing the route which Charlotte had embarked upon, might have found it herself.

The night was very cold. Charlotte pulled a scarf from her coat pocket and tied it over her head, hesitating, wondering whether to turn back. She had not expected to be out long and had left no note explaining where she was; Imogen, however, if she returned first, would not realise she had gone out so she would not be alarmed, but if she had come this way and got lost, or worse, Charlotte might find her. She crossed another stile, shining the torch ahead. There were rustles in the field, and a sleepy heifer loomed towards her. Several of her sisters came sidling up, their eyes gleaming in the darkness. Charlotte kept on. They were mild, bemused creatures and would not hurt her. At last she reached a stile in the post and rail fence which ran through the hedge at the end of this field, beyond which lay the river. She would walk along the bank to the bridge, and work her way back to the village from there. She was tired now, and discouraged. If Imogen had suffered some misfortune while walking through the night, she could have used that mobile phone of hers to summon help, providing she had it with her, but Charlotte's fear was not of a simple accident; Imogen was emotionally upset and she might have decided on drastic action.

The path here ran close to the river's edge, curving sharply at a bend. Charlotte shone the torch ahead, briefly looking up, calling Imogen's name. She heard a faint sound which could have been one of the heifers lowing softly, or might have been something else, and turned, failing to watch where she was stepping. She put a foot in a hole, stumbling and toppling sideways, dropping the torch which rolled away from her as she slipped again, this time on some mud. All sense of direction lost in the sudden darkness, and her balance gone, Charlotte fell backwards into the river.

14

Jerry had rung for a taxi while Imogen was dressing. She kept his blue shirt on, pulling her sweater over it.

When she went downstairs, he was wearing clothes he had taken from a pile in the kitchen waiting to be ironed.

'You'll hate me now,' she said. 'You won't want to come and do the garden.'

'I'll finish it,' he said. For his own satisfaction, and for the money he would earn, he would complete it; besides, Mrs Frost would be a good referee for him when the work was done. 'I can't let Mrs F. down,' he went on. 'And I don't hate you.' He was sorry for Imogen; he was even flattered that she had cast him in the role of prospective father of her child. 'Here's the taxi.'

He went with her. He was afraid, if he didn't see her into Mrs Frost's house, that she might take off again and get herself into more trouble, which might involve him. They sat in the back of the cab, Imogen curled up, arms crossed over her body, giving occasional shuddering sighs. The pair were otherwise silent, and the driver formed quite the wrong impression of what was going on.

In Granbury, Jerry asked the driver to wait at the end of the close while he walked with Imogen along the road. She stopped him some way from the door.

'Don't come any further,' she said, and she thrust at him the rest of the money she had with her. It was quite a lot.

'For the taxi,' she said. 'Sorry.'

Jerry's hand closed over the notes. Maybe he needn't finish the garden after all; he didn't like leaving a job half done, but putting plants in was easy enough. Mrs F. and Imogen could finish that. As he hurried back to the cab, he heaved a huge sigh of relief. She really was a nutter and he was better out of it.

Imogen saw no significance in the hall light still being on when she entered the house. She put the torch back on the shelf, then crept upstairs and into her room. She was cold again. Shock and shame swept over her as she pulled off her clothes. Jerry's shirt came off with her sweater and she bundled both into a drawer, then put on the long tee-shirt in which she slept and got into bed, where she lay shivering, reliving what had happened.

Jerry had been very kind. She knew it, and lying against him, tucked up together, warm beneath the duvet, had been, for a few brief minutes, wonderful, but how could she ever look him in the face again?

It was a very long time before, at last, she dropped into a troubled restless sleep, finally submerging into a series of frightening dreams which she could not remember when, at twenty past nine, she woke up.

The house was quiet. On all the previous mornings, Charlotte, though not noisy, could be heard moving about but today there was nothing. Maybe she'd gone shopping. Imogen decided to have a bath; she was still cold, and she felt dirty, soiled by her own lies, as she told herself when lying in the water. Today she must confess the truth to Charlotte, and wait for her punishment.

She couldn't be sent back to school, or not yet, as the term was over, and she wouldn't look as far ahead as next term.

She drowsed a little in the bath, then freshened it with hot water before washing her hair, sinking down with the long strands floating around her. It was half-past ten when she finally got out of the water, dried herself, wrapped a towel round her head and got dressed, putting on some of the clean clothes which kind Charlotte had ironed. Then she went downstairs.

The blind was still drawn in the kitchen, which was strange. Imogen pulled it up; she felt thirsty, though not particularly hungry, and she put the kettle on and found a mug and the jar of instant coffee. There was milk in the refrigerator. The house around her was still silent and while the kettle boiled, Imogen went into the other downstairs rooms, where the curtains were still drawn. Charlotte must be sleeping in, and why not? Imogen's mother often did; just because Charlotte hadn't done so on any of the other mornings during Imogen's stay didn't mean she couldn't now. Imogen pulled the curtains back, and because Charlotte would often have the kitchen radio on, usually tuned to Classic FM, she turned it on now, keeping the volume low so as not to disturb Charlotte. That was more normal.

The coffee cleared her head, and she made herself some toast, then drank another cup, her mind a blank. She could avoid Jerry by not going to the garden centre this afternoon, though Charlotte would think it strange. Perhaps Nicholas would come over. If she told him the truth, he might tell Charlotte for her.

At that thought, she cheered up, and went out into the garden.

It was raw and cold; the fine weather of the previous few days had gone but it wasn't wet. Looking up at Charlotte's window, she saw the curtains were still drawn and felt guilty. Because of her, Charlotte's routine had been disturbed and now she was tired out, but this unusual behaviour meant that Imogen could postpone revealing her deception. Virtuously, she went into the dining-room and pulled out her books to attempt some work; however, she began to wonder if Charlotte might be ill when, by half-past twelve, she had still not appeared. Imogen hadn't heard her going to the bathroom, but she could have done that while Imogen herself was having breakfast. She had better go and see if she should take Charlotte some lunch.

There was no reply to Imogen's gentle knock on Charlotte's door. She opened it carefully and looked in. The room was in darkness. Imogen called Charlotte's name softly; then, when there was no reply, she felt a surge of panic. Charlotte had died – she had had a heart attack during the night and had been lying upstairs dead all this time. Almost sick with fright, Imogen turned on the light, prepared to discover a lifeless body, but the room was empty.

She took some deep breaths, walking forward, staring. The bed had been slept in; the duvet was thrown back, the pillows dented, but there was no Charlotte. Slowly, Imogen took in the fact that Charlotte's nightdress lay on the bed. She must have dressed and gone out somewhere.

Imogen raced downstairs to see if the car had gone, but it was in the garage.

Where could she be? Perhaps something had happened to her son – an accident at sea – some emergency – but wouldn't she have left a note? She'd left one when she went shopping. Panicking now, Imogen ran all round the house looking for a message. There was none in the kitchen or any of the downstairs rooms, nor was there in Charlotte's bedroom.

Charlotte must have been taken ill and been whisked off to hospital in an ambulance, and she was so bad that she hadn't been able to get up to call Imogen to help her, or to leave a message. Or had she called, and when there was no answer because the house was empty, decided that Imogen was so deeply asleep that she hadn't heard? Even then, she'd have had to be very bad not to have asked the ambulance people to wake her.

Imogen went all round the house looking for anywhere that Charlotte could possibly be, but there was nothing to explain her absence. What was she to do? Should she call the police? If she did, would she have to tell them that she had left the house herself?

In the end, Imogen rang her brother.

Nicholas's advice was to telephone Captain Smythe. Perhaps he had been taken ill, telephoned Charlotte and she had gone down there.

'She'd have taken the car,' said Imogen. 'And she'd have left a note.'

'Well, try him, and if he hasn't got a better idea, ring the police,' said Nicholas. 'Or the hospitals. Or both. Anyway, didn't you hear her go out?'

'No,' said Imogen.

'I'm surprised she didn't wake you and tell you where she was going, or at least leave a note,' said Nicholas, feeling cross with Charlotte for such thoughtlessness. 'Look, I'm busy now. I've got to pick up some washing – we've got going already with our ironing service – ring me back in a bit.'

Imogen knew that Charlotte might not wake a girl she thought was pregnant.

'Leave your phone on,' she pleaded, but he had rung off.

A chance to tell him what had really happened had gone, but he had told her what to do. Imogen looked up Captain Smythe's telephone number and dialled it.

He took a long time to answer the telephone, and then he had trouble understanding what Imogen was saying, for she burst into tears, becoming almost hysterical.

'I'll come over at once,' he said. 'Try to calm down, Imogen.'

He had heard the telephone as he came in from the garden, hurrying when it went on ringing. He had been walking around looking for signs of spring and finding plenty of shoots appearing. Each year he expected never to see another, yet round the months went again, and soon it would be April. Methodically, he locked the house and set off towards the village. He still walked briskly, but it was uphill until he reached the High Street and he was always a little short of breath when he reached the top. At best, it would take him ten minutes to reach Charlotte's house.

He refused to speculate about what had happened until he got there and could persuade Imogen to give a rational account of what seemed to be Charlotte's disappearance during the night. She might have returned by the time he arrived.

Imogen was watching for him, and opened the door as he came up the path. Her face was white and she looked terrified.

'Oh, thank you for coming, Captain Smythe,' she said, in a gabble.

'Let's sit down, Imogen, and you tell me calmly what has happened,' he said, ushering her in front of him into the house.

Imogen explained that she hadn't come downstairs herself until after half-past ten, and it was only then that she realised Charlotte must have slept in because the curtains were still drawn. Much later, when Charlotte still hadn't appeared, she had gone to her room to discover it was empty.

'There was no note? And you heard nothing during the night?'

'No.'

'You're sure about the note? You've looked in every possible place?'

'Yes.'

He had to take her word for it. She wasn't a child.

'The car's here,' she said.

'I see.' Howard pondered for what seemed to Imogen an age but was only seconds. During their brief acquaintance, Charlotte had seemed calm and controlled, but who knew what she was really feeling, recently bereaved, and with this troubled and possibly troublesome girl now thrust upon her, not to mention the tearaway youth, Jerry, at large in her garden? 'What is missing?' he asked. 'Has she taken a coat? Boots? What was she wearing?'

'She was dressed,' said Imogen. 'Her nightdress was on the bed, just tossed down, not folded or anything.'

Howard understood her. Charlotte was tidy, a nightdress folder rather than a bundler.

'Let's see what coat she had on. There was that nice red

one, and she had a green padded one,' said Howard. 'Let's see if either of those is missing.'

They established that the padded jacket was not in the downstairs cloakroom, where it was normally kept, and, just to make sure, Imogen went upstairs to look in Charlotte's cupboard in case she had hung it there for a change, but no. Her strong shoes were missing, as far as Imogen could tell.

'Perhaps she couldn't sleep and went out for a walk, and had some sort of accident,' said Howard. 'That's the most likely explanation.' People did that sort of thing, occasionally. 'You didn't hear her?'

'No.' It had been nearly two o'clock by the time Imogen returned herself. She did not mention that. 'Perhaps we should go and look for her?' she suggested.

'We don't know where to start,' said Howard. 'First I'll ring the hospitals, and then, if we don't find her, we'll call the police.'

It was what Nicholas had suggested.

'Make some tea, Imogen, while I telephone,' said Howard, who had had no lunch and nor, presumably, had the girl. It would give her something to do.

The two local hospitals took a little while to check their records, but neither had admitted a possible accident victim called Charlotte Frost in the past twenty-four hours, and neither had an unidentified woman in any ward.

Captain Smythe had some difficulty in explaining to the police that this was a genuine case of a disappearance, not someone who had gone off on a whim.

Or was it? Had she flipped and vanished? She had not taken her handbag, nor her spectacles. Both were in her bedroom, into which, feeling himself a gross intruder, Howard had gone in Imogen's wake. It was only when he asked to speak to the detective constable who had come out to Rose Cottage after the break-in that he persuaded them to take his concern seriously, and he was told an officer would call round.

He had a real sense of foreboding. Charlotte was not in hospital, but if she had gone walking during the night, she might have been hit by a car and fallen into a ditch.

'Do you think someone's kidnapped her?' Imogen said, as she assembled bread and cheese.

'No,' said Howard. 'I think she went for a walk and had some mishap.' He feared she lay out of sight, hurt and unconscious; last night had been cold and she could be suffering from exposure.

'She took a torch,' Imogen said suddenly, looking up at the shelf from which she had taken the small one. She was in such a state when she put it back that she hadn't noticed the larger one was missing. 'There were two kept there – a big one and a smaller one.'

She seemed very sure.

When WPC Cornish arrived twenty minutes later and heard what they had to tell her, the fact that Charlotte had taken no money or spare clothing, nor the car, convinced her that Mrs Frost had either met with an accident or, though she did not say it, gone out with the intent to commit suicide.

Both Howard and Imogen picked up the implication.

'She wouldn't,' said Imogen, bursting into tears, for she, with her presence, rude and ungrateful, and a liar, would have been the direct cause, the last straw.

'There was no note,' said Howard.

'She might have posted one,' said the officer.

*   *   *

Jerry had not gone straight home. He got the taxi to drop him off near Becktham station and from there he went to the bungalow where Tracy lived. He tapped on her window, and she let him in as she had done many times before. He'd slip out the same way in the morning, no one the wiser.

His mother was already back when finally he returned; she had sensed that the house was empty and it wasn't the first time. She would ask no questions, simply hoping he was with a girl. He was a grown man. Perhaps he was with Imogen, though if so, Mrs Frost might be none too pleased. Tired after her night shift, she went to bed and did not wake when he came back to shower and change for work. By now he had put Imogen out of his mind, but as the chip shop closed for the afternoon, he remembered that he was due at the garden centre. Mrs F. could do with his advice, even if he didn't do the planting, and it was all money. The best thing was to go on as if nothing had happened. After all, it was the truth. Imogen might well be embarrassed at seeing him, but he'd be easy with her so that she'd think no more about it. On reflection, and as he didn't know Nicholas's mobile phone number, he'd leave the business about the baby. It was nothing to do with him, after all.

His mother, wearing a pink quilted dressing-gown, had been in the kitchen eating a cheese sandwich when he went home, and she was expecting him to take the car. She was going back to bed, she said.

'I've promised to see this job through for Mrs Frost,' he told her. 'We're picking up some plants this afternoon and I'll put the lot in tomorrow. An old guy she knows has given her some other stuff.'

'That's all right,' said Angela. 'Just don't be late for the shop.'

'I won't be,' Jerry promised.

But when he reached the garden centre on the outskirts of Nettington there was no sign of Mrs Frost's Fiat. Jerry, who had arrived on the dot of when they had arranged to meet, locked his mother's car and wandered off to look for climbing roses. Even if Mrs F. didn't recognise the car among the others parked outside, she'd realise that he was there ahead of her. Or them. He supposed that Imogen would come with Mrs Frost. He selected several pot-grown specimens, loading them into a trolley; Mrs Frost would accept his advice on what to grow, he felt sure. When she still had not arrived after he had been there twenty minutes, he was annoyed. She knew his time was limited; he had been punctual, so why wasn't she?

She hadn't expected him to come and pick her up, had she? Jerry was sure they'd arranged to meet at the garden centre. All the same, maybe he'd better go back by way of Granbury in case there had been a misunderstanding, though soon he'd run out of time. He abandoned his laden trolley near a pile of paving stones; someone else could put the plants away. Then he went back to the car and drove to Granbury.

Turning into Vicarage Fields, he saw a police car outside Number Five.

Jerry drove straight past. Now what had that mad girl gone and done?

15

There was no need for anyone to know that she had been out so late, nor was there any need to lie, for no one suspected her absence. Imogen said that she had not heard Charlotte leave the house, which was true. She related how she had gone to bed early leaving Charlotte watching television – also true. She truthfully described her surprise when Charlotte was not up at her usual time, and the gradual growth of her unease.

'We were going to the garden centre today, to buy some plants,' she said. 'Charlotte has been getting the garden sorted.' She did not mention Jerry. The less said about him the better, for he was the only person who could give her away, though if he did, people might wonder about him, since he had a record, and there was the question of his mother's car being parked overnight in Granbury when Captain Smythe was burgled. For both their sakes, the less said the better, but if Captain Smythe told the police that Jerry was due to meet them, no one could imagine that the arrangement was connected in any way with Charlotte's disappearance.

'I can't understand why she went out, apparently in the

middle of the night, without leaving any sort of message,' Captain Smythe declared.

But Imogen could. It took her rather a long time to work it out. If Charlotte had not committed suicide – it was unthinkable that she might have done – she could have looked into Imogen's room and, finding her gone, set out to search for her.

But why had she not returned? Wouldn't she give up eventually and come home, if only to report Imogen's absence?

That afternoon, Charlotte was found by a man and his two small sons who had started to play pooh-sticks on the bridge over the river and had seen her body caught in reeds near the bank.

The nightmare began then. Imogen stuck to her story; if she confessed to leaving the house, she would have to say where she had gone.

Howard Smythe had explained his presence in the house as a friend and fellow resident in Granbury.

'Mrs Frost has a son and daughter,' he told Sergeant Beddoes, who had come to break the news that the body of a woman answering Charlotte's description had been found but had not yet been positively identified. To spare Imogen, he volunteered.

'Perhaps it isn't her,' said Imogen wildly. Charlotte couldn't be dead. It wasn't possible.

'The sooner we find out for sure, the better,' Howard stated. The chance of its being someone else was too remote to be seriously entertained, and this was one fact that could swiftly be established.

Beddoes agreed. The body had not yet been moved from the river bank, where life had been pronounced extinct by the police surgeon; a forensic pathologist was at the scene, for foul play could not be ruled out until after a full examination of the site, as well as of the body. It was a short walk from the nearest road, across the bridge and along the path. Captain Smythe could go there; it would be quicker than waiting for the body to be taken to the mortuary.

He went off in a police car, promising Imogen that he would return as soon as possible, but suggesting that meanwhile she telephone her father.

WPC Cornish, left at the house with Imogen, urged her to take this advice, and Imogen, still snuffling weepily, dialled Felix's number, but the answerphone was the only response. She hung up.

'Why didn't you leave a message?' Rachel Cornish asked.

'He doesn't care. He'll be no help,' sniffed Imogen. 'He sent me here to Charlotte to get me out of the way.'

'Why so?' asked Rachel Cornish.

But Imogen decided not to tell her the whole truth.

'He's split up with my mum. There were problems,' she said.

Rachel Cornish had established that the missing woman was not Imogen's real grandmother.

'Where do Mrs Frost's son and daughter live?' she asked.

'Her son's in the navy and her daughter is in America.'

If the body was that of Charlotte Frost, they would be her next of kin and must be informed.

'Do you know their addresses?' Rachel asked.

But Imogen didn't even know what Charlotte's surname had been before she married Rupert. Dry-eyed now, she lapsed into a silence which the police officer, who was prepared to make some allowance for shock, nevertheless deemed sulky. She tried a few calming overtures, commenting on the garden, saying it was neat, realising that the lawn had been freshly laid and sparsely planted beds awaited filling. She had seen the boxes of plants from Rose Cottage waiting on the path beside the garage.

'Your grandmother must be a keen gardener,' said Rachel, not using the past tense because, technically, it did not yet apply.

A shrug was Imogen's response. Then she said, 'She's not my real grandmother.'

'You were staying with her. That means she was – is – fond of you,' Rachel said, falsely, for it did not follow.

'She had to have me,' Imogen said. 'They made her – Dad and my aunt.'

Rachel decided not to pursue this contentious line. If the girl was always as ungracious as this, Mrs Frost must have found her a difficult guest.

'How about some tea?' she asked briskly.

'I'm not bothered,' said Imogen, adding, in a surly tone, 'You have some if you want.'

Anything to escape for a few minutes from this tiresome girl, thought Rachel, going into the kitchen, which was tidy, with no unwashed dishes on the drainer. From Imogen's sullen behaviour, she would have expected lack of domestic ability, but all was as orderly as if the grandmother had just popped out of the room. She put the kettle on to boil and found the teapot, setting out some mugs. When the old man came back, he might appreciate a cup. He wouldn't be away much more than an hour, if that; there'd be the walk along the bank to the scene, but it wasn't far, and he seemed fit enough. Once there, identification would be a matter of seconds rather than minutes, unless the dead woman's face had been disfigured. She could not have been in the water long enough for it to have had much effect. Old Captain Smythe had doubtless seen many drowned bodies during his wartime service; he would not disintegrate at the sight of one more. Returning to the sitting-room, she picked up the colour supplement from the previous weekend's *Sunday Times* and began reading it.

To Imogen, the wait seemed endless, but while it lasted she could tell herself that Charlotte would walk in at any minute; the woman in the river must be someone else. Sitting here in silence with that cow of a policewoman callously reading a magazine was almost unendurable. She put on the television. On Saturday afternoon there was always sport to watch; several choices, usually.

'Completely heartless,' reported Rachel Cornish later.

Howard looked rather grey when he returned. He was glad of the officer's tea, and could have done with a dash of brandy in it.

'I'm afraid there's no doubt,' he said to Imogen. 'Charlotte is dead, my dear.'

Imogen did not react at all. There were no tears and no hysterics, but she, also, drank a cup of Rachel's tea.

She was calm enough to give her father's name and address, but it was Charlotte's relatives who must be found before news of her fate leaked out.

Howard Smythe, who carried a card with his daughter's address on it in his wallet, suggested that she probably had something in her handbag which might reveal her next of kin, and sure enough, there was an engagement diary in her bag. It gave her son Tim's address in Dorset, and her daughter's in

New York. Now the police machinery could grind into action, routine dictating how they would be told about their mother.

'Her son's at sea,' Howard said.

During his naval career, it had sometimes been his lot to give men and women serving under his command bad news, and it was never easy. Tim Paterson would be given compassionate leave to return home as soon as it could be arranged. He told Imogen this, but it drew no response. The girl was in a state of shock, and the sooner her own family came to care for her, the better.

'Why don't you ring your brother up and see if he'll come over?' suggested Howard.

'You've got a brother?' Rachel Cornish pounced.

'Yes, she has. A twin,' said Howard. 'Nicholas Frost. He lives in Oxford.'

'Her father isn't answering his phone,' said Rachel. 'But now that his stepmother has been identified, he will be informed.'

'She's close to her brother,' said Howard. 'He's got a car, and it isn't far. I'm sure he'll come over if he can.'

Imogen thought it would be wonderful if Nicholas were to turn up.

'I wish you wouldn't talk about me as if I wasn't here,' was, however, what she said.

Eventually Howard persuaded her to give the police officer her brother's mobile telephone number, but there was no answer. However, a message asking him to call his sister as soon as possible was accepted.

He would have to be located.

'Tell us his address,' said Sergeant Beddoes.

Imogen gave him Nicholas's address, but she did not know Phoebe's, nor her telephone number, and that afternoon

Nicholas was at her flat, dealing with enquiries for their ironing service. The telephone was in his car and it was some time before he received the news.

As routine, the police called at Charlotte's neighbours asking if they had heard anything unusual during the night. When had they last seen Mrs Frost?

Charlotte would have been surprised to know how many of her neighbours had noticed her; the couple on one side with the children, and the pair who went off to work so early, knew her well by sight, and had observed the work being done in the garden. Jerry had been seen laying turf; a woman opposite had even witnessed its arrival and could name the supplier. Mrs Frost seemed quite reserved, everyone said; she had not been there long and there had been no social contact. Imogen's presence had been noted; she had helped the young man who was doing the garden work and one neighbour had seen them kiss.

The woman opposite, whom Charlotte could not have described if she had been asked, and who was married to an air steward who was on a flight to Australia, had seen Imogen enter the house early on Saturday morning. It must have been getting on for two, she said; she had been unable to sleep and had come downstairs to make some tea. Looking out of her window, she had noticed the hall light on in Mrs Frost's house much later than was usual, and then she had seen the girl – she thought it was the girl, not Mrs Frost – open the front door and slip inside. She could not swear to which upstairs lights were on, if any; the curtains were lined and fitted well, and though chinks might be visible, she was not aware of any showing at that hour.

She had not waited at the window, going back to bed and falling asleep quite quickly. The girl had probably been out clubbing, she said tolerantly.

Slowly details of life at Number Five, as observed from outside, were disclosed as more enquiries were made at other houses in the close. Because it was the weekend, people were at home and several had seen Jerry arriving; two were sure he drove an old red Metro.

'Who was this man who was working in the garden?' Imogen was asked eventually.

'What man?' asked Imogen.

'The man who laid the turf. A young man. Your neighbours have described him,' Rachel Cornish said impatiently.

'I don't know. Someone Charlotte found,' said Imogen.

But Howard, who had refused to leave Imogen on her own with just a police presence in the house until he had handed over responsibility for her to some member of her family, even if it were to be only Nicholas, knew his name was Jerry and that he lived in Becktham.

'He's a friend of yours, isn't he?' he said to her. That was how Charlotte had come to employ him. 'You must know his other name, Imogen.'

She said she didn't. In her world, only first names counted.

Rachel Cornish noted that she had lied about not knowing who the gardener was. Now, why had she done that?

Howard wondered why Imogen was being so obstructive. Shock, he supposed. The fact that Jerry had a record did not mean he was involved in any way with Charlotte's accident – for it was an accident: it had to be. He kept his counsel about that.

He wanted to go home. Seeing Charlotte's pale, sodden

corpse had been most distressing; he grieved for her, and he was weary. All the same, he owed it to Charlotte, if not the girl herself, to do what he could for her. While WPC Cornish was conferring with Sergeant Beddoes in the kitchen, and Imogen was apparently watching television, he went into Charlotte's dining-room, looked in the sideboard where, among her small stock of wine, he found glasses and some brandy, and poured himself a tot, which he drank. Feeling better, he followed the officers into the kitchen.

'Imogen has had a bad shock,' he told them. 'It's natural that the sudden death of someone she was fond of should upset her.'

'But she's not upset,' said Rachel Cornish. 'She's watching television.'

'She's frightened,' Howard said, and he left them, returning to the unhappy girl he now thought of as his charge.

'She's acting guilty,' said Rachel Cornish.

'Guilty of what?' asked Beddoes.

'I don't know. She's hiding something. She said she didn't know the gardener but Captain Smythe said they're friends.'

At this point PC Daniels, who had been carrying out door-to-door enquiries in Vicarage Fields, came in with the information about Imogen's excursion in the night.

Imogen would have to tell them where she'd been. Beddoes went to ask her.

But she refused to say.

Howard was startled when he heard. Nevertheless, something was explained.

'Mrs Frost must have discovered that Imogen had gone out

without telling her, and went to look for her,' he said. 'She'd be worried. After all, the girl is pregnant.'

'Pregnant?' Beddoes glanced at WPC Cornish. 'Did you know?'

She shook her head.

'Who's the father?' she asked, not that it made much difference.

'Imogen won't say,' said Howard, wishing that he had not been the one to tell them. Still, perhaps they would now make some allowance for her present conduct. 'It's obvious what happened,' he went on. 'Mrs Frost found her room empty and went to look for her. During her search she somehow slipped and fell into the river.'

Charlotte must have gone that way because she feared the girl might have done something stupid, but it was Charlotte who had acted foolishly.

'What if Mrs Frost found Imogen meeting some young man down by the river, and they had an argument?' Rachel said to Beddoes, after Captain Smythe had left the room. 'That girl comes from a dysfunctional family. She's dysfunctional. She could have killed her grandmother.'

'Yes, she could,' said Beddoes.

Imogen had walked away from everyone and was in the garden. She had put on Charlotte's wellington boots and, glad that Jerry hadn't finished doing it, was putting in more of the plants from Rose Cottage. Howard Smythe went out to see how she was getting on.

Her face was tear-stained, and muddy marks showed where she had wiped her hand across her eyes.

'They might as well go in,' she said. 'Else they'll die.'

'Quite right,' he said. Physical labour was an excellent remedy for grief, anxiety, almost anything.

'I don't know what they are or where they're meant for,' she said. 'But it doesn't matter now. Dad can sell the house and cash in.'

'Your father owns the house?'

'Yeah. He calls it Charlotte's grace and favour residence,' said Imogen. 'He'll be mighty glad to cash it in.'

'Hm.' Howard had not known about this arrangement.

'I expect someone will snap it up quite quickly,' Imogen said, fiercely digging out a hole in which to put some roots of phlox.

'I expect so,' Howard said.

'So he won't be sorry about Charlotte.' Imogen brandished a slip of winter jasmine. 'Where shall I put this?'

'Against the fence, perhaps,' Howard suggested.

'He's not really my father, I'm glad to say,' said Imogen.

'Isn't he?'

'Nick and I think we're test-tube babies. Or else Mum had a fling. She's always having them,' said Imogen. 'We're not a bit like either of them, but we're not adopted.'

'If it's worrying you, you'd better talk to them about it,' Howard advised.

'Nick tried with Dad. He wouldn't give a straight answer,' said Imogen.

'This viburnum slip would look good in the corner at the end of the plot,' Howard said. 'It will grow quite tall and it has pale pink flowers throughout the winter.'

'Oh, all right,' said Imogen, and went off to the corner of the garden with her spade.

Howard thought of asking her where she had gone last night, but what difference would it make if she told him? She went out without Charlotte's knowledge and her absence was discovered. That had to be the sequence of events. He was tired and he was distressed. He wanted to go home, but he had lived a life devoted to his duty and his ways would never change. In silence, he handed her the few remaining plants, and watched her put them in. The light was going when they were called into the house because Detective Inspector Fleming had come to talk to Imogen.

They were still talking when Lorna arrived.

Charlotte's daughter-in-law, Victoria Paterson, had tele-phoned her after a police officer had arrived at her house to tell her about Charlotte's death. Victoria could e-mail the ship, and this she did; then, while waiting to hear from Tim, who would telephone as soon as possible, she knew, she called Jane, her sister-in-law, in America.

Officialdom had not yet reached Jane with the news. Victoria told her all she knew herself, which was not a lot. It seemed to be a ghastly accident which had happened during the night.

'Shall I go over there, Jane?' asked Victoria, who wanted to stay put until she had heard from Tim. 'That girl's there. Imogen. Rupert's granddaughter. The spot of bother, Tim called her, because she's in one.'

'Oh – yes. Poor kid. How dreadful for her, on her own with this,' said Jane, who was still trying to absorb the news that her mother was dead. 'I'll come over as soon as I can fix a flight.' But however fast she moved, she could not be in England until the next day. 'Get Lorna,' she said. 'She'll see to Imogen. It was Lorna who got Mum to take her in. That family can't walk away from this. Mum was their father's widow, after all. Felix is useless at the moment. Apart from Zoe taking off, his business is in trouble.' She'd heard this from her mother the last time they spoke on the telephone. Jane had meant to call this weekend to see how things were going. Now it was too late.

'Ben's there?' Victoria asked. 'You're not on your own?'

'Yes. It's all right,' said Jane. 'He'll fix things for me at the office if I can't get hold of anyone.'

'Do you need to come right away?' asked Victoria. 'There's nothing you can do for Charlotte, is there? Not now. Not for a few days. There has to be an inquiry,' she explained.

'I'll come. It may take Tim a day or two, and someone must hold the vultures off. I'll telephone when I know my flight.'

'I'll meet you if I can, or I'll organise someone,' Victoria said. 'Be in touch. I'm sorry, Jane.'

'Yes. I know.' Jane's voice cracked. 'See you soon,' she said. 'Get Lorna,' she repeated. 'And don't let her wangle out of this.'

'I won't,' Victoria promised.

On a Saturday afternoon, Lorna was not at home but her husband was. Shocked by Victoria's news, he promised to find Lorna, who had gone to show some clients round a property to let but who had a mobile phone, and something would be done about Imogen.

'Wretched girl,' he said. 'Causing so much grief.'

Replacing the receiver, he feared that they would have to take her in until her maternal grandmother returned from her cruise. She couldn't be left alone in Charlotte's house during the police investigation of a suicide. For what else could it be, happening in the night? Mature widows did not go walking round the fields and byways in the dark simply for exercise. Charlotte had become unbalanced – not altogether surprising in her situation, except that she had always seemed so calm and level-headed, but those were the very people who hid inner turmoil.

He traced his wife immediately, and she said that she would go to Granbury as soon as she had finished with her clients.

16

Imogen did not like the questions she was being asked.

'Were you on good terms with your grandmother?' Detective Inspector Fleming wanted to know.

'She's not my grandmother. She married my grandfather,' Imogen said, yet again.

The interview was taking place in Charlotte's dining-room. Imogen's school folders were stacked at one side of the table, and she was sitting opposite the officer, a lean, dark man with greying sideburns. With him was a detective sergeant, a fatter, younger man with cropped hair, acne scars and a scratch across his face.

'Were you on good terms with Mrs Frost?' asked Fleming patiently.

'Yes. She was very good to me,' said Imogen curtly.

'In what way?'

'She was kind. She took me in when my own family had no time for me. She ironed my clothes. I wasn't very nice to her,' Imogen said.

'In what way were you not nice?'

'I was rude and ungrateful.'

'Rude enough and ungrateful enough to make her want to get away from you?'

'She never said so. Anyway, she could turn me out. It's her house. Well, not exactly.'

'How do you mean, not exactly?'

'It belongs to my father. And my aunt. They let her live here. They have to. It was in my grandfather's will,' said Imogen.

'So she leased it?'

'She doesn't pay rent,' said Imogen.

'She was having the garden made over. Who was doing the work?'

'Just a guy.'

'What guy?'

'A guy she knew.'

'His name?'

Imogen shrugged.

'You must know his name.'

'I forget,' said Imogen.

A huge sense of unreality was swamping her. This could not be happening. Charlotte couldn't be dead. It was all a dreadful dream and she couldn't be sitting here discussing her relationship with Charlotte with this weedy, skinny man who was trying to look trendy with his sideboards.

'Why were you staying here with your – with Mrs Frost?'

'I told you. She took me in because my own family wouldn't. My dad and mum have split up and my mum's in America with her boyfriend.' Imogen burst into tears as she spoke.

It brought the interview to a halt.

'We'll continue this at the station,' Fleming decided.

The sergeant thought the interview should have been done there anyway, since Fleming was taking such a hostile stance.

While they were conferring, the telephone had rung twice and had been answered in the sitting-room. Now Rachel Cornish came in to report that Imogen's aunt was on her way to Granbury, and Charlotte's daughter would arrive from America as soon as she could get a flight.

'A word,' said Fleming to the woman officer. 'Keep Imogen company for a few moments,' he told Detective Sergeant Morris, leaving his colleague to deal with Imogen's tears, and he left the room, drawing Rachel Cornish into the hall where they could not be overheard by the pair in the dining-room or by Howard Smythe, who was in the sitting-room. 'What do you make of that young lady?' he enquired.

Rachel Cornish told him.

Howard Smythe, meanwhile, who would not desert the girl, weary though he was, drew encouragement from the news that her aunt was coming. He could honourably leave after this saviour arrived. The police, also, were relieved; if Imogen were to be left alone overnight, an officer would have to stay with her, lest she, like Mrs Frost, do something stupid, but meanwhile she could be taken to the police station to make a formal statement.

Rachel Cornish had told Fleming that in her opinion Imogen knew more than she was saying.

'She met some boy last night. Maybe Charlotte flushed them out,' she had said.

'Hm. The father of the kid,' Fleming suggested.

'Or this gardener. One of the neighbours saw them having a snog,' said Rachel.

'You don't like her, do you?' Fleming asked.

'Not a lot,' said Rachel.

Detective Sergeant Morris, in spite of his unappealing appearance, was more tolerant. Left alone with Imogen, he spoke gently to her.

'You've had a nasty shock,' he observed.

Imogen did not answer. She sat staring at the window, not wanting to look at Morris's stubby hands, with their short, blunt fingers, resting on the table opposite her.

'This has to be done. All these questions,' he said. 'We have to find out what Mrs Frost was doing down there by the river. How she came to leave the house.' He paused. 'You were out on a date, weren't you?'

Imogen did not answer.

'She heard you go out and followed you.'

Still Imogen said nothing.

'You were seen coming back. One of the neighbours saw you.' Morris's tone was silky.

Imogen stiffened in her chair. If this was true, the neighbour couldn't have seen Jerry because he hadn't come right down the road with her.

'If you haven't got anything to hide, why don't you explain?' asked Morris, reasonably enough.

But Imogen had a lot she wanted to conceal.

Lorna arrived to find that the only person in her stepmother's house was a distinguished-looking, tall, thin, elderly man.

She wasn't sure what she had expected: a weeping Imogen being cared for by a neighbour, or by a policewoman, perhaps.

Howard had been listening for her car ever since the police had left the house with Imogen. He had suggested to Detective

Inspector Fleming that surely her statement could be taken in the morning, after her aunt had arrived and she had had a night's sleep, but Fleming had said it was best to get it over. In fact, he wanted to question Imogen while she was still overwrought and unsupported. The post-mortem was already in progress, not held over till the next day or even Monday, as could happen in such circumstances.

There was no evidence, yet, to suggest that Charlotte's death had been anything other than an accident, but the girl's behaviour had been suspicious and, in his opinion, not consistent with genuine grief. An experienced officer, and a cynic, he knew that there were often dark compelling forces behind apparent calm.

If suicide were ruled out, what was a respectable widow in her sixties doing at night, by the river bank? Where had the plain, uncooperative and pregnant granddaughter been at the relevant time? When had Mrs Frost left the house? And whom had Imogen met, other than her grandmother? Used to dealing with splintered and extended families, the detail of Charlotte's being a relative only by marriage did not hinder Fleming's speculations. And who was the father of Imogen's expected child? Was he involved?

'You must be Imogen's aunt,' said Howard, opening the door before she had time to ring the bell.

'Yes. Lorna Price,' said Lorna.

'Howard Smythe,' said Howard, ushering her in. 'I am – was – a friend of Charlotte's. When they left, I stayed until you arrived, to explain.'

'When they left? Who's left? Has Imogen gone off again?'

'Imogen is at the police station in Nettington,' he said. 'Fleming – the man in charge – insisted that she go there without waiting for you to arrive.'

'But why?'

'Won't you come in, Mrs Price, and I will try to explain. I don't really understand why the police couldn't leave it until the morning,' said Howard.

He stood back to let her precede him into Charlotte's sitting-room. All was orderly; the bossy policewoman had washed up the mugs used for the tea that had been consumed, but Howard had tidied up the cushions and the newspapers. Everything was shipshape.

He gave Lorna a brief account of what had happened, as he knew it.

'But surely Charlotte's death was an accident? Or do they think she killed herself?' Lorna, driving to Granbury, had had time to wonder about this.

'They don't know. They'll know more after the post-mortem, I imagine,' Howard said. 'I don't think she did,' he added.

'Surely even Imogen couldn't drive her to such desperate straits,' said Lorna, not sure herself if she meant the remark to be a joke.

'One can't tell what makes a person snap,' said Howard gravely. 'I agree that Imogen was not likely to have been the final straw, but Charlotte had had a difficult time, nevertheless, with the brief marriage to your father, then his death, then her move to an area where she knew no one. I met her in the butcher's shop,' he added. It was less than two weeks ago.

He explained that Imogen had, it seemed, left the house on Friday night after telling Charlotte she was going to bed.

'She won't say where she went. The police think that Charlotte went to look for her.'

'That's probably correct,' said Lorna. 'Why won't she say where she was?'

'They think she was meeting someone. Some young man.'

'The father?'

'It's a reasonable supposition,' said Howard.

'Do they think Charlotte found them by the river and there was a row?'

'They haven't said so, but I suspect that is their theory,' Howard said.

'But if Imogen had seen Charlotte fall into the river, she'd have got her out,' said Lorna. 'She's an excellent swimmer. And the young man would have helped, surely?'

'One would imagine so,' said Howard. He added, 'Imogen was extremely upset when she found that Charlotte was missing. She rang me up – that's how I came to be here. It was about twelve-thirty. She'd thought that Charlotte was having a late morning, but that was unusual, I gather.'

'I really didn't know her well enough to say,' said Lorna, somewhat sheepishly. 'I didn't see a lot of her, after she married my father. But when I did go to White Lodge – his house – she was always up and about early.'

His house, she had said, Howard noted.

'Her daughter is coming over as soon as she can get a flight,' he said. Presumably this woman knew that her stepmother had a daughter in America. 'And her son will come as soon as it can be arranged.' He spoke sternly. That family had not cared a jot about their father's widow. 'We can't do much for Charlotte now,' he added. 'But Imogen needs help. That's why you've come, isn't it? Should you go to the police station and try to get her home? She could be interviewed tomorrow.'

He was right.

'Where's Nicholas in all this?' she asked. 'Does he know about it?'

'He wasn't answering his telephone,' said Howard. 'Nor was Imogen's father,' he could not resist adding.

'No – well, Felix is difficult to get hold of at the moment.' Lorna rose. 'Thank you so much, Mr Smythe, for helping out,' she said coolly. 'Will you make sure the house is locked before you leave? I have a key to let myself in when I return.'

With Imogen, I hope, thought Howard grimly. He had been going to ask her if she would drop him off at Rose Cottage on her way to Nettington, though it would mean a small detour. Now, nothing would make him do so, but he had been feeling slightly faint and he knew he would be wiser not to walk.

It was less than a mile, but he would ring up for a taxi after Mrs Price left. He often used them.

Lorna, rescuing Imogen, was missing an evening dining with friends in Richmond. There had been no option about going to Granbury; Brian had unenthusiastically offered to go with her, but he still had work to do on a big case he was handling; he could put in several hours before he had to leave for the dinner engagement, and it hadn't seemed necessary for both of them to deal with the immediate situation. They agreed that Charlotte's own children would have to take over as soon as they arrived. Meanwhile, since Imogen's parents were neglecting her, someone must do something for her, even if it meant Lorna bringing her back with her to London until Felix could be made to see that he really must take care of his daughter.

At Nettington police station she was not allowed to see her niece immediately, so she made a fuss.

'What is happening?' she demanded. 'Surely Imogen has told

you what she knows about Mrs Frost's movements? She was found hours ago, I believe – it can't be taking all this time.'

'Someone will come and see you shortly,' said the desk sergeant, urging her to take a seat, and Lorna waited, fuming at the delay, then gradually beginning to feel anxious. If what Mr Smythe had said was right, there could be reason for concern.

By the time she was taken into the interview room where Imogen, with a white and tear-stained face, sat at a table, she was ready to consider any theory, and seeing her, Imogen started to weep again, but she was not sobbing in hysteria. Silent tears coursed down her cheeks in a seemingly endless stream and Lorna, angry though she was – for at the best, Imogen had been stupid – went to her and hugged her.

Imogen responded by clinging to her and now the tears became great gulping sobs.

'You've been bullying her. How dare you – a pregnant eighteen-year-old girl,' stormed Lorna, glaring at Fleming and Morris. 'Perhaps she should see a doctor.' Lorna held Imogen away from her and looked at her keenly.

'I'm all right,' said Imogen. 'I just want to get out of here.' She took a deep shuddering breath. 'They seem to think I pushed Charlotte into the river.'

'Do you?' Lorna turned to challenge the two detectives.

'Not as such. Not yet,' said Fleming. 'But Imogen won't tell us where she went last night.'

'She will tomorrow,' Lorna promised. 'She's exhausted. Can't you see that? She's not fit to be questioned. I'm taking her home.'

Fleming had been taking a chance, trying to push Imogen into an admission, if not of guilt concerning Charlotte's death, at least of revealing where she had been and with whom. He let them go, promising to be in touch the next day.

By then the post-mortem results would be through.

When they were in the car, Imogen could not stop shaking. She was shuddering and trembling, seriously shocked, as Lorna realised, putting the car heater on full blast.

Finding the police station had been rather a matter of luck; as she came into Nettington she had seen a patrol car entering the town and had followed it, hoping those in it were going back to base, which they were. Now she was not sure of the route back to Granbury and Imogen was in no state to direct her, but she saw a signpost at a junction just in time to avoid going the wrong way, and eventually they returned to Vicarage Fields.

There was no question of taking Imogen back to London yet. The girl had to be put to bed as soon as possible; moreover, that foxy-faced detective would be wanting to talk to her in the morning.

Imogen's teeth were still chattering as she stumbled into the house after Lorna.

'Now come along,' said Lorna. Thank goodness the house was warm. Thank goodness, also, that there was a gas fire in the sitting-room. Lorna bundled Imogen on to the sofa, then ran upstairs to fetch blankets or a duvet. The room she went into was Imogen's and she pulled the duvet off one of the beds, running down with it and wrapping the girl up in it. Then she lit the fire, and after that, put the kettle on. A hot drink would help, but, as Imogen went on shivering, she decided that she must call the doctor.

First she made the tea, adding sugar.

'Now Imogen, you must drink some,' she said. 'Come along, dear. I know it's dreadful. Poor Charlotte. But you must try to calm down.'

She held the mug to Imogen's lips, coaxing her to sip, and the girl managed to swallow some of the tea. Her shaking slowly eased a little, and her icy hands felt warmer, but when Lorna judged she could leave her long enough to telephone, she was still trembling.

Lorna took Charlotte's telephone book into the kitchen, closing the door. She looked under D for doctor; if Charlotte had not listed her GP there, she would have to go through the whole book, but there it was: the village health centre was listed. Lorna dialled the number, but as it was a Saturday, and getting late now, she had to call the duty doctor.

She explained the situation as quickly as she could.

'The girl's very shocked. She's pregnant. No, I can't bring her anywhere. She must be put to bed and kept warm,' said Lorna firmly.

Some instinct told her that it might be useful if a doctor could testify that Imogen was in no state for further questioning, and, indeed, should not have been subjected to the cross-examination she had just endured.

The call made, she went upstairs to see if Charlotte had a hot-water bottle, and found a blue rubber one hanging on the bathroom door.

Imogen had drunk the tea and was looking marginally pinker when her aunt returned.

'Thank you,' she managed, as Lorna helped her to undress, put on the long tee-shirt in which she slept, and get into bed.

'The doctor's coming soon,' Lorna told her. 'He may give you something to calm you down. I'm going to ring up Brian now, to explain what's been happening and that I will be staying here tonight.'

She did not notice Imogen's swift look of alarm, but she did pick up her trainers and her coat and took them downstairs. She couldn't flit far without a pair of shoes.

Lorna left the bedroom door ajar, too.

17

Jerry, busy in the chip shop on Saturday evening, was annoyed at having wasted his afternoon, and he was worried because of the police cars parked in Vicarage Fields. Imogen hadn't gone and swallowed pills or something crazy, had she? She'd been in quite a state when he took her back, shivering like a shaken jelly. He was thankful that at least he'd made sure she got home. After that, anything that happened was down to her, but what was she thinking of, pretending to be pregnant when she'd never even done it?

'Why would a girl say she's pregnant when she's not?' he asked his mother, over a late Sunday breakfast. He was dressed, but Angela was still in her pink dressing-gown.

Angela was surprised by the question. She pondered for a moment.

'To get her bloke to marry her?' she suggested.

He hadn't thought of that, but it couldn't be Imogen's reason as there was no bloke involved.

'Maybe,' he said. 'Any other ideas?'

'To get attention?'

That was more like it. Imogen was certainly getting plenty,

sent to her grandmother in disgrace, and with Mrs Frost fussing over her like a hen with a chick.

'Why do you want to know?' his mother asked.

'Oh – nothing special,' Jerry said. His mother didn't know about Imogen's pretence.

'She might do it to get a flat,' Angela said. 'Pregnant girls can get them. But I should think they'd check. Wait till it showed or even till she'd had the baby. I don't really know.' It hadn't worked like that for her; the system came in later. She'd spent some time in a hostel with other pregnant girls, then in a mother-and-baby home run by a charity and that had been good; there was company and support. It must be scary, as it had been for her when she had to leave, being in a flat on your own with an infant when not much more than a child yourself.

'Are you going over to Granbury today?' she asked. 'You met them at the garden centre yesterday, didn't you? Did they buy a lot of stuff?' The more plants Mrs Frost bought, the more lawful work there would be for Jerry, putting them in.

'No,' he said. 'Mrs Frost must have changed her plans. She didn't turn up.'

'Oh! But you were there?'

'Yeah. Waited about, didn't I, wasting time and petrol.'

'And she didn't let you know?'

'No.'

'Well, I am surprised. I wouldn't have thought that nice lady would be like that.'

'Nor would I,' said Jerry.

'Maybe she's ill,' Angela suggested. 'Are you going to ring them up to find out why they weren't there?'

'No,' said Jerry. 'I've got better things to do.'

Like what, his mother almost said.

'I might paint the lounge,' Jerry said. 'You know it needs doing.'

It did, but Angela was surprised at this sudden proposition.

'All right,' she said meekly. He might change his mind if she said this wasn't a convenient time.

'Get dressed, Mum, and we'll go to B&Q to choose the paint,' said Jerry.

They'd just returned, and Jerry, with the furniture piled into the centre of the room, had begun filling in the cracks around the window frames when Nicholas arrived.

'What's been going on?' he demanded.

Jerry, in an old tee-shirt and jeans, looked up from his pot of filler as Nicholas came bursting into the sitting-room ahead of Angela, who had answered the door. She had no idea who this white-faced angry young man could be and was terrified that he was some former prisoner with a grudge against Jerry. He'd stormed past her at the door, saying, 'I want a word with Jerry.'

Jerry also turned pale and put down his tin.

'Who are you?' Angela was quavering in the background.

'I'm Imogen's brother and I want to know what's been going on,' Nicholas said. 'I suppose you do know Imogen, do you, Mrs – er –?' he turned to glare at Angela.

'Yes, of course. How is she?' Angela relaxed, all smiles now.

'Practically in prison,' Nicholas answered. 'Haven't you heard?'

Mother and son looked at him in bewilderment, but Jerry felt the start of panic.

'In prison?' he repeated.

'Charlotte's dead. They found her in the river yesterday, and the idiot police seem to think Imogen put her there on Friday night.'

'Oh no!' Jerry exclaimed.

'My Christ!' said Angela, sitting down. 'Oh, that nice lady!'

'Yes, she was. Imogen would never hurt her,' said Nicholas.

'But what's happened? Why do they think Imogen —?' Angela could not finish and Jerry was so startled that like his mother, he had to sit down.

Nicholas had calmed down slightly.

'I only heard about it this morning,' he said. The previous evening, he had been at his waiter's job until nearly midnight and he hadn't checked his messages. His father, traced eventually by Lorna's husband to a hotel in Belgium where he was hoping to raise money for his own financial rescue, had got through to him on the telephone, telling him that Charlotte had had some accident and Imogen was in a mess; would he go and sort it out? Nicholas had telephoned the house in Granbury and got no answer, so he had driven straight to Rose Cottage, hoping that Captain Smythe might be able to explain.

Howard had done his best. Nicholas now knew as much as he did, including that Imogen had been seen returning to the house sometime after midnight on Friday night and discovered Charlotte to be missing on Saturday at around midday.

'Do you know where she was?' Nicholas now asked Jerry. 'She hasn't any other friends that I can think of, except the guy who's landed her with a kid, if he's around.'

Jerry had some choices. Imogen was weird, but it seemed

she hadn't said she was with him, for if she had, the police would have already been to question him, and she couldn't have pushed Mrs Frost into the river. She wasn't as far out of it as that. Besides, when could she have done it?

'Why did Mrs F. go to the river?' he asked, reasonably enough.

'No one knows, unless she meant to jump in,' said Nicholas. 'The police think she was looking for Imogen, who'd gone out somewhere. They think Imogen met someone by the river – some bloke – and Charlotte found them and there was a row, and she fell in or was pushed. At least, that seems to be the general idea.'

He'd gone from Captain Smythe's house to the police station, where he had found his aunt, Lorna. She told him that Imogen was being questioned and that Brian, her husband, was with her in his legal capacity. Though not a criminal lawyer – his field was financial litigation – he had decided that if she were being aggressively questioned, as seemed likely, she must have a solicitor present. He would be at least as effective as someone plucked at random from those available, and he'd managed to learn some of the post-mortem findings.

'I know who the gardener is,' Nicholas had said. 'I'll go and see him. Maybe he can tell us something.'

Captain Smythe had known his name was Jerry, but no more.

Nicholas did not know his surname, either, but he knew where he lived.

'But this is dreadful,' Angela said. She had taken in the fact that Imogen was pregnant. 'The poor girl.' Then she remembered

Jerry's earlier question and warning bells began ringing in her head. Jerry couldn't be responsible, however; he'd only just met the girl: or had he? 'Was it you, Jerry?' she accused.

'What? Oh – shit, no,' said Jerry. 'I only met her a week ago, or less. And you,' he said to Nicholas. This was what came of being nice to people, welcoming them into your home. He forgot that Nicholas had driven him to search for his mother's missing car.

'That's true, Mrs – er –' said Nicholas. 'What is your surname?' he enquired, much calmer now. It was obvious that though Jerry had been at Charlotte's, working in the garden, as Captain Smythe had revealed, neither mother nor son knew anything about Charlotte's death. His news had shocked them both.

'Hunt's our name,' said Angela.

'Mrs Hunt,' Nicholas repeated. 'Well, I'm sorry if I alarmed you but Imogen is in a lot of trouble and I need to find out what's been happening. You've been doing the garden, haven't you, Jerry?' He'd get this fact confirmed.

'That's right.'

Nicholas was remembering his suspicions about Jerry's knowledge of where his mother's missing car might be found. Jerry might not be whiter than white, but unless he was a maniac, he couldn't have killed Charlotte. Why should he want to do such a thing?

Jerry was thinking that he might well have been tempted to push Imogen into the river had they been near it on Friday night but not her grandmother, who had all her marbles. Now he knew why Mrs Frost wasn't at the garden centre yesterday, and why the police car had been outside her house. She was already dead.

'But what happened? Could she have killed herself?' Angela asked.

'I don't know. Who knows why people do things?' said Nicholas. 'But she could swim – she used the pool at my grandfather's house while they were married. And Imogen's an excellent swimmer. Really first class. She'd have hauled Charlotte out if she'd fallen in, but Charlotte should have been able to save herself, anyway. Captain Smythe said the river isn't very deep.'

'Why can't Imogen just tell them where she was?' asked Angela.

'I've no idea,' said Nicholas.

So she really wasn't saying. Jerry hoped she'd stick to that. He must keep out of this. Earlier, he'd wanted to get hold of Nicholas to tell him that Imogen wasn't pregnant, but he would not do it now. The less he claimed to know, the better. Even so, why wasn't she telling?

Jerry did not realise that Imogen's silence was due to shame.

'The only part that seems clear is that Imogen went out during the night – a neighbour saw her coming back – and the police think Charlotte discovered she was not in the house and went looking for her. They think she found her near the river and there was some sort of row and Charlotte ended up in the water. Then Imogen came home and reported her missing next day. Lorna – my aunt – seems to think this is what the police have decided happened. When they started to search for Charlotte, they realised she'd gone out because her boots and coat had gone, and a torch. She didn't take the car.'

'It's difficult to get the police to change their minds, once they've decided something,' Jerry said feelingly. 'It's all about collaring people. Never mind if they're innocent. Have they found the torch?'

'I don't know. What does it matter?'

'If someone did push her, they might have nicked it,' Jerry said.

'I suppose they might,' Nicholas allowed. 'And I suppose the police will have thought of that.'

'You can't be sure what they'll be thinking – not if they're thinking Imogen had something to do with it,' said Jerry. Imogen had been in no state to do anything that night except get herself into bed.

'Poor girl,' said Angela again. 'And pregnant, too. I wonder if it could have been the father, though why should he do such a thing?'

'I can't see Charlotte and him having a prearranged meeting by the river,' Nicholas said. 'My uncle is sure it was an accident, but even so, it needs explaining.'

'When is her baby due?' Angela asked. She avoided Jerry's gaze as she spoke.

'Oh – I don't know.' Phoebe had asked the same question. 'In seven or eight months, I suppose,' Nicholas hazarded.

'You're sure she is pregnant?' Angela asked.

'Well, of course. She ran away from school before they found out.'

'Did she like that school?'

'No. She hated it.'

'Well, maybe she just said she was pregnant to get away. Or to get attention,' Angela said carelessly, and when Nicholas stared at her incredulously, she said, 'Girls do strange, silly things, sometimes.'

'I can't believe she'd do that,' Nicholas said at last. 'Can you, Jerry?'

Jerry simply shrugged.

Imogen sat mutely in the interview room at the police station. Beside her was her uncle by marriage, Brian Price.

She and Lorna had arrived at ten o'clock that morning, as requested by Detective Inspector Fleming the previous evening. Lorna, not wanting to share with Imogen in the twin spare room, had spent the night in the third bedroom, which was small but warm and comfortable. Charlotte's room was off bounds for now. The relief doctor who had come to see Imogen was a middle-aged man who accepted what he was told by Lorna and was unafraid of prescribing a mild sedative for a shocked pregnant young woman. He had gently palpated her abdomen and asked her if she was in pain. Imogen muttered 'No,' and was silent when he asked her when her baby was due.

'There's no point in trying to talk to her now,' he had told Lorna. 'She's in no state to answer questions.'

'I was afraid all this might bring on a miscarriage,' Lorna said. But if it did, would that be such a bad thing? It would solve one problem.

'I don't think there's any risk of that,' said the doctor. 'How many weeks is she saying she's pregnant?'

That was the nearest he could go, bearing in mind patient confidentiality, to casting doubt on the veracity of the girl's condition. Imogen had been wearing a long cotton tee-shirt. He had not inspected her above the waist, and she was a plump girl, so he could not be certain, but she had no obvious signs of an established pregnancy.

'I'm not sure. Two or three months?' Lorna guessed. 'She won't talk about it. Or anything,' she added.

'She's in shock. That's the immediate problem,' said the doctor. 'I'm sure you'll get her to your own doctor as soon as possible − or her own,' he added, remembering that this was the aunt, not the mother.

'Of course,' said Lorna. 'Thank you for coming out.'

'Not at all,' said the doctor, anxious to get home.

Imogen had slept for several hours, but this morning she still felt as though she were acting in a play or dreaming; however, Brian's presence beside her was reassuring. She did not know him very well but she liked him; at family gatherings, unlike Felix, he always had time to talk and even seemed interested in what she said, though that was never much.

'I'm here to help you, Imogen,' Brian said. 'What were you doing when you went out on Friday night?'

'Nothing special,' said Imogen.

'Well, where did you go? Did you meet anyone? Is there anyone who can say where you were?'

There was, but she would not bring Jerry into this. No one else must know what had happened. He could have raped her but then, just when she began to wish he would, he hadn't. She'd been awful but he'd been great, even making sure she got safely home, and he was the only person who knew she wasn't pregnant.

'No,' she said.

'Imogen, my dear, you are not helping yourself by this silence. I'm acting as your solicitor now; what you tell me is confidential. I won't reveal it to anyone − not the police − not your aunt − not your parents.'

'I didn't go anywhere in particular,' she said. That was only a tiny lie.

'Had you planned to meet anyone? Your boyfriend?'

'No.' That was true, anyway, and Brian noticed how she said the word with conviction.

'You just went for a walk? At half-past nine at night? On a cold, windy night?'

'Yes.'

'You never thought of telling Charlotte you were going out?'

'She wouldn't have let me go,' said Imogen. 'I didn't think she'd know. She was watching television when I left.' Then she added, 'If she'd respected my privacy and kept out of my room, she wouldn't have known I wasn't there.'

That was probable.

'She was concerned for you,' said Brian, also wishing that Charlotte had been less conscientious, for, after all, Imogen had returned and if Charlotte had simply gone to bed, this tragedy would not have happened. And Felix, his brother-in-law, by abandoning his wayward daughter at a crisis in her life, had set the whole sad business in motion.

At this point, Fleming and Morris came back into the room. Uncle and niece, or solicitor and client, whichever way you chose to define it, had had plenty of time for their confidential consultation.

Brian had seen that Fleming had formed a poor opinion of Imogen, who was looking particularly unattractive this morning. There was an angry spot which she had picked at on her chin; her skin looked sallow and she had shown a truculent defiance towards the detective as she gave minimum details of her movements on Friday night. She was overweight, too, but some of that might be the baby. All she would admit to, when Fleming resumed the questioning he had begun the day before, was to leaving the house around half-past nine or ten, and returning some hours later; she was not sure of the time.

The neighbour had said she came back at about two o'clock in the morning.

'Well, if they say so.' Imogen shrugged.

'That's four and a half hours. Where did you go?'

'I just walked around.'

'For four and a half hours? That's a long time to be walking around,' said Fleming.

Imogen did not answer.

'Plenty of time to see your grandmother leave the house, follow her and have an argument,' said Fleming.

Still Imogen did not reply.

'Mr Fleming, is that a serious suggestion?' Brian asked.

'We only have Imogen's statement that she closed her bedroom door. If she had left it open, or ajar, Mrs Frost would have seen that she was not in the room.'

'Are you implying that my client waited for Mrs Frost to emerge, then set off in pursuit?'

Put like that, it sounded ridiculous and Fleming knew it, but he also knew that there was a whole lot the girl could say if she were pushed hard enough.

'What possible motive could Imogen have had for such behaviour?' Brian asked.

'Who knows what goes on in young women's heads?' Fleming responded.

'You have had the post-mortem report in. Surely the findings indicate an accident?'

The findings indicated sudden heart failure due to shock.

Mrs Frost had not drowned. A fright could have caused her to die and then fall in the river.

'The findings offer various interpretations,' Fleming said.

'Imogen, why don't you simply tell us where you were, and whether anyone saw you who can confirm it?' This was Detective Sergeant Morris.

'No one notices you when you're just walking around,' said Imogen.

But someone might. Not everyone was tucked up in bed by midnight, and if she left the house at half-past nine, as she claimed, people would have been about, even in Granbury.

Imogen was eventually allowed to leave, but Morris and a detective constable followed her and Lorna back to Vicarage Fields. They wanted to remove for testing the clothes she had worn on Friday night. Brian remained behind, saying he would join them after he had had a talk with Fleming. The man was like a terrier with a rat; he had taken a dislike to Imogen – and it was understandable, as she had revealed none of her qualities while in his presence. What were her qualities, Brian wondered briefly: academic excellence, sporting prowess, but a disposition that was often sullen. Brian and Lorna had two sons, one in his first job as a systems analyst, the other in his final year at university. The problems daughters could pose might be more serious than those boys manifested, he reflected, but Felix and Zoe had a lot to answer for; particularly Felix. Perhaps Zoe's flight into other arms was understandable.

He was in the midst of challenging Fleming to explain why he was treating Imogen as a suspect in the matter of Charlotte's obviously accidental death, when the telephone on Fleming's desk rang.

'Right. Bring him up,' Fleming told his caller, then turned to Brian. 'It's Nicholas Frost,' he said. 'Perhaps he can tell us something useful.'

Brian sat back. Perhaps he could.

18

They went through all Imogen's things, though she had not brought much with her to Granbury. Morris stood by while the woman detective did the searching. From time to time he handed her a transparent bag into which she put what she was removing.

In the top drawer of the chest in Imogen's bedroom were the sanitary pads which Charlotte had discovered; one pack had been opened and several pads had been removed. Bundled in another drawer, not neatly folded as were the rest of Imogen's clothes, was a dark sweater, with, as the officer soon discovered when she removed it with her gloved hands, a blue shirt tucked inside it. Imogen moved abruptly when she glimpsed the shirt, then looked away, aware for the first time that it was a football shirt.

They took Imogen's trainers, so that she was left with only a pair of flat-heeled pumps, and they took the soiled washing she had put in the bathroom bin – some underwear and a tee-shirt. Then the detective who had found the pads returned to the bedroom and pulled back the duvet. On the lower sheet was a tiny bloodstain.

She looked at Imogen, who glared at her.

'I'll leave you these,' she said pleasantly, indicating the remainder of the packet. 'You OK?'

'Yes,' said Imogen sourly.

'A word,' said Morris to his colleague, drawing her outside.

Detective Constable Patsy Wilson followed him on to the landing, where they muttered together.

Lorna, meanwhile, was alarmed.

'Imogen – are you bleeding? Are you in pain?' she asked anxiously.

'No – I'm all right. It's nothing,' Imogen answered. 'Just a drop,' she added wildly. Her period, often irregular, had come on that morning.

Morris had returned to the room.

'We'd best get you to hospital,' he said. If she miscarried, and police harassment were to be alleged as the cause, there could be serious trouble.

Imogen saw the plain, cropheaded detective regarding her with an expression of concern; he was ugly, like her, but it didn't mean he wasn't a nice person. Her aunt and the woman detective were also looking anxious, but she sensed that Morris's gaze was truly sympathetic. If she let them take her to hospital, they'd discover that she wasn't really pregnant.

'Can I talk to you in private?' she asked him, and though she tried to speak calmly, the words emerged aggressively.

Morris nodded.

'Let's go downstairs,' he said, aware that being alone in the bedroom with the girl could later lead to accusations even more unjustified than those his boss was planning to level at Imogen.

They went into the garden, where DC Patsy Wilson and Lorna Price could see them from the window. Overhead, the sky was overcast; soon it would rain.

Imogen stood on the new lawn, beside a small senecio shoot she had planted. Gazing at its grey leaves, she confessed.

'I'm not pregnant. I never was,' she said.

'I see,' said Morris. He maintained his calm demeanour. 'And did Mrs Frost find out?'

'What? You think she did and I pushed her in the river to stop her telling?'

'No. As it happens, I don't,' said Morris. Those others might, if they knew. 'Your walking around in the night makes more sense now. You'd told a lie, for some reason, and it got bigger and bigger and you didn't know how to stop it. Is that more or less right?'

It was, except that she had wanted to make it into fact rather than admit to her deception.

'Sort of,' she said.

'So you walked around and meanwhile Mrs Frost found you'd gone out and went looking for you.'

'I suppose she did,' said Imogen.

'Could she have found those pads? Could she have suspected you weren't telling the truth?'

'I don't know. She might have, I suppose. She ironed my washing but she didn't put it away. And I might have had the pads anyway, in case of trouble, even if I had been pregnant,' Imogen said.

Morris saw what could have happened. Mrs Frost had meant to put the washing away and had seen the pads. If she acknowledged her discovery, she would have had to challenge

Imogen, and she could have decided to give the girl time to own up herself.

'A doctor saw you last night,' said Morris.

'Yes, but he didn't examine me. Just gave my tummy a bit of a feel. He didn't ask awkward questions. Charlotte took me to the doctor here, and I said I'd come about my weight. The doctor told me to eat more fruit and vegetables, and cut out chips and chocolate,' said Imogen, and at last a hint of a smile crossed her face. 'Will it be all right now?' she asked.

'I'm afraid not,' said Morris. For now there was a motive. If Charlotte had discovered the truth, it could be alleged that Imogen, a girl with serious problems, might have wanted to stop her from revealing it.

'Must you tell them?' Imogen asked him.

He saw that it was almost more than she could do herself; she was like someone who had dug a large pit and jumped in, then could not clamber out unaided.

'Someone has to,' he told her.

'I can't,' she whispered. 'They'll be so angry.'

'Well, you've caused a lot of bother,' he pointed out.

'I know. And now Charlotte's dead.'

'If you tell your aunt, I'll tell Mr Fleming,' he said.

At least he could spare her, but not for ever, the wrath of that bitter man.

She nodded.

'I'll do it now,' she said. 'I haven't got to go back to the police station, have I?'

'Probably,' he said. 'But maybe not right away.'

*   *   *

'Where's Imogen?' Nicholas looked at the two men, Fleming and his aunt's husband Brian, who were seated facing one another in a small bare room with a table between them.

'She's gone back to Granbury with Lorna,' Brian said.

'Surely she told you everything she knew yesterday,' said Nicholas. 'Why have you been talking to her again? She must be very upset.'

'She is,' said Brian.

'She won't tell us where she was on Friday night, when Mrs Frost went walkabout,' said Fleming.

'Wasn't she the one who went walkabout? Didn't Charlotte go looking for her?'

'It's possible,' said Fleming.

'Of course it's possible. Imogen was bloody stupid to go wandering about in the night, and poor old Charlotte fell into the river and drowned. Rotten luck. Why couldn't she clamber out?'

'She didn't drown, Nicholas,' said Brian. 'It seems she died of shock. Vagal inhibition, it's called, due to the water rushing up her nose. Like the brides in the bath.'

'Who on earth were they? Well – never mind – so she didn't drown, but it was an accident.'

'Of course it was,' said Brian.

'We have to investigate every possibility,' said Fleming. 'Your sister has not been at all cooperative.'

'Well, what do you expect? She's had an awful shock, and she's pregnant.'

'Oh, is she?' Fleming sneered the words. 'I've just had a message from my sergeant,' he continued. 'She's been telling porkies. It seems she isn't – never was.'

Nicholas looked from him to Brian.

'Is this true?' he asked.

'So it seems,' said Brian. Fleming had received the call from Morris a few minutes before Nicholas had arrived.

'She told my sergeant the dreadful truth,' said Fleming.

Nicholas couldn't see what was dreadful about it. It was good news.

'What made her do such a crap thing?' he asked. 'What a prat.'

'We don't know why,' said Brian. Maybe Imogen herself didn't really know.

'She's upset about Mum and Dad,' said Nicholas. 'They've split up,' he told the sly-looking detective.

'People split up all the time. You're not little kids,' said Fleming.

'Nick, this isn't really helping Imogen,' said Brian. 'You had a reason for coming here. What was it?'

'Oh yes!' Nicholas put himself back on track. 'It's the gardener. Charlotte's gardener. I know who he is. Jerry Hunt's his name – lives in Becktham. He works at the chip shop, but not on Sundays. To tell you the truth, I had thought there was something a bit dodgy about him. His mother's car got nicked and he had an idea where it might be, so I took him there, and it was. How did he know?'

'And where was that?'

'Well, it was in Granbury, parked in that area outside the shops.'

'What sort of car was it?' Fleming was enjoying this.

'A red Metro.'

'Just when was this, Nicholas?' Fleming asked. 'Can you tell me the date?'

Nicholas could.

Fleming did not believe in coincidences. He left the room and asked a constable to do some checking.

No red Metro had been reported missing from Becktham on the date in question, but the previous night there had been an attempted burglary at Captain Howard Smythe's house in Granbury. Jerry Hunt had a record, and he'd been banged up with Pete Dixon, charged with the offence. There could be a connection.

Imogen and Lorna were in the sitting-room at Charlotte's house.

While Morris and DC Patsy Wilson were driving back to Nettington with Imogen's clothing, Lorna had rung Brian but their conversation had lasted only seconds. Lorna feared Imogen might be taken in for further questioning but she was going to try to get some explanation out of her first. Meanwhile the girl was upstairs in the bathroom.

She came downstairs eventually. Her face was pale but she was more composed than Lorna had ever seen her.

'It's time we had something to eat,' Lorna said. Even when the world was falling apart, people had to eat. She looked sharply at Imogen. 'I expect it's a relief in a way that you've been found out,' she added.

Imogen nodded. In fact she felt almost purified, washed clean by the shedding of her load of deception.

'I'm sorry,' she mumbled.

It was no good lecturing her.

'Do you know why you did it?'

'Not really. It seemed a good idea,' said Imogen.

'Well, let's not worry about that now,' said Lorna. 'Let's see what Charlotte's got in her freezer.'

She led the way into the kitchen and began poking about in the small refrigerator which Felix had considered large enough for just one lady's needs.

'Dad'll be able to sell the house now,' said Imogen. 'He never wanted Charlotte to have it, did he?'

'He's a bit pressed for cash at the moment, I believe,' said Lorna. 'But Charlotte was your grandfather's widow. She had to be looked after.'

'What Dad did was awful. Turfing her out of White Lodge with Granddad barely dead and not giving her a chance to decide where she wanted to be.'

Lorna had found a frozen cottage pie large enough for two which Charlotte had recently bought at Waitrose. She peered at the packet, trying to read it without her glasses which were in her handbag in the other room.

'I wonder how long this will take.' She slipped the sleeve off the dish and put it in the microwave. 'I'll give it ten minutes,' she decided. 'But I'd better get my specs and make sure.'

'I'll get them.' Imogen was eager to be helpful.

'Thanks. They're in my bag. It's on the chair.'

Imogen rushed to get it, stumbling against the table as she went. Lorna sighed. She was like a clumsy puppy. Something must be done about her; she'd have to see a shrink or other sort of counsellor. She took her bag from Imogen and found her glasses, setting them on her nose and scrutinising the instructions on the packet.

'There's some lettuce,' Imogen said. 'I'll get it, shall I?'

'Oh, yes. Good idea.'

'What will happen now?' Imogen asked.

'I don't know,' said Lorna. This wasn't the end of it, by

any means; Charlotte's death must still be explained to the satisfaction of Detective Inspector Fleming.

'Will I get into trouble?'

'What do you expect? You know where the knives and forks and things are, Imogen. Find some, will you?'

'With the police, I meant.'

'I can't answer that. You still haven't said where you were on Friday night.'

'Wandering about. That's all,' said Imogen.

It might just possibly be true, Lorna thought, searching back through memory to her own teenage years.

Detective Inspector Fleming had separated Nicholas from his uncle. Impatient, but reluctant to leave the police station while the situation regarding Imogen was unresolved, Brian was in one room while Nicholas was in another. Each had been brought a cup of tea which neither wanted.

After an interval, Fleming entered the room in which Nicholas sat fretting.

The policeman was smiling.

'Well, Nicholas, your information about Jerry Hunt has been useful,' he said. 'And perhaps you can clear up some other problems for me.'

'Like what?'

'Your father owns Mrs Frost's house. He'll get his cash back if he sells it now?'

'I suppose so. Him and Lorna. My aunt.'

'And with your parents splitting up, he's short of cash?'

'Yeah – I suppose.' Nicholas sensed danger in the question.

'Imogen would know this?'

'Probably. Yes – she would.'

'So Mrs Frost's death would free up some money which would come in useful for your dad.'

Now it wasn't a question, simply a statement. Fleming, whose own marriage had recently ended with the selling of the couple's mortgaged house and his wife's acquisition of the larger part of the resulting funds, now lived in a stark flat in a new block in Nettington while his wife and their two children had moved in with the man who had supplanted him.

Nicholas made no comment. He couldn't see why the detective inspector was so interested in his parents' finances. Fleming, however, had not finished with him.

'Fond of football, is she? Your sister?' he asked. 'Follows a team?'

'What?'

'Plenty of women are keen fans. Chelsea or Arsenal would be her favourites, I'd guess,' Fleming said.

'She barely knows the first thing about it,' Nicholas replied. 'It may surprise you to know that more people go to art galleries than to football matches.'

The arrogant young bugger.

'Your sister does that, then? Goes to art galleries?' he snapped.

'I don't know. Maybe. If it's easy,' said Nicholas. He couldn't see Imogen making much effort but their racy maternal grand-mother had taken both of them to the Tate, though primarily to have lunch and enjoy the Whistler murals. 'She's keen on tennis. Follows that,' he added helpfully.

'So she's not an Everton supporter?'

'No. What's given you that idea?'

'She had an Everton shirt in her possession,' Fleming said.

'And as she isn't pregnant after all, the obvious answer doesn't spring to mind.'

'There could be a boyfriend, though,' said Nicholas.

'Oh yes.' Fleming was willing to admit that.

'Or there was one,' Nicholas said. 'For her to get herself into this tangle over.'

Fleming was now intent on finding out who owned the shirt, unmistakeably that of an Everton supporter. He could start by picking up Jerry Hunt and asking him about the break-in at Captain Smythe's. Had he been driving his mother's car that night? A red Metro's ownership had been traced to Angela Hunt, who lived at the same address as Jerry. Nicholas had even noticed the number of the house. He would be a good witness against his sister and Jerry Hunt, if it turned out that in some way they had conspired to bring about the death of Charlotte Frost.

There was a financial motive now. Imogen, undeniably a naive girl, not very streetwise, and concerned about her father's money problems, had seen that selling the house could be the solution. Jerry Hunt might not be involved, but they were acquainted.

There were some questions to be answered. Now he must speak to the girl again, but before her brother had a chance to talk to her.

19

Jerry was getting on well with his refurbishing of the sitting-room when a plain-clothes police officer rang the bell that afternoon. With his radio on and his back to the window as he painted the rear wall, he did not hear her, nor did he see her coming up the path, and his mother, opening the door to DC Patsy Wilson, did not recognise her for what she was.

Patsy, smiling pleasantly, produced her warrant card, and Angela's heart began to pound. She immediately thought Jerry must be in trouble again, but then she remembered poor Mrs Frost. Jerry had known her; it was natural that the police would want to talk to him about her.

'Jerry in?' asked Patsy.

'Yes. He's doing some painting for me,' said Angela. The sitting-room door was shut and Jerry's music could be heard in the hallway.

'It's you I want a word with, Mrs Hunt,' said Patsy. First, anyway, she thought. Fleming had been crafty sending her and not a man. Jerry might have got the wind-up if a male detective had arrived. Two officers could not be spared; Morris had got others out tracing taxi drivers after a tip-off during door-to-door enquiries that a taxi had been seen waiting for a fare on the corner of Vicarage Fields, its engine running, round about half-past nine on Friday night.

As she walked up the path, Patsy had observed the industrious scene within.

Angela led her through to the kitchen.

'Yes?' she said. 'It's about that Mrs Frost, is it?'

'No,' said Patsy innocently. 'It's about when your car was stolen, Mrs Hunt.'

'Oh! Wasn't I lucky to get it back so soon, and quite undamaged. It was ever so kind of you to bring it back,' said Angela. 'I wonder where you found it? You never did tell me.'

Beyond blinking slightly, Patsy did not betray surprise.

'Let's see, when exactly did you report it missing?' she said calmly. She had intended to ask Mrs Hunt where she had been on the night of the break-in at Captain Smythe's, and if she was not using the car herself, to enquire whether Jerry could have borrowed it and if she knew where he might have gone, but here she was, giving spontaneous information.

'It was missing on the Friday morning,' she said. 'That's not last Friday – the one before. Jerry said he'd report it – I hadn't time – I had to rush off to catch the train to work but I was going to need it to get to my evening job. There it was, when I came back from Denfield,' she added. 'And with the tank filled up.'

Patsy took down the details of Angela Hunt's jobs and made sure she had the dates and times correct. She didn't even have to work round to ask about Jerry's contact with Mrs Frost for Angela asked her if there was any news about what had happened.

'Poor lady, whatever was she doing down by the river?' she said.

'You've heard about it, then?'

'Yes. Nicholas came to see us. He and his sister – Mrs Frost was their grandma – are friends of Jerry's.'

'I see.'

'Mrs Frost came here once. She and Imogen gave Jerry a lift home. She was ever so nice,' said Angela. 'Jerry's been helping her in her garden.'

'Has he?'

'Yes. He works in the chip shop here, but he loves gardening,' said Angela.

Patsy made movements indicating that she was about to leave.

'Does Jerry follow any particular football team?' she asked, as if she'd just thought ot it.

'Everton,' Angela said promptly. 'He got keen –' She was about to say, when he was in prison, but, although the police would know he had a record, she thought better of it. 'A year or so ago,' she ended sedately.

'I'm a Manchester United fan myself,' said Patsy.

She went away without seeing Jerry at all. She'd got what she came for, and more.

Detective Sergeant Morris had not told Fleming about his taxi-tracing project.

The inspector had got it into his head that Imogen knew more than she was saying – which was true – and it was accepted procedure not to take an apparently accidental death at face value; alternative scenarios had to be investigated thoroughly to satisfy the coroner, and when you had a member of the deceased's circle acting strangely, questions must be asked. Nevertheless, often the simplest explanation turned out to be the right one.

Fleming had unearthed a motive. Because of his marriage break-up, the girl's father needed money. Fleming could sympathise with this predicament. When he asked Brian Price who would benefit from Mrs Frost's death, he learned that Price's wife and her brother owned the dead woman's house, for which she paid no rent. It followed that now the property would be released, capital could be realised, and the father's financial problems solved. What he had not learned was why Imogen had pretended to be pregnant, but Morris intended to discover that.

When Patsy Wilson returned from her visit to Becktham, he intercepted her before she could report the results of her enquiries to Fleming. He needed to know them first.

'It probably is Jerry Hunt's shirt,' she said.

'Doesn't prove the pair of them pushed her in the river,' Morris said.

'No,' said Patsy Wilson. 'It may prove that they're an item. But Jerry is involved with the burglary in Granbury. He's going to have to explain how he knew where his mother's car was, and why he didn't report it missing, as she thought he had.'

'Sounds as if Jerry's in trouble either way,' said Morris. 'What's Fleming doing now?' He didn't want to see the man himself; Fleming might order him to arrest Imogen and before then he wanted another chance to talk to her.

'He's not let Nicholas Frost leave yet. Doesn't want those twins getting together and cooking up a story, but the uncle will soon start kicking up a fuss.'

'Hm.' Fleming, always a difficult man, had grown very bitter since his marriage break-up; his irascible temper had become more unpredictable and he had always leaned towards seeking evidence to fit his theories, instead of the other way about. Now, in his eagerness to make swift arrests, he had become more stubborn and intractable. If he'd cast Imogen as a scapegoat and could find enough circumstantial evidence, he was capable of charging her. 'I'm going to see Imogen,' Morris told his colleague. 'At the house, with the aunt there. She's got to have a chance to save herself.'

'Fleming'll bring the Hunts' car in,' Patsy said. 'There may be evidence to link Jerry Hunt with the Granbury break-in, and there were those thefts before, with a lad calling at the door selling stuff while his mate went round the back. Jerry and the lad Captain Smythe collared, Pete Dixon, were in the nick together. That fits.'

'Yes,' Morris agreed. 'Well, Jerry Hunt can look after himself. Imogen Frost needs a bit of help.'

He left before Fleming could discover he was in the station and prevent him from attempting to provide it.

Lorna opened the door to him.

'Ah –' This was the detective who had somehow got through to Imogen and found out about her faked pregnancy. 'Come in,' Lorna said.

'I'd like a word with Imogen,' said Morris.

'She's in here.' Lorna led the way into the sitting-room, where the television was on, turned to a sports programme.

Imogen was curled up on the sofa, almost dozing. She looked up as Morris entered, and he saw fear in her expression but it changed when she recognised him. Imogen smiled. Lorna was astonished: this was a rare phenomenon. 'I'll leave you to it,'

Lorna said, and did so, going into the dining-room with the Sunday paper which had been delivered that morning.

Imogen turned the sound down. A football match was on the screen.

'Like football, do you?' Morris asked.

Imogen shrugged.

'Not really. It's all that's on today,' she said.

'Mm. That's Tottenham playing Leicester,' Morris said. 'The Worthington final.'

'Oh.'

'Doesn't interest you?'

'No.'

'What about the boyfriend? Is he keen?'

'What boyfriend?'

'Well, I thought you had one,' Morris said.

'You mean, because of what I said?'

'Yes.'

'There's no baby and there's no boyfriend,' Imogen said.

'So how did you come to have an Everton shirt in your possession?'

Imogen stared at him, not understanding.

'There was an Everton shirt in your drawer,' said Morris.

'Oh!' Imogen went pink. Then she rallied. 'I didn't know that's what it was,' she said. 'I borrowed it from someone.'

'I see,' said Morris. 'Well, I think you borrowed it from Jerry Hunt. He's an Everton supporter.'

'What if I did?' Now Imogen looked defiant.

'Imogen, I'm not here to trap you.' Morris spoke gently. 'You and Jerry made friends. There's nothing wrong in that. So you borrowed his shirt. Why turn it into a mystery?'

'Jerry's got nothing to do with this,' said Imogen. 'He's just a friend Nick and I met by chance, buying fish and chips from where he works. It ended with him coming to work in Charlotte's garden. That's all.'

'And in the course of your friendship he lent you his shirt?'

'Yes. He knew I hadn't brought much stuff with me,' she invented.

'And when was this? Which day?'

'The day I went there and met his mother,' Imogen was inspired to say. 'It was about a week ago. That's right. It was on Saturday. The next day Jerry came to lunch and made the plan about the garden.'

'You're fond of Jerry.'

'I told you, we're friends.'

'He hasn't been to see you since Mrs Frost died.'

'He doesn't know about it,' Imogen retorted. 'She's only been dead a day,' she said, and the tears began again.

'He does know. Nicholas has told him,' Morris said.

'Nick? Where is he?'

'At the moment he's at the police station with your uncle,' Morris said. 'I'm sure he'll be here soon, once Mr Fleming has finished talking to him.'

'But Nick can't know anything about it either. We couldn't get him on the phone.'

'In the end your father told him,' said Morris. 'Nicholas thought Jerry might know something useful.'

'Why should he?' Now Imogen was frightened. It seemed that Nick had somehow blundered in, involving Jerry.

'Only because he'd been working in the garden. No one knew who the gardener was, except that his name was Jerry. You weren't saying anything. All this has happened very fast, Imogen, and you haven't made things easy for your-self.'

She and Jerry had been seen kissing. More than just the movement of a shirt might have passed between them.

'What's going to happen to me now?' Imogen asked. 'You don't think I killed Charlotte, do you?'

'No, I don't,' said Morris. 'But unless you can prove you were somewhere else, Mr Fleming will find it difficult to agree with me. Ring me, when you decide to tell the truth, Imogen,' he said, and gave her his card. 'Every little lie leads to a bigger one, you know.'

Soon after Morris left, Nicholas and Brian arrived in their separate cars. They muttered together outside the house, and then came walking up the path.

Lorna let them in, but Imogen hung back as Nicholas fol-lowed his uncle into the sitting-room which suddenly seemed very full of people, and came over to give her a hug.

'It'll be all right, Imogen,' he said. 'It must have been awful for you, with that smarmy copper making snide remarks.'

Brian sank down in an armchair. A cautious man, by nature and profession, he did not hasten to endorse Nicholas's comment, though he agreed with his description of Fleming.

'He has a duty to eliminate all possibility of foul play,' he said portentously.

'What evidence is there to support such an idea?' asked Lorna.

'Nothing. It's all in his head, but if Imogen could prove that she was nowhere near the river because she was somewhere else, it would help.'

Three faces turned to look at Imogen.

'I was just walking around,' she insisted. Then she took a deep breath.

'I'd got into a mess and I was wondering how to get out of it,' she said, studying the carpet. There was a muddy mark on it; that was from where Sergeant Morris had stood after being in the garden when she told him the truth. The big lie had already been admitted; some of the smaller ones might not have to be revealed.

Lorna knew that her explanation might be true. The girl might even have got as far as the river and been contemplating drastic action on her own account, except that she was such a good swimmer that she'd have failed.

'Did Charlotte find you? Did you have a talk?' she said, not adding, ending in an argument.

'No.' Imogen denied it fiercely. 'How could I know she'd go poking into my room and be stupid enough to follow me?' she said, at last showing some emotion.

'We'd left you in her care, Imogen, and she thought you were pregnant,' Lorna said.

'Well, I should have been in my father and mother's care,' said Imogen. 'Why didn't they come when I needed them?'

'Is that what this is all about, Imogen?' Brian asked her. 'Did you think that if you were in trouble – in other words, pregnant – they would get together again?'

'I thought it might work,' Imogen said sadly. 'If they really are our parents. Dad, anyway.'

'What do you mean?' Brian asked.

'Imogen's got this idea that we came out of test tubes,' said Nicholas. 'She thinks we've got an unknown father and that's why Dad doesn't like her – at least she thinks he doesn't. I'm sure he does.' As he spoke, Nicholas longed to be back in Phoebe's shabby flat, with her steadily ironing at one side of the living-room while her children watched cartoons on television, and where the only tears were theirs. Phoebe was magically calm.

'Why don't you speak to your father about it, if it's on your mind?' said Brian, avoiding his wife's gaze as she marginally shook her head.

'We did, when he came over here, but he didn't give us a straight answer,' Nicholas said.

'You didn't come from test tubes,' Lorna said. 'I promise you that.'

This conversation was making Nicholas feel uncomfortable.

'I've got to go,' he said. 'I'm on duty in the restaurant this evening.'

'Can I come with you? Would Phoebe put me up?' said Imogen. She turned to Lorna. 'You've been so kind, considering I'm not really your niece at all. I know you've got to get back home. I've wrecked your day.'

Not just our day: the next weeks, quite probably, even months, if that pigheaded inspector didn't change his attitude, thought Brian, who intended to get hold of Felix and, however grave his misfortunes, make him come back to face his responsibilities.

'No.' That wouldn't do at all, Lorna decided. 'I'll stay overnight again,' she said. 'I can go up to the office in the morning.' Imogen could come too. If the police knew where to find her, they couldn't object.

But before either Brian or Nicholas had left, Charlotte's daughter Jane arrived, offering a different solution.

*   *   *

She came from Heathrow airport in a taxi. Tim would probably arrive on Monday, Victoria had said, when Jane had telephoned her sister-in-law from New York before she left. As their mother was, in fact, dead, the urgency was less acute than if she were critically ill, and though no ship in the Mediterranean was ever far from land, there were logistic problems.

In the taxi, Jane had wondered whether she would be able to get into her mother's house but if Lorna had gone, a neighbour might have a key. Victoria had said that Lorna was there with Imogen. Seeing lights on and cars outside, Jane was glad she would be able to gain entry, but she wanted the Frosts out. This was still, technically, her mother's house. When their father died, the Frosts had behaved in a callous, mercenary fashion, bundling his widow unceremoniously out of White Lodge, then instantly putting it up for sale. Tim and Victoria had been indignant, and so was Jane, when she understood the perfidy of Charlotte's step-family. Until her possessions had been removed from Granbury, her memory must be respected and Jane meant to see that everything was dealt with properly.

There was the problem of Imogen, too, she realised, when she was led in to the sitting-room and saw the twins there, with their aunt and uncle. Charlotte had mentioned her arrival the last time they had spoken on the telephone: last Sunday. Of course Imogen was still here, but no doubt they'd soon remove her. A week ago Jane had spoken to her mother, and heard the reason for Imogen's visit; now Charlotte was dead.

Jane was very tired, but she was not going to let those Frosts be witness to her distress. Not a tear should escape her eyes in front of them, she resolved.

They were all hanging back, even Lorna, who at their only previous meetings – the wedding and Rupert's funeral – had seemed extremely poised; Jane deduced that they were more embarrassed than sad. Then Lorna took control and offered tea.

It seemed a good idea. Tea-drinking gave you time to think, and it could even make you feel better.

She had never been in this house which for so few months had been her mother's home. Suddenly tears threatened, and abruptly she said that she would like a wash after the journey.

'Imogen will take you up to the bathroom,' Lorna said severely, and Imogen, in silence, led the way.

Jane followed her upstairs, and Imogen pointed to the bathroom.

Once safely locked inside, Jane gave way to tears, burying her face in a large, peach-coloured fluffy towel hanging on the rail and which she imagined was her mother's. She spent some time in the bathroom and Imogen, reluctant to return to the troubled group downstairs, waited anxiously for her in her own room, with the door ajar. When Jane emerged at last, she asked which was her mother's room, and Imogen pointed silently to its door. Jane went inside, fumbling for the light.

Downstairs, the others were unnerved, and Nicholas decided to leave. He didn't want to lose his waiter's job. He bounded up the stairs calling softly to his sister, and she met him on the landing, gesturing to show where Jane had gone.

'It'll be all right,' he said, giving her a hug.

But would it? What had she really done? Where had she really been? Suppose she and Charlotte had met on their nocturnal walk, or even gone on it together, and for some reason Charlotte had slipped into the river, surely Imogen would not have walked away? Had Charlotte found out she wasn't pregnant and fear of the truth coming out had made Imogen do something dreadful?

That man Fleming thought this and money needed by Felix provided a motive. Nicholas couldn't believe that Imogen would do anything so outrageous, but her pretence pregnancy had been pretty wild.

They couldn't talk about it now, nor about Jerry's possible involvement in the burglary at Captain Smythe's. He drove back to Oxford and his job. And Phoebe.

When Jane came out of Charlotte's room, Imogen managed to say, 'I'm so sorry. Charlotte was very kind to me and my grandfather really loved her.'

'Thank you for that, Imogen,' said Jane, calm now. 'You've had a bad time, too. This must be shocking for you.'

'Yes,' said Imogen. Then she added, 'I must tell you quickly, before they do – I'm not pregnant. I never was. I don't really know why I pretended to be.'

'You must have had a reason,' Jane said. 'Maybe we can work it out later. Let's get the next bit over,' and she went downstairs, into what she thought of as the lion's den, although she swiftly found that neither Lorna nor her husband were in a fierce mood. They plied her with tea and biscuits, and explained that the police were still making extensive enquiries into the circumstances of Charlotte's death.

'But it was an accident, wasn't it?' said Jane.

They had to fill in the details, explain about Charlotte's late walk and that Imogen had been out of the house.

'It's all my fault,' said Imogen. 'If I hadn't gone out, she wouldn't have, either. But she shouldn't have gone looking in my room,' she added, still defiant.

Jane's head had cleared and she tuned in to the conversation with the sharpness that sometimes comes with extreme fatigue.

'Why did my mother have to look after Imogen at all?' she asked. 'Why couldn't she go home?'

Charlotte, when she spoke to Jane on the telephone, had been afraid of Imogen overhearing the conversation; she had said very little, simply that the girl was pregnant and had run away from school while Zoe was in California and Felix away on business. Now Lorna repeated this, and explained that Zoe's mother, with whom she had stayed at first, had gone on a cruise.

'I'm going to get hold of Felix and see that he comes over,' Brian said now. 'He is needed here.' There was no need to tell Jane about Detective Inspector Fleming's suspicions; she would find out for herself, soon enough.

'Jane, I'll stay here tonight,' said Lorna. 'Imogen will probably have to talk to the police again tomorrow as there are some points to be cleared up. I can go to the office in the morning.'

'But there's no need for that, since it's difficult for you,' said Jane. 'I'm here now. My mother was looking after Imogen. I'll take over. This is still her house, I take it, until at least the funeral?'

That barbed remark went home.

'Of course,' said Lorna, and then, 'Would you, Jane? Just for a short time? It would be simpler.'

'I can see that,' said Jane. 'My mother's car is in the garage, I suppose? Imogen and I can use it. We shall need to get about. She can show me the way.'

Brian and Lorna left ten minutes later, having written down

every relevant telephone number they could think of, and after they had gone, Jane looked at her watch.

'Look at the time, Imogen. You must want your supper, and I want lunch. Let's ring up for a pizza. It must be possible. Where are the Yellow Pages?'

20

Jerry had finished painting the ceiling and two walls of his mother's sitting-room. Angela was wondering whether papering them would have made a nice change, though it was a messier and longer job, and was discussing it with him when the doorbell rang again.

She hadn't told Jerry about the visit from DC Patsy Wilson. He'd had his radio on so loud that he hadn't heard her, and after the policewoman had gone, Angela realised that she still didn't know where the Metro had been found; DC Wilson hadn't said. She hadn't said a lot, really; she'd seemed only to want to verify the date when it went missing, and then she'd said it hadn't been reported after all. Something was wrong; the detective must have made a mistake. Angela had a feeling that the date coincided with Pete Dixon being caught trying to rob someone's house in Granbury. Jerry had stopped going out at nights with Pete some time before that date. He couldn't have been involved, but maybe Pete had stolen her car and Jerry guessed it and had got it back. She wouldn't mention it, or not just yet.

This time the callers were two male detectives. They wanted

to take a look inside her car, and they wanted to ask Jerry a few questions.

Under the matting in the boot of Angela's car they found a gold chain-link bracelet. It must have slipped down there after Pete had stolen it on one of their excursions, Jerry thought, his stomach lurching with sick fear. Its owner could identify it.

He was taken in for questioning.

At the police station, Fleming was delighted. While he was working on one case, a sudden death in Granbury, a thief acquainted with the girl he suspected of knowing more than she had said about that incident had been nicked. The case against Pete Dixon was watertight; he had been apprehended in the act by the besieged householder, a man of exemplary character. For all Fleming knew, deprived by Pete's arrest of his usual partner in crime, Jerry Hunt could have enlisted Imogen as an assistant and that was why she was being so cagey about her whereabouts on Friday night. Maybe she wasn't pushing her grandma in the river; maybe she was out thieving.

He floated this idea to Morris.

'She's no need to steal. She comes from a comfortable background,' Morris said.

'Does it for kicks, maybe. Likes a bit of rough with young Jerry Hunt.'

Fleming was getting a buzz out of this.

'Would you be so sure that she's mixed up in something if she was a pretty girl?' asked Morris, all his life the butt of animosity and even suspicion because he was an ugly man who had been an unattractive child. Added to her plain looks, Imogen had a brusque, off-putting manner; she made a negative impression.

'Plenty of pretty girls are crooked,' Fleming said. 'We'll go and interview young Jerry Hunt and see what he can tell us.'

Jerry had had to leave his paint roller and his gear in mid-task. He had not been allowed even to clear up.

'It's all right. You'll soon be back,' his mother had said, as he was driven off, but as soon as he had gone she burst into a torrent of tears. He'd promised, and she'd believed him. She still believed in him.

Neither could have known that, as a form of insurance, Pete had deliberately dropped the bracelet, one of no great value, which he had kept back from an earlier burglary, in the Metro before he went to rob Captain Smythe. If he were caught, either on this occasion or another, and he wanted to bring Jerry down, it would be easy.

'Look in the car,' was all he would have to say. He hadn't done it yet, but he might.

'I drove the car a few times with Pete,' Jerry admitted now. 'That's all. I never did the thieving.' This was true. All he did was ring the doorbell and chat up whoever answered. Eventually, desperate to save himself, he described how meeting Captain Smythe and Mrs Frost, both of whom had told him he should change his ways, had convinced him he must break his association with Pete Dixon. Mrs Frost had even given him a job.

'What do you know about her death? Mrs Frost's?' demanded Fleming, pushing his thin, angry face towards Jerry's round, ingenuous one.

'Nothing. Only that she is dead.'

'How did you hear about it?' A local radio broadcast had reported the discovery of a woman's body in the river but she had not been named.

'Nicholas Frost told me.'

'Ah – so you do know the family?'

'Yes. I worked for Mrs Frost, in her garden,' Jerry said. He'd best stick to the truth as much as possible.

'Where were you on Friday night?'

What a bit of luck that after he'd dropped Imogen off, he'd visited Tracy. She fancied him rotten and she'd say he'd been there, he was sure. Besides, it was true.

'With a girl,' he said.

'What girl?'

'A girl I went to school with.'

In the end he gave her name. He couldn't say he'd been with Imogen first.

While Jane and Imogen were waiting for their pizzas, Captain Smythe telephoned. Jane answered the telephone. It might be Ben ringing from New York, or her brother Tim.

'Jane Paterson speaking,' she said.

'You're Charlotte's daughter.' The male voice was deep and steady.

'Yes.'

'My name's Smythe. Howard Smythe. I'm – I was a friend of your mother's,' he said. 'Can I be of any help? Is Imogen all right?'

'Sort of,' said Jane.

'Are her parents there?'

'No. Her aunt and uncle were, Lorna and Brian, and Nicholas, her brother, but they've gone now. We're on our own. I haven't been here long,' said Jane.

'You've come from New York?'

'That's right.'

'I live in the village. I don't want to intrude, but would you like me to come round?' he offered.

'That sounds a very good idea. May I just have a word with Imogen?' said Jane. Here was a link with her mother. She covered the mouthpiece with her hand and said, 'It's a Howard Smythe. Friend of Mum's. Sounds nice. Shall he come round, he says?'

Imogen nodded vigorously.

'Yes, please. We'd like that,' Jane told him.

'I will be there in about fifteen minutes,' Howard said.

'He's pretty old,' warned Imogen. 'He was Charlotte's friend, but they hadn't known each other long.'

She told Jane that he had caught a burglar in his house.

'Sounds a great guy,' said Jane.

'I'll have to tell him about the baby.'

'The non-baby,' Jane said. 'There wasn't one. Don't give it an existence it never had. Will he drink wine or something stronger?'

'I think he might like something stronger,' Imogen said.

'Let's see what Mum's got beside wine,' said Jane.

They found brandy, and a bottle of Famous Grouse.

'Mum enjoyed a nip now and then,' Jane said. 'And so do I. Drink can be a friend, but it can also be an enemy.'

'I know. I don't drink much,' Imogen said.

'You stick to that. All the same, a glass of wine with

your pizza won't hurt you. It might make you sleep,' said Jane.

'You're being so nice to me,' said Imogen. 'And if it hadn't been for me, Charlotte would be alive.'

'We won't even think about that now,' said Jane, but probably it was true. 'For all you know, she might have had a car accident next week, or been stricken by a dreadful illness. From what my sister-in-law told me on the telephone – I rang her from Heathrow – she can't have known much about it.' Punctilious, anxious to keep Charlotte's family fully informed, for his wife's had much to answer for, Brian had telephoned Victoria about the post-mortem results.

Howard carried a torch to light him on his way. It had rained during the afternoon but it had stopped now; however, there were puddles on the road. He walked carefully; it would be easy to slip and at his age a fall could be seriously damaging. Less resilient with every year, he still felt tired and he was worried about Imogen. Nicholas, calling that morning, had said that the police had been harassing her, as he put it.

'She's a difficult girl,' he had said. 'Thinks the world's against her.'

'Well, you're not, and nor am I, and nor was Charlotte,' Howard had replied. 'Better get that into her head, if you can.'

Imogen opened Charlotte's door to Captain Smythe.

'Ah – Imogen,' he said. 'How are you?'

'All right,' she said. 'Let me take your coat.'

He shrugged off his oiled jacket and gave it to her, with his old tweed hat, and she hung them up beside

Charlotte's raincoat in the cloakroom. Then she led him into the sitting-room where Jane waited. They had decided that this was how they would do it, rather formally.

'This is Jane. A sort of aunt,' said Imogen. 'Captain Smythe,' she added, in a mumble.

Jane held out her hand, and as Howard took it, looking at her, small and neat, with brown hair and arching brows over deep blue eyes, he said, 'You are very like your mother.'

'So they say,' said Jane.

'You've got here very quickly.'

She had, securing a last-minute standby seat on a flight that had been delayed.

'It was necessary,' she said. 'My brother will be here soon. I haven't seen the police yet. I know there will be formalities – an inquest – all that.'

'I'm afraid so. I'm so very sorry,' Howard said. 'Charlotte was a new friend and I was looking forward to seeing more of her. She was a kind and charming woman.'

'I'm glad that she had met you,' said Jane. 'She was very lonely. She was bundled here by the Frosts.' Saying this, Jane frowned.

'It's true,' said Imogen. 'And Dad resented her being here, rent-free.'

'She intended to insist on paying,' Jane revealed. 'She knew the arrangement would cause bad feelings, but there wasn't time to make a different plan when White Lodge was sold so quickly. She meant to look into things with a solicitor and see what could be done to regain her independence.'

'Granddad would have been very angry if he'd known what they'd done,' said Imogen.

'She did have a pension,' Jane pointed out. 'From his estate, I mean.'

'I should hope so,' said Imogen.

And she had her own, as well as the state pension.

'She wasn't badly off,' said Jane. It was time to change the subject. 'Won't you have a drink, Captain Smythe? What would you like?'

She moved like Charlotte, he noticed, purposefully and economically, as she poured them both considerable whiskies. Without asking her, she gave Imogen a glass of white wine. He wondered what her father had been like.

'I expect the Frosts will want to sell the house as soon as they can,' Jane continued. 'Sorry, Imogen, but it's the truth. However, for the time being, I regard it as my mother's. I shall stay here for as long as it's necessary, and I'll look after Imogen, too, as my mother did, till some member of her family takes over.'

'They'd made good friends, your mother and Imogen,' Howard said. 'Hadn't you, Imogen?'

'I was a trouble,' said Imogen. 'Captain Smythe, I have to tell you, I'm not pregnant. I made it up.'

'Really, my dear? That was a silly thing to do, wasn't it? Couldn't you have found another way of telling your parents how unhappy you were?'

'They wouldn't listen,' Imogen said. Then, 'You don't seem shocked.'

'It takes a lot to shock me, Imogen,' he answered. 'Charlotte's death has shocked me – and shocked you. And Jane, and her brother. Even your family.'

'They'll be glad in the end,' said Imogen. 'It solves Dad's problems.'

'Oh no, Imogen,' Captain Smythe replied. 'You're wrong.' It was such a waste, he thought; here was this bitter, angry girl who might have been the catalyst for these events, but it was her family's denial of her that had involved Charlotte, who, it now appeared, they had treated shabbily. 'What is the present situation?' he asked.

'The police think I pushed Charlotte in the river,' said Imogen. 'I did cause her death, by going out that night.'

'Imogen, my mother wasn't very sensible to go roaming off in the dark over fields – she went across fields, didn't she? The river path was in a field, wasn't it?' said Jane.

'She took a torch,' said Imogen.

'Well, I'm glad to hear it, but really, unless she had some reason to think you'd gone down to the river, why didn't she stick to the roads or call the police?'

'Perhaps she thought I was going to jump in, because of being pregnant,' Imogen said.

'All the more reason to call the police. They might not have come if she'd just said you'd gone out – they can't go looking for every girl who's simply out late – but if they knew there was a particular reason to be anxious about you, they might have taken it seriously. Though I suppose they couldn't do a lot in the dark. What a pity she didn't just go back to bed and wait till morning to look for you,' she added.

'Imogen, you must be mistaken, surely,' said Howard Smythe. 'Have they suggested you were there when Charlotte fell into the river?'

'Sort off,' said Imogen. Oddly, she did not feel like crying now. She felt grown-up and sensible. 'There was something about Charlotte not drowning. Like the brides in the bath, someone said. I don't understand that part.'

Howard did.

'There was a man who went in for serial marriage, as it's called today. This was years ago – in my childhood. He insured them heavily and then each one drowned in the bath. It was suggested that he caught hold of their feet and tipped them up, causing the water to rush up their noses so that they died from sudden heart failure. You must have been told to hold your nose when jumping into water, Imogen. It's a crucial precaution – you can do it like this,' and, separating his thumb from his fingers, he put his hand under his nose, the soft skin against his nostrils. 'It's important if you have to abandon ship.'

'And they think something like that happened to my mother? But if she'd been pushed in, it wouldn't have, would it?' Jane said. She would have struggled, fought against the water or her assailant, taken time to die. She shuddered.

'It's difficult to say,' said Howard. 'It would depend on how she fell.' He hesitated. 'If you want to go there, Jane, we could tomorrow, when it's light. Perhaps we could work it out.'

'It's true about holding your nose,' said Imogen. 'I had a swimming instructor when I was very young who was paranoid about it, making us do it whenever we were jumping off the diving board or even the side of the pool.'

The doorbell rang.

'That'll be our pizzas,' said Imogen.

But it wasn't. The pizza courier, who came from Nettington, was having trouble finding Vicarage Fields and it was the driver of the taxi Howard, fearing weakness on his part or further rain, had ordered for his return before he left his house.

Imogen opened the door to him.

'Well, hullo,' the driver said. 'You're OK then? I was

worried about you the other night. I've called for Captain Smythe,' he added.

He was the man who had taken Imogen to Becktham on Friday.

21

Imogen shot away from the front door into the house.

'It's not the pizzas – it's a taxi for you, Captain Smythe.'

'Oh – thank you,' said Howard. He looked at Jane somewhat sheepishly. 'I walked up, but I ordered a taxi back for two reasons – one, to stop one of you from feeling you should escort an old man, and two, because the lane is dark and if I slip and fall, I could be a nuisance and might even cause someone else to have an accident.'

'I'd have driven you,' said Jane. 'Mother's car is here.'

'You've had a long journey,' he said. And a drink or two, he did not add. However innocent of causing any accident, a driver could be breathalysed and hounded by the law. 'I no longer drive,' he told Jane.

Imogen had fetched his coat. The driver, she saw with relief, had returned to his car.

'I'll telephone in the morning,' he said, putting on his coat. Imogen handed him his hat, and he patted her shoulder. 'You have got friends, my dear,' he said.

'Thank you for coming,' Jane said, heartened by his visit.

The taxi driver had driven Captain Smythe many times,

usually for short journeys round the area but also to meet some of his grandchildren for lunch in various places.

'That young girl all right, is she?' he asked now, as they moved off down Vicarage Fields to join the main road. Here was the spot where he had picked her up on Friday night.

'Under the circumstances, not too bad.' Howard was surprised by the question. 'You've heard about it, then?'

Now it was the driver's turn to be surprised.

'About what?' he asked.

'Her grandmother – step-grandmother – had a fatal accident. She was found in the river yesterday,' Howard told him.

'I did hear there'd been a drowning,' said the driver. 'Very sad. I didn't know who it was.'

'Why did you ask about Imogen?'

'I drove her to Becktham on Friday night,' the driver said, negotiating the turning into Meadow Lane.

Howard stayed entirely calm.

'Oh yes,' he said, as if he knew about the trip.

'Picked her up on the corner. She was in a bit of a state and I was anxious. Young girls, you know.' He did not mention Imogen's generous tip.

'Quite,' said Howard. Nicholas had said that Jerry lived in Becktham. The fog of subterfuge was clearing, and if Imogen had been in Becktham on Friday night, she couldn't have been down by the river. 'Was it you who brought her back?' he tried.

'No. Maybe she got a lift. Or a local cab,' said the driver, drawing up outside Rose Cottage. 'It's all happening in Granbury, then,' he added. 'I'm sorry about the girl's grandmother. That's bad. All right, sir, yourself, are you, after the burglary?'

'None the worse,' said Howard.

'Glad you caught the little monster,' said the driver.

But Pete hadn't been a monster. He was a greedy, undisciplined, lazy boy, the sort that, if he were directed down a route with purpose, might be turned around.

Howard paid the driver, bidding him goodnight. In the morning he would have to decide what to do with his new knowledge – whether to confront Imogen and give her a chance to speak up before telling the police, for of course it cleared her. She was unlikely to have gone down to the river after a trip to Becktham. If she wasn't pregnant after all, the situation was very different and there could have been something between her and Jerry.

He would sleep on it. In wartime, snap decisions must be made, but this was not one of those occasions. Things might look different in the morning.

Jerry had been cautioned and questioned.

He denied involvement in the burglary at Captain Smythe's house and disclaimed knowledge of the bracelet discovered in the Metro, but he agreed that he had not reported his mother's car missing because he suspected that Pete might have taken it. Pete was already on remand awaiting trial and there was no way he was going to get off since Captain Smythe had caught him.

'I did go round with Pete, selling dusters and that.' Jerry had admitted this already. 'I didn't have nothing to do with the stealing. I just talked on the doorstep.'

'But you knew what Peter was doing. You shared in the profits,' said Detective Sergeant Beddoes, the officer who had charged Pete. He was conducting the interview but because of Jerry's connection with the Frosts, Fleming had decided to be present.

'Pete wanted to borrow Mum's car. I said no,' said Jerry. 'He could have taken the spare key when he came to our house. I guessed that was what had happened and I found the car and brought it back. No harm done. I didn't want to waste your time,' he added, winningly.

'Don't waste your smiles on me, Jerry,' Fleming snapped. 'I'm not a gullible pensioner you can charm, nor a silly young girl like Imogen Frost.'

'Imogen's got nothing to do with this,' Jerry said.

'No?'

'Captain Smythe's place was done before she ever got down here,' said Jerry. 'I met her next day, in the chip shop. Her and her brother.'

This could be checked. Beddoes knew – as the whole CID team did – that Fleming had taken a dislike to Imogen Frost and had convinced himself that she was the active cause of her grandmother's death. Fleming was a good detective and he had solved many awkward cases, largely through perseverance, but he was stubborn, and he wanted convictions. There was no single piece of substantiated evidence to connect Imogen with the river death, nor a motive that would stand up in court, but there could be grief along the way – and for Fleming as well as the targeted girl. If he went too far, there could be a complaint and it wouldn't be the first time he had overstepped the limits with a witness. Beddoes and his colleagues were sure that Mrs Frost's death was due to misadventure. There was no crime to investigate: only suicide or accident. But theft was different. Jerry had a record; he was the confidence trickster who had kept victims talking while Pete took the stuff.

In the end they locked him up for the night. He could be charged in the morning.

Jane had not noticed Imogen's reaction to the taxi driver. The pizzas arrived soon after he left, the courier apologising for the delay.

They needed warming up. Jane put them in the oven, then said she'd have a shower and change her clothes before they ate.

'I'll sleep in Mum's room,' she said.

'I'll find some clean sheets,' said Imogen.

'Don't worry, Imogen. That's OK. It's my mother's bed, not some stranger's. I'll just feel at home.'

Jane hurried, however, not wanting to steep herself in grief, and she wanted to call Ben, who would be wondering about her. Wrapped in the towel she thought was Charlotte's but which had been used by Lorna, she rang him from the telephone in the bedroom. They had a short talk. She explained that she hadn't yet spoken to the police but there were unresolved problems concerning Imogen, who had been out of the house when Charlotte went for her midnight walk. Before she left America, Jane had been convinced that Charlotte had not taken her own life; that would not be her way, unless she had had a total breakdown, which no one had suggested. Now she was still more certain. She promised to ring Ben again when Imogen, whose timetable was five hours ahead of theirs, had gone to bed.

There would be a great deal to sort out in the morning,

but Tim would soon arrive, perhaps even tomorrow, and lend a hand.

'The good news is, I didn't let those Frosts walk all over me,' she said, not telling Ben that an encounter with Felix was yet to come. Lorna had been quite nice, she conceded, though swift to accept Jane's offer to take temporary charge of Imogen.

She dressed in clean clothes and went downstairs, where Imogen had laid the table in the dining-room. The salad which Charlotte had bought on her last shopping expedition had kept fresh in its sealed bag in the fridge, and there was the wine Jane had already opened. Imogen had even found table napkins, and candles, which she lit when she heard Jane on the stairs.

'Oh, Imogen, that does look nice,' said Jane.

Imogen glowed.

'I know you're sad, but Charlotte would want you to feel it's home,' she said.

'You're right,' said Jane, pouring the wine. She took a gulp. 'The garden's looking good,' she said. 'I didn't expect that.'

Of course, she didn't know about Jerry.

'Charlotte had some help,' Imogen said. 'A friend of mine and Nick's. He did most of it this week.'

'Oh?'

'And Captain Smythe gave us a lot of plants. We were going to get some more yesterday.' They were to have met Jerry at the garden centre yesterday. What had he done? He wouldn't have known about Charlotte. Had he gone there, as arranged?

'Mum had said it was a mess,' Jane said. 'Some moth-eaten lawn clawed up by dogs and cats. Or children, possibly.'

'We put down new turf,' said Imogen.

'I expect she was pleased.'

'Yes.' Imogen was glad she had put in the plants. 'Captain

Smythe was burgled, just before I got here,' she said. 'Well, it was the night before. He caught the thief and hung on to him till the police arrived. He's a great old bloke.'

'He seems to be. What sort of captain was he?'

'He was in the navy.'

'Was he? Tim would like to meet him.'

'Well, he will, when he gets here,' said Imogen. 'How long will you stay?'

'I don't know. Between us, if we can, till everything's settled.'

'You mean the funeral? Perhaps she can be buried near Captain Smythe's wife, in the graveyard here,' said Imogen.

'Perhaps,' said Jane.

After Rupert's death, Charlotte had said she wanted to be cremated. Should she look in her mother's desk for a will? Had she made a new one after Rupert died? It might be complicated, if she hadn't. There was no point in worrying about that now, but it would be a good idea to find a solicitor who wasn't Brian, a Frost connection. Captain Smythe could advise them.

There were some pears which needed eating. Jane and Imogen had one each for their dessert, and Jane told Imogen about the flight and a man who sat next to her on the plane and talked about planting a vineyard in Lancashire.

'I told him it might not be his best choice because of the climate,' said Jane. 'Too little warm sun. He was possessed of a dream. Not a bad thing, in fact.' Had Imogen a dream? Hers at that age had been to get good exam results, a degree, and an interesting career, with maybe marriage and a family along the way. She'd achieved the first three of these ambitions; marriage and a family had eluded her, but her relationship with Ben was mutually sustaining and, she believed, would last.

'Jerry has a dream of being a proper gardener. A horticulturist,' said Imogen. 'Charlotte thought we could help him find out how to do it.'

'He'll have to do that for himself now, won't he?' Jane said. 'It won't be difficult. The internet, for starters, you could suggest.'

But Imogen did not expect to see Jerry again.

They watched television later; it saved talking. Neither took in much of what was on, and, when they went to bed, alone in their rooms, both wept bitterly, one from grief, the other from fear and remorse. After Jane had dried her tears and spoken on the telephone to Ben, she propped open her bedroom door and put a chair across the landing at the top of the stairs, just in case Imogen decided to go walking in the night again. With any luck, she would hear her either falling over or removing the obstruction.

Jane woke next morning to a tap on the half-open door.

It had taken her some time to go to sleep, lying in her mother's bed wondering what Charlotte's thoughts had been as she lay here. There were two books on the bedside table, short stories by Carol Shields and Alice Munro. Jane had given her both of them; when she was in England for Rupert's funeral she had recommended the authors to Charlotte. There was a marker in the Carol Shields; this must have been the last of her mother's reading. How lonely she must have felt, uprooted from all that was familiar, forced to readjust again. Jane and Ben had tried to persuade her to visit them, and she had agreed to come when Jane could take time off to be with her. Victoria had been concerned about her, wishing she would visit them more often, but Jane knew her diffident mother had been anxious to avoid being thought pushy and interfering; perhaps she had erred too much the other way. At least she'd met that nice old man, Captain Smythe, through whom she might have made other new friends; Jane did not realise that he was also isolated.

She had been deeply asleep when the knock came, and struggled back to consciousness, trying to remember where she was, without Ben beside her, and why she was being disturbed in the middle of the night.

But it was morning here. She was in England in her dead mother's bed, and responsible for a disturbed, unhappy girl.

'Yes – what –?' she called out groggily, blinking, pulling herself into the present.

The door opened and Imogen came in, carrying a tray.

'I know it's night for you, but it's nine o'clock here and we're going to meet Captain Smythe,' she said. Though no time had been arranged, Imogen wanted to be out of the house before the police came for her again, as she feared they would.

'Oh – that's sweet of you, Imogen. How lovely,' said Jane, heaving herself up as Imogen set the tray down on the dressing-table stool and carried it over.

'I thought you'd want coffee but I can easily make tea, if you'd rather,' said Imogen anxiously. 'Here's the paper.' She had *The Times* tucked under her arm. 'There's just toast. Would you like an egg?'

'Coffee's fine. I won't be long,' said Jane. 'Thanks, Imogen.'

A few minutes later the sound of the vacuum cleaner could be heard as Imogen set about clearing up after yesterday's incursion of visitors. Poor kid, she was certainly doing all she could to be a ray of sunshine now, but she bore a lot of responsibility for the tragedy that had taken place.

'I do blame her,' Jane had said to Ben, last night. 'But it wasn't sensible of Mum to go off like that in search of her. And now Imogen says the police think she may have pushed Mum into the river.'

'Do you think so?'

'No. She's troubled and disturbed. But she was fond of Mum. She can't really believe what's happened and nor can I.'

'I wish I could be there with you,' said Ben.

'So do I. But Tim is coming. Meanwhile, I mean to rout the Frosts – except for Imogen.' Ben knew what she felt about their treatment of her mother.

'You do that,' Ben encouraged. As she had the wayward Imogen to keep an eye on, she wasn't alone, and this elderly acquaintance of her mother's, Captain Smythe, was good news.

Howard Smythe telephoned just as Jane, carrying her tray, came downstairs. They arranged to meet almost immediately, as soon as Jane and Imogen could get to Rose Cottage. They would come by car, Jane said, aware that as he had used a taxi the night before, he was perhaps more fragile than he appeared.

They had just left when Detective Inspector Fleming called them on the telephone.

Howard intended to challenge Imogen. He was sure the police would interview her again today, and Jane would have to talk to them about the inquest. Probably it would be opened the next day, or on Wednesday, he thought, and even though it would be adjourned to a later date, by then the investigating officer would hope to be able to satisfy the coroner as to whether it was an accident or something more sinister.

There had been cases where, because an involved person had an unfortunate manner, was brusque or surly, or even simply ugly, an impression of guilt could be created and the investigation became geared, not to discovering the truth, but towards finding evidence to support the prejudice. It would be dreadful if for this reason Imogen were considered to be under suspicion. Such people often gave a poor account of themselves under cross-examination, alienating juries. Now, though, there was a taxi driver who could reveal where she had gone.

Imogen sat in the back of Charlotte's car as Jane, directed by Howard Smythe, drove the short distance round the lanes to the nearest point where they could leave it before crossing a stile and walking to the narrow footbridge. There was a police car by the verge, and as they drew closer to the bridge they saw a lone constable on duty beside tapes marking off an area a hundred yards or so further along the bank.

None of them spoke. Imogen hung back while Captain Smythe, with a word to Jane, led the way. Straight and tall, he walked across and paused to let them catch up. The path was narrow, and they had to go in single file. This was where Charlotte had come that night, but had she approached from the road, as they had done, or across the fields? Could the answer ever be discovered?

The constable stood forward alertly as they came towards him.

'I'm sorry, sir. I'm afraid you can't come any further,' he said.

'Officer, this lady is Mrs Frost's daughter,' Howard said.

'Oh. Well, even so, Scenes of Crime may be coming back,' the constable replied.

'But there was no crime, officer,' said Howard gently. 'It was an accident.'

'That may be so, sir, but I have my orders,' said the policeman.

'And you must obey them,' Howard said.

He looked past the man, aware from walks here himself that some way beyond where the constable was standing the path curved, and the bank was steeper, cut away. There would have been nothing for Charlotte to clutch at if she had slipped there, and the current could have moved her body to the spot where, caught up in reeds and grasses, it seemed that it had come to rest. However, she had had a torch.

'Has the torch been found?' he asked.

'I can't answer that,' said the constable. After all, he was uniform, not CID.

'It could have fallen in the river or it could have rolled away,' said Howard. 'Be good enough to glance up and down in the grass beside the path further away from us, constable, where it bends, and also in the water. We'll wait here.'

Faced with Howard's quiet authority, and seeing no chance that he might contaminate the crime scene, if that was what it was, any more than those who had trampled it when removing the body from the water, the constable did as he was bid, while Jane thought that surely the area would already have been carefully examined and the torch found, if it was there.

The constable saw it, some distance from where he had been standing, half-hidden in the grass, a heavy, black rubber torch. His boredom fled; here was evidence. After the rain, his own footsteps had left marks on the path, but there were others, not wholly obliterated, by a pothole close to the edge above the river, where the bank was high and steep above the water.

He called the station straight away, gesturing, thumb up, to Howard as he did so.

Howard glanced at the two women.

'I think this means that Charlotte entered the water further along than this roped-off area. You'll be able to come back later, Jane, after the significance of what the constable has found is assessed and the police have gone. We would be wise to leave the scene before reinforcements arrive.'

22

Felix had returned to England late the night before. His answering machine was filled with urgent messages, some about business and others concerning Imogen. Zoe had tried to get him; who, she asked, was looking after Imogen now that Charlotte was dead?

Bit late to start worrying about that, thought Felix, listening to Brian telling him that Jane had taken on this role. He wondered who had told Zoe about Charlotte; he hadn't.

Brian's final message mentioned, in no uncertain terms, that Imogen was in a dicey situation.

Bloody girl, thought Felix. The stupid little cow had never done him credit. He'd given her his name, brought her up as his, and no one knew who her real father was. Nicholas was different; he was a boy any man could be proud of and it had not been difficult for Felix to convince himself that he was his real son. Perhaps their real father had been a stupid, shiftless idiot, like Imogen. Thinking that was less painful than imagining him to be an accomplished lover. Felix had tortured himself with such speculation.

He would have to go Granbury and sort out this mess.

Surely even Imogen couldn't have been crazy enough to push Charlotte in the river? But you couldn't be certain. What about criminal genes? Who knew what she had inherited? A promiscuous disposition, evidently. He would like to know what the two of them were doing, roaming round the countryside in the middle of the night. Charlotte must have been behaving very irresponsibly towards the girl. There was no denying that with her off the scene, his financial situation would be much improved; the house would be easy to sell, and he might persuade Lorna to let him use her share of the capital, short term. Though Brian wouldn't approve; he'd advised Felix against going ahead with a merger that had proved a sad mistake, leading to his company's present trouble, and now Zoe had escaped.

Felix had very little feeling left for Zoe. She had been happy when the twins were born, and had seemed fulfilled, but once their baby stage was over – even Imogen had been no plainer than many other babies – she had begun to distance herself from Felix. Perhaps she was also haunted by that unnamed man, wanting him again. Living comfortably, both busy with their careers, they had seemed to have an enviable life, but in fact it was, increasingly, a sham. His mother had sensed the truth, but she had died, and all too soon, Rupert married Charlotte.

Felix telephoned Brian at seven o'clock on Monday morning, and he did not enjoy hearing what Brian had to tell him, nor did he thank his brother-in-law for his efforts to protect Imogen's interests.

'You'd better get over there, Felix,' Brian told him. 'And be careful with Inspector Fleming. He's developed an antipathy to Imogen and she hasn't helped herself by refusing to say where she went on Friday night. See if you can get her to tell you, and keep cool with Fleming.'

Fat chance of either result, Brian thought, as the conversation ended, leaving Felix more angry and astounded about Imogen pretending to be pregnant than any other detail.

Felix showered and shaved. Next, he made telephone calls and sent some e-mail messages. He had secured a loan of several hundred thousand pounds, but at high interest; perhaps bankruptcy would have been a wiser action, for after an interval he could start again, but to do so meant conceding defeat and he was too stubborn to do that. He put on a dark grey suit and a pale blue shirt and tie. Let Fleming see that he was a man of consequence. Then he got into his Mercedes and set off towards Nettington.

He had picked quite the wrong image to impress Fleming. Jeans and a sweater, and a show of parental emotion, might have pierced the inspector's hostile armour; not city slicker presentation; and Fleming, foiled by getting no reply when he telephoned to warn Imogen that a police car would shortly call for her, was about to leave for Granbury to look for her when Felix arrived.

As it was, Felix's interruption meant that Fleming was still at the station when the constable on the river bank rang in to report the discovery of the torch.

'Why didn't someone calculate that the body would have been carried by the current?' Fleming barked at Morris, when the significance of the find and of the nearby scuff marks was made plain.

Because you didn't think it relevant, and you didn't order the search to be extended along the bank, thought Morris, who yesterday had raised both these points and been shouted down for his pains.

'You've gone soft on that silly girl,' Fleming had said. 'She's a liar. She could have got up to anything.'

Now it was raining, and vital marks could be expunged. Morris went off with protective sheeting to preserve what could be saved, if anything. Let the girl's father and Fleming join battle, as clearly they were about to do, while he looked for evidence in Imogen's defence.

'What is going on?' demanded Felix, looming over Fleming. 'Where is Imogen?'

'You tell me,' said Fleming. 'I've just telephoned the house to say we want her in here, and there's no reply. I'm on my way to get her.'

'If they're not answering the phone, you won't find her, will you?' Felix snapped.

'That sort of attitude isn't going to help,' said Fleming.

'You've been harassing a young girl. One who's had a shock,' said Felix, who though furious with Imogen had picked up on some of the points Brian had made.

'She's lied and wasted police time,' said Fleming.

'She's entitled to legal representation if you're questioning her,' said Felix.

'And she had it,' Fleming replied.

'My brother-in-law isn't available now. Another solicitor must be found. Whoever is available,' said Felix. 'She'll qualify for legal aid.' Felix could not pay legal fees.

'You seem to agree that she has a case to answer.'

'You are putting her in that position.'

'She's done it herself, by refusing to answer questions and by proving herself a liar over saying she was pregnant.'

'That's not the point,' said Felix.

'Oh yes, it is. Mrs Frost may have discovered that it was a lie and Imogen wanted to stop her from talking.'

Brian had warned Felix that once the groundwork of a prosecution theory had been laid, tiny circumstantial straws and bits of grit could be added to build up the edifice, blinding those constructing it to other possibilities, so that opposing facts and theories were never aired, let alone discussed, and Imogen's own conduct, with her not immediately appealing appearance, as he put it in an attempt at tact, her brusque manner and her refusal to talk were the cement that bound the whole. Now Felix saw a man obsessed with a theory, worrying it like a dog with a bone. Fleming had made up his mind and would not look for other explanations.

'She'd better be found,' Felix muttered.

Both men thought she might be doing something stupid. In fact she and Jane were in the kitchen at Rose Cottage, having coffee with Howard Smythe.

'You haven't seen the police yet, have you?' Howard asked Jane. 'Apart from the constable we met just now, I mean.'

'I don't suppose they've realised I'd arrived,' Jane said. 'I suppose I can't put it off much longer. I ought to call them.'

'Ring from here,' said Howard. 'And while you're gone, Imogen can stay with me – if that will suit you, Imogen?'

Imogen nodded.

'They'll want me, as well. That creep Fleming will third-degree me and start twisting everything I say,' she muttered.

'Aren't you exaggerating, Imogen?' said Howard. 'The problem seems to be that you won't say anything.'

Imogen had the grace to smile, though in a shamefaced way.

'There's no need for you to go over there unless they ask you to,' said Jane. 'And I doubt if they'll think of looking for you here.' She didn't want to leave the girl alone, and Howard's was a good suggestion. The two got along, Jane saw, and the wise old man was skilled at handling people; the constable on the river bank had instantly done as he had been asked.

'Will you find the way?' asked Imogen.

'Once I get to Nettington, anyone will tell me where the police station is,' said Jane. Howard gave her some directions, Imogen lent Jane her mobile phone, and Howard wrote down his telephone number.

Jane felt apprehensive, driving off, after telephoning to say that she was on her way. What would she hear? Had her mother struggled and suffered or had Brian been correct when he said that death came suddenly?

She passed Felix on the road, but neither recognised the other's car.

Fleming had planned to grill young Imogen this morning, but he had barely parted from her father when news came that a taxi driver who had taken her to Becktham on Friday evening had been traced.

Fleming would not let this information alter his construct of what he was convinced was a crime. Imogen could have gone to Becktham and come back in time to lure Charlotte Frost from the house to the river.

Meanwhile, a resident of Becktham, a youth with whom Imogen was on very friendly terms, since they had been witnessed kissing, was conveniently locked up in one of his cells. Questioning Jerry Hunt about his relationship with Imogen might produce interesting results.

But Jerry wouldn't say a word: only that of course he knew her, working as he did in her grandmother's garden.

After Jane had left for Nettington, Imogen asked Howard what would happen when she arrived at the police station.

'The formalities will be explained,' he said. 'And she may want to see her mother. It's natural. When someone dies suddenly, it can be difficult to believe unless you see them. It happened a lot like that in the war, when ships were sunk and relatives received telegrams, and there was no funeral.'

'She'd never been to the house,' she said. 'Jane hadn't, I mean. She was never there with Charlotte, and I was. It's so unfair.'

'Life is, Imogen. You know that,' Howard answered. 'The police will explain about the inquest – there will have to be one, I feel sure. Afterwards, they will be able to arrange the funeral.' He thought about sailors dying of their wounds, their bodies buried at sea, and sighed.

'I hope her brother comes soon. I'm no help – I'm just a nuisance,' said Imogen.

'I'm sure you're not being a nuisance now, Imogen, and you are company for her. That's good. You may have been the last person to see Charlotte alive. That will mean something to Jane and her brother.'

'You don't think I pushed her into the river, do you?' asked Imogen.

'You know I don't,' he answered. 'But why don't you tell Mr Fleming that you went to Becktham on Friday night?'

Imogen's face turned ashen as she stared at him.

'How do you know?' She spoke in a whisper.

At least she hadn't denied it.

'The taxi driver who brought me back last night drove you there. He recognised you.'

'Yes – I knew that, when he came to the door,' she said. Then she got angry. 'He had no right to tell you,' she stormed. 'It's my business.'

'He was worried about you. He thought you were upset, that night,' said Howard. 'You went to see Jerry, didn't you?'

Imogen remained silent, and Howard sighed again.

'Imogen, I'm not trying to trap you. I'm trying to help you but you are doing nothing to help yourself,' he said.

'Jerry was out,' Imogen said. 'And his mother.' It wasn't a lie; they were, when she arrived.

'So you came home?'

'After a bit.'

'In a taxi?'

Imogen debated whether to say she had hitched a lift, but that would provoke a heavy lecture about the risks of hitching. In the end, she stayed silent, an answer in itself.

'I see,' said Howard, and he fell silent too, meditating on what line to take next.

Imogen broke the silence.

'But for me, Charlotte wouldn't be dead,' she said.

'Charlotte was unwise to go over the fields at night, alone, searching for you, if that was what she was doing,' said

Howard. 'But she had had a difficult time herself latterly, and she may not have been thinking very sensibly. She'd been married to your grandfather for only a short time, hadn't she? She'd had to adapt to that, and then he died and almost at once she moved here. That's right, isn't it?'

'Yes.'

'It must all have been very distressing and difficult for her,' he said. 'Your coming to stay must have been a mixed blessing. I could see she was fond of you, but to have a girl to stay who was causing her own family a lot of worry must have been a strain.'

'Do you mean I was the last straw and she committed suicide?'

'No. I don't think someone like Charlotte would take such a step. She would know it would cause a lot of sorrow and make other people feel guilty.' Unless she really had snapped, he thought, and had a breakdown. Desperate people did not always show outward signs of acute distress.

'What must I do?' said Imogen.

'I think you should tell Fleming what you've told me – that you went to see Jerry but he was out, and so after a while you came back,' he said.

Unless Jerry told, no one would know that she knew where the key to his house was kept, and that she'd used it.

Imogen didn't know that Jerry had been arrested.

'Must I go and tell Fleming now?' she said.

'I think he'll be busy with Jane. Probably he'll want to see you anyway but he doesn't know you're here. Let's wait a bit and see what happens,' Howard said.

He wondered how to keep her occupied, but Imogen, restless, got up and walked about his study, where they had